So... field emanated from him.

I... hrouded her, energizing her from head to toe.
... was it? Charisma? Raw, animal sex appeal?
... ...ever it was, she could see why he'd become
a movie star.

H... stared at her, his eyes black pools in the
sh...dows of his face. Even wreathed in darkness
li... this, he was beautiful.

... zinging between them built until she thought
... would explode.

"...y something," she whispered. "You're making
... nervous." Not nervous in the way he was
... ...ng to think, but what he didn't know wouldn't
... ...t him.

"...y grandmother likes you."

... like her, too. I bet you I could convince her
...'re dating."

... exhaled a gust of laughter. "You could convince
... without too much trouble."

...a blinked up at him in shock. Her and a movie
...? The notion of the two of them as a couple
...cked words completely out of her brain.

... blurted the first thing that came to mind.
...iss me."

HIGH-STAKES BACHELOR

BY
CINDY DEES

Published in Great Britain 2014
by Mills & Boon, an imprint of Harlequin (UK) Limited,
Eton House, 18-24 Paradise Road, Richmond, Surrey, TW9 1SR

© 2014 Cynthia Dees

ISBN: 978-0-263-91427-6

18-1114

Printed and bound in Spain
by CPI, Barcelona

Cindy Dees started flying airplanes while sitting in her dad's lap at the age of three and got a pilot's license before she got a driver's license. At age fifteen, she dropped out of high school and left the horse farm in Michigan, where she grew up, to attend the University of Michigan. After earning a degree in Russian and East European studies, she joined the US Air Force and became the youngest female pilot in its history. She flew supersonic jets, VIP airlift and the C-5 Galaxy, the world's largest airplane. During her military career, she traveled to forty countries on five continents, was detained by the KGB and East German secret police, got shot at, flew in the first Gulf War and amassed a lifetime's worth of war stories.

Her hobbies include medieval re-enacting, professional Middle Eastern dancing and Japanese gardening.

This RITA® Award-winning author's first book was published in 2002 and since then she has published more than twenty-five bestselling and award-winning novels. She loves to hear from readers and can be contacted at www.cindydees.com.

Chapter 1

Anabelle Izzolo looked around at the gorgeous young women waiting their turn to go out on the mat and wrestle with a stuntman. At barely five foot two, she noticed how her eyes were at chest height to the mob of leggy, boobtacular, Hollywood-starlet-wannabes who'd shown up for this audition. Crud. She had no business being there. It had seemed like a good idea when she'd signed up for it. But now that the moment was upon her, she felt a giant humiliation coming on.

Thing was, the write-up on the open casting call had been specific in saying that a fight sequence would be auditioned. She was trying to break into the business as a stuntwoman, so a fight was right up her alley. Of course, she wasn't going to get the acting part, but she was hoping to catch the casting director's eye and nab a bit part for some stunt work.

Yet another blonde bombshell went out onto the green gym mats and prissied her way through the fight sequence. God, none of the girls could even make a proper fist, let alone throw a decent punch. You had to drive through the elbow and down the arm into the knuckles. Put your weight behind it. Of course, this fight sequence was more about grappling and falling than throwing punches. Still, Ana was embarrassed on behalf of all women to watch the other girls muff their way through fake fighting.

The stuntman and casting director looked bored out of their minds. Whenever a superhot blonde with impressive cleavage came along, they perked up a little. But that was the extent of it.

"Next!" an assistant with a clipboard called.

"Hold up," the stuntman complained. "I need to piss."

The casting director huffed. "Make it fast."

A male voice, familiar to her from movie theaters, piped up. "I'll take over fighting until he gets back."

Ana turned, gaping. *OMG. Jackson Prescott in the flesh.* The star of the movie being cast stepped out of the shadows beyond the stage lights. He was a muscular, bronzed god of a man with sun-bleached hair and golden-hazel eyes that leaped off a movie screen and melted hearts all over the movie-going world. And in person…well, he was even hotter. Squeals, followed by an audible series of sighs, went up from the crowd of starlets. Ana was a little ashamed to realize she'd contributed to the collective swoon.

"Who's next?" Jackson asked the clipboard girl.

"That would be Number 127."

Oh. Crap. That was her. Ana lurched forward. She caught her foot on the edge of the raised stage and narrowly avoided face-planting as she stumbled into the wash of down lighting.

"You sure you want to try fighting?" Jackson joked. "Maybe you should master walking first?"

A titter of laughter went up from the Barbie doll brigade, and her face erupted in heat. She opened her mouth to make a clever quip back, but no sound came out. Instead, she raised her hands defensively in front of her and settled into a fighting stance.

"Okay, then," Jackson murmured. He stepped up to her, and she was abruptly struck by how much taller and more muscular than her he was. The guy had to be pushing six foot four. And he was so pretty she had trouble tearing her stare away from his face. The combination of boyish charm and masculine confidence was mesmerizing, and his eyes were a warm golden-green that almost seemed lit from within.

"Let's do this," he rumbled low and sexy.

Her insides twisted with shocking lust that distracted her just as he pounced. She barely dodged in time as his fist flew at her face. Wow, he was fast. The swiftness of the leg that swept her feet to the side caught her by surprise, too, and she slammed to the ground on her back as he jumped on top of her.

Her breath whooshed out on a grunt of shock and pain as she fought to draw the next one. Jackson straddled her stomach, pinning her down with his superior weight.

A brief look of disappointment crossed his face. She was supposed to have swung back at him with her fists and rolled aside before he could land on top of her, but she'd blown the move and let him pin her arms. He looked like he'd already mentally checked her off the list and moved on to the next starlet in the audition. In fact, seeming supremely bored, he went off script and reached down to wrap his hands around her neck as if to punctuate her failure.

But as his fingers tightened around her larynx, panic roared to the fore. Black night closed in on her, and she gasped for air as other big hands tightened around her neck. *Dying. She was dying.* Helplessness washed over her. She had to find a way to fight off her would-be killer. Had to live—

Fight, Ana. Live. She kicked her right leg up frantically, jamming her toes into the back of his head sharply enough to make him turn her neck loose and block her next kick with his forearm. She dragged in a rasping breath.

Get. Off. Me.

She fought like a tiger, twisting and turning violently between his knees, wrenching an arm free. She threw a punch at his face and connected solidly with his jaw. He lurched back and she tore her other arm loose. She flailed at him like a wildcat, unreasoning rage joining her panic.

He blocked her blows, which flew at him thick and fast, until he managed to catch her left wrist in his right hand. He yanked it over her head. She got in one last body blow with her right fist before he snagged that wrist, as well. He yanked it up, stretching her out flat beneath him. He sprawled on top of her, using his superior weight to physically subdue her.

Not that she went down without a fight. She wriggled and writhed beneath him, seeking a weakness, desperate to throw him off.

A chuckle vibrated in her ear. "Fiery little thing, aren't you?"

Startled, she froze beneath her attacker—no, wait.

Beneath Jackson Prescott. Audition. Movie. Fake fight. Not trying to kill her.

She went limp beneath him, and his big body pressed down on her, overwhelming in its hard planes and bulging muscles. One of his thighs pressed intimately between hers, and his chest crushed her breasts until she couldn't draw a full breath. His face was about eight inches from hers. And the bastard was grinning down at her.

If sparks could actually fly from a person's eyes, then they were crackling forth from his, all gold and green and smoking hot, snapping back and forth between the two of them as she glared back at him. She registered disbelief as something deep and unwilling inside her responded instinctively and powerfully to the man's raw sex appeal.

"Thank you, Number 127," the casting director called.

With a quick flex of muscular arms, Jackson did a push-up over her and jumped to his feet. "Nice fight."

Vague shock at having survived the attack washed over her…no, not an attack. Just pretend. She sagged against the mat, emotionally exhausted. *She'd made it. She was still alive.* "Thank you, Mr. Prescott."

Memory of that horrible night retreated back into its dark little cave in her mind. The lime color of the green screen set replaced the impersonal blackness of a cold night sky.

"Call me Jackson." His gaze slid down her body as she lay between his feet, taking in every detail of her appearance with disconcerting thoroughness. He held a friendly hand down to her. Embarrassed, she skipped his hand and jumped to her feet, shooting him a patently fake, everything's-peachy-keen grin.

"You're not what I expected," he commented thoughtfully.

"Um, neither are you. I thought I'd be fighting one of the stunt coordinators. I was hoping to pick up some stunt work."

"I think you may be destined for more than that," Jackson replied, his voice a purring caress down her spine.

Ho. Lee. Cow. Was he flirting with her? With a soundstage full of Playboy Bunny blondes to choose from?

"I'll put in a good word with the producers for you," he remarked drolly as if it was some kind of inside joke.

She frowned, not sure how to take that. Confused, she dusted off her rear end and headed offstage. The other stuntman returned from the restroom and took Jackson's place on the mat as the other actresses closed in around Ana aggressively, demanding to know what it was like to roll around with Jackson Prescott.

One especially gorgeous girl hissed, "You think you're so special getting to audition with Jackson Prescott. This job's mine and no one's going to steal it from me."

Wow. Venom much? Ana sidled away from the nasty woman and slung her cheap nylon gym bag over her shoulder. She turned for the exit, but clipboard girl was right behind her. Ana drew up, startled.

"Is the phone number on your head shot the one Mr. Prescott should use to call you?"

Ana blinked, stunned. "Yes. That's my cell phone."

"Keep it turned on," the assistant murmured under the background noise of the last audition finishing and the mob of auditionees dissolving into chatter.

She nodded at the assistant, uncomfortable. She had

no desire to be the flavor du jour for a megastar who would use her and throw her away like a soiled tissue.

"Oh, good. You're still here." She looked up to see a handsome man. Early thirties if she had to guess. Shaved head. Nice physique under a tight T-shirt. Was he talking to her? "Hi, Miss…"

"Izzolo," clipboard girl supplied.

"Miss Izzolo," he said. Apparently, he *was* talking to her. "I'm Adrian Turnow. I'll be directing the movie—"

The rest of what he said faded out as shock rendered her numb. Adrian Turnow in the flesh? He was one of the hottest directors in the business. Every film he worked on was movie gold. Dang. When Jackson Prescott said he would put in a good word for her, he wasn't kidding!

"—time this afternoon for a test shot? We'd like to see you on camera."

Her? They wanted a test shot with her? She was just looking for some stunt work. "Um, sure," she mumbled.

Cameramen were moving around the set, shifting a boom camera out over the green mat and setting up two big cameras on rolling rails along two sides of it. The last of the blondes were filing out. Lighting guys were talking about technical stuff that might as well be Greek to her, and a half dozen people were running around with rolls of extension cord over their shoulders and tablet computers in hand. In short, it was chaos.

A tall, lean, African-American man stepped up to her. "Number 127?"

"That's me. Although I usually go by Ana," she replied, flummoxed.

"I'm Tyrone. Makeup. Let's get you over to my chair and make you smashing for your screen test."

"Can you tell me what's going on?" she asked in a small voice as he stared critically at her.

"Callback, sweetie. You blew Jackson's socks off in your audition."

"Callback? Me?" The notion refused to compute.

Tyrone smiled warmly as he dabbed her face with bronzing powder. "Great skin. Too pale for the camera, but we can fix that. You're whiter than Wonder Bread, girlfriend. I bet you blush beet-red at the drop of a hat."

"Sometimes I blotch, too," she confessed.

He tsked and instructed her to look up and not blink as he deftly applied eyeliner and mascara. "Your bones and coloring could take a full glamor face and heavy color, but I'll let you in on a little secret. Adrian and Jackson both go for the natural look. I'm going no makeup with your look."

"Thanks," she mumbled behind unmoving lips as he applied lip gloss. For doing a no-makeup look, he sure was putting a lot of makeup on her.

"Take a peek."

She turned in the chair and looked at the lighted mirror behind her. *Whoa.* "Is that me?" she breathed. She looked fresh, young…and kind of beautiful.

"It's not a trick mirror," Tyrone retorted.

Her shoulder-length blond bob, which was not at all like the current fashion of long, flowing, wavy locks, swung around her face, the tips turning in a bit to frame her jaw. Her gray-blue eyes looked huge, and her lips were just pink enough not to get lost beneath her cheekbones.

"Camera's gonna love you, baby," Tyrone said encouragingly.

"Thanks. Let's hope the director does, too."

"Jackson's coproducing this film. You gotta impress both him and Adrian to get this gig."

Ahh. Hence Jackson's earlier joke about putting in a good word with the producers. "Got it. Thanks, Tyrone."

"Go get 'em, kid."

She stepped out onto the bright green mat and looked around. The atmosphere was electric. She could get hooked on this. Choosing to reinvent her life in the film industry had been a great decision.

A cell phone rang, and she looked up in time to see Jackson Prescott scowling down at his caller ID. He rolled his eyes and moved away from the mat to take the call. She figured it must be a woman to have elicited that look of disgust. Last night's lay, maybe?

Her stomach dropped in disappointment. It wasn't like she was ever going to be in his league, though. And if she got a part in the movie, he'd also be her boss. This put him firmly off-limits. She couldn't recall which actress the tabloids had him matched up with this week. But he went through women like chewing gum.

Clipboard lady from before came over to her. "Hi, I'm Sheila. Adrian's assistant. The guys want to shoot a combat sequence with weapons. I see from your résumé that you've studied kendo, so I assume you're okay with that."

Ana had obsessively studied various martial arts ever since the attack two years ago. The fast-moving Japanese form with bamboo swords was, in fact, one of them.

On cue, a kid who must have been with the prop department trotted up to her and handed her a foam club. It looked like driftwood on steroids. She swung the craggy piece experimentally. It had about the same heft as a baseball bat. "It's heavier than a kendo sword, but I can handle it."

The brunette moved away, and a man approached her. "I'm Crash. Fight choreographer."

"Not a reassuring name for a man with your job," she responded drily.

He grinned. "I specialize in car stunts. But today, I'm gonna teach you a quick fight sequence with that toothpick."

She paid close attention as he walked her through the choreography until she had the sequence memorized. Gradually, they sped it up to full-out. It was a dance between the two of them, really.

Adrian signaled that he was ready to shoot, and Jackson pocketed his phone. He joined her on the mat and someone passed him a king-size club, which he swung a few times, getting the feel of it. Apparently, he already knew the choreography.

"Places, everyone!" Adrian called. "Quiet on set, please."

She stepped into the middle of the mat and took up a fighting stance, feet apart and knees bent. Jackson did the same, towering over her. Lord, just being close to him made her heart beat faster. The guy was like a high-powered electromagnet.

"Almost doesn't seem fair to beat up a squirt like you," he teased.

She snorted back, rising to the bait. "Big, clumsy lunk. You're gonna have to catch me first."

He grinned at her taunt and leaped at her. He was flipping *fast* for a guy his size. *Step. Swing. Dodge, slide left. Spin. Jump. Swing. Swing.* She chanted the choreography in her head by rote.

Ka-pow.

Her arm jarred from the impact of her club on Jackson's face.

"Jackson!" she cried out as he doubled over, swearing. "You were supposed to spin right, not left!"

"Yeah, I got that memo just now," he muttered in a voice muffled by his hands.

She spied blood dripping from between his fingers. "Medic!" she shouted. Adrian was backing away from Jackson, looking sick to his stomach. No one responded immediately to her shout, and Jackson was bleeding all over the place. A sports trainer in high school, she leaped into action. She whipped off her green camo T-shirt and wadded it up. "Here. Use this to catch blood while I find a first aid kit."

Good thing she'd worn a camisole under her shirt today. She looked around frantically and spotted a big red cross on the far wall. She raced over to the first aid kit, yanked the briefcase-size metal box down and sprinted back to Jackson.

"What did I hit? How hard?" she asked urgently.

"Nose. Clocked me good."

"Lemme see." He was reluctant to take her shirt away from his face, and she had to physically peel his fingers loose. She reached up to gently squeeze the spot she'd hit.

"Youch!" he yelped.

Nothing crunched or wiggled under her fingertips. If his nose *was* broken and she'd pinched it like that, he'd have howled to the rafters, not just squeaked a little. Crud. She was going to get sued into the Stone Age if she'd just ruined the prettiest face in Hollywood.

"It doesn't feel broken," she announced. "But you've got the mother of all nosebleeds." She stuffed his nostrils with gauze and ordered, "Tilt your head back." She called out to no one in particular, "Is there somewhere he can lie down?"

"My office," Adrian replied thickly. *Guy must get queasy at the sight of blood.*

In stunt work, guys got banged up all the time. Cuts and scrapes were all part of a day's work. She guided Jackson's hand to her shoulder and followed Adrian's assistant to the director's office. His big palm gripped her bare skin lightly, and her bones felt oddly small and fragile under the heat of his hand. A shiver of something unidentifiable ran through her.

"Okay, Jackson. We're at the couch." She guided him down to a leather sofa. "On your back."

"Let me guess, you've been dying to get me flat on my back on a casting couch," he joked.

"Oh, baby, oh, baby, oh," She intoned as she tucked a throw pillow under his head. *Keep it light. Impersonal. He's a freaking movie star.*

"Don't make me laugh. It hurts."

She took a closer look at his nose. It was swelling across the bridge and turning red. His left eye was puffing shut, too. "You're lucky that club was covered in foam. Looks like you may still get a shiner, though."

"Great. A black eye from a *girl*. I'm never gonna hear the end of this."

"I'm so sorry—" she started.

He cut her off immediately. "My fault. I wasn't paying attention and zigged when I should have zagged. I was distracted."

"That phone call?" she asked sympathetically.

He huffed in obvious exasperation at the memory of the offending phone call. She recognized that sound from countless times listening to guys grouse about their re-lationships. "Woman trouble?"

He scowled. "You could say that."

"Anything you want to talk about?" She winced as soon as the words left her mouth. That was her. Ole shoulder-to-cry-on for every guy she knew. They *all* went to her for advice about chicks. Apparently, hav-ing the same reproductive apparatus as their girlfriends made her some kind of expert.

Which was a load of crap, by the way. She didn't know squat about women. Hell, she hardly knew how to be one, herself. And she had no idea how to do a relationship. It wasn't like her own past had given her any sterling examples to go by. After the disaster—God, was it two full years ago now?—she'd pretty much sworn off men.

Jackson rolled his eyes. "My grandmother is harangu-ing me to settle down, find a nice girl and get married. She's just antsy to get a great-grandkid, and figures that, out of all my brothers and sisters, I'm her best prospect. She's being a total pain in the ass."

Jackson Prescott was looking to get hitched? Wow. Talk about an eligible bachelor.

"I don't even have a girlfriend." He added, scowling, "No matter what the damned tabloids say."

Really? Interesting. Oh, get over yourself. He'd never take a second look at you. Aloud, she commented, "You could have an actress friend fake an engagement with you to shut up your grandmother for a while. Or, you could just skip the wife and go straight to the baby. People don't have to get married to make babies."

"So I should, what? Pick up some random chick in a bar and get her pregnant to shut up my grandmother?"

She shrugged. This flavor of woman trouble went well beyond her ability to give advice on it.

"I don't even like going to bars," he grumbled.

Shut the front door. "Seriously?" she blurted.

Someone barged in just then with the plastic bag of ice she'd asked for on the way in there. She stole a hand towel from the sink in Adrian's bathroom, wrapped the ice in it and laid it gently on Jackson's face. She felt for the guy; she would have no idea how to go about picking up a woman if she were a man.

In an attempt to be helpful, though, she commented, "There are other places besides bars to meet women. I hear there are good pickings in the produce section of grocery stores. Apparently, if you act clueless when a hot girl comes along, she'll stop and help you."

Jackson retorted, "I would have to actually be in the market for a girlfriend for that to work."

Oh. Something way down deep inside her deflated at the news that he wasn't interested in dating. It was nothing personal, of course. She was just reacting on behalf of her entire half of the species. Jackson Prescott was a hell of a hunk that some woman ought to get to enjoy.

She replied cautiously, "I have to say, I doubt you'd have all that much trouble finding a woman willing to have your baby."

Warmth uncurled inside her at the thought of holding his baby in her arms, shocking her into momentary silence. Where in the hell did *that* come from? Had her biological clock just started ticking? Heck, she wasn't in the market to have a kid any more than he was.

He lifted aside the ice pack to stare up at her. Was that a speculative gleam in his gorgeous eyes? Surely not.

A little panicked at the direction her thoughts were

taking, she pushed the big ice bag back down onto his nose, which also had the effect of covering his eyes and taking his distracting hazel gaze off her.

Thoughtful silence was all that emerged from the towel for the next couple of minutes. Then, "What's your name, 127?"

"Ana. Anabelle Izzolo."

"You have zilch by way of acting credits, Anabelle Izzolo."

She didn't need a box-office giant to point that out to her. She was well aware of her lack of credits. She'd been taking acting classes as part of her plan to become a stuntwoman, but it was hard to get work if you hadn't already had some previously.

"But the chemistry between you and me is exactly what we're looking for."

"For...what exactly?"

"The lead actress in our film. Assuming you can act."

Lead? Actress? Her mind went completely blank. He was right. She was totally unprepared to do anything like that. But what kind of idiot would she be to say so? Chances like this came along once in a lifetime. Once in a very lucky lifetime.

"I can act," she blurted, then added hastily, "I bet I could convince your grandmother I was having your baby."

He started to snort with laughter but cut the sound short with a groan of pain.

"Quit moving around so much. I almost had the bleeding stopped, but now you've got it going again."

"Pushy, aren't you?"

"No. Just trying to stop a nosebleed. That only makes me sensible," she declared.

He laughed again, but carefully. "So here's the thing. We're going to have to convince the primary investors in the film to go with an unknown leading lady. My name should carry the box office…we'll have to spin it as the debut of an exciting new star. It could work if we market it right…"

"Am I supposed to know what you're talking about?"

"Nope. Just keep being you. Oh, and I'm going to need to have supper with you, tonight."

"Why?" She was immediately suspicious. It probably didn't help that her last real date…that fateful one two years ago…had started out as a dinner invitation from a big good-looking guy. He'd been the star of the high school football team, and all the girls had swooned over him, too. Ana had kept in touch with him after graduation, as he'd attended the same college as her on a football scholarship.

"Consider it part of your callback."

The hallway door opened before she could come up with a polite way to turn him down but still get the dream acting job. "How are we doing in here?" Adrian asked from the doorway. He seemed leery of charging in and finding pints of blood spilled on his floor.

Nervous, she jumped to her feet. "Good. I think we've got things under control," she declared with false cheer.

"Thanks for your time this afternoon, Miss Izzolo," Adrian said politely. "We'll be in touch."

Oh, God. The classic Hollywood brush-off. *Don't call us; we'll call you.* She'd clobbered the star of the movie and wrecked her shot at fame and fortune, after all. It had been a fun fantasy for the five minutes it had lasted. Ah, well. Maybe she could still break into stunt work, someday.

She headed for the locker room to retrieve her cheap nylon gym bag and get back to her regularly scheduled life. She threw open the locker door and stared in dismay. Her bag was shredded. As in literally shredded. Her extra audition clothes were in tatters, and what little makeup she had was smeared all over the rags formerly known as the only decent clothes she owned.

What the heck? Who would do a thing like this? And *why?*

Chapter 2

Jackson had no idea what to do about casting the lead actress part in the film. His gut shouted at him to go with Anabelle Izzolo, the unknown with the wild talent. But just as surely, the movie's investors were going to want him to go with a more established actress. Someone like Shyann Brooklyn.

The tall blonde had been last to audition today. Although Shyann looked great on film, he doubted there was room for him on the silver screen with her and her ego. She was nasty, self-centered and not all that bright, either. He doubted she would have long-term staying power in the business. A few films from now, after the public got its fill of looking at her, it would dawn on everyone that she couldn't act her way out of a paper bag.

His phone vibrated. It was a text from his grandmother to call her. Meddling woman. Oh, Minerva was well-meaning enough, but a royal pain sometimes. Too bad he loved her so damned much.

His father, a soldier, had died on active duty, and his mother had drowned in her grief and wasted away on sleeping pills until she'd finally OD'd. Gran had taken in the whole passel of Prescott kids, him, his three brothers and his twin baby sisters, and raised them all. Minerva had married young herself, and his parents had married right out of high school. As a result, Gran was far from ancient and was energetic, nosy and felt within her rights to boss all of them around. She was a classic iron-fist-in-a-velvet-glove type.

And right now, he was ignoring her.

He shoved his phone into his pocket and stepped out into the studio's parking lot. The blistering California sun slammed into him. The soundstage he and Adrian had built was inland far enough not to catch the ocean breezes that cooled the California coast. But the price had been right on the sprawling piece of property. Beads of sweat popped out on his brow as he threw a leg over his Harley and cranked it up. The powerful engine revved between his legs and, as usual, gave him a bit of a hard-on.

He rolled out of the parking lot and spotted a familiar figure standing at the bus stop in front of the studio. Ana Izzolo looked about ready to burst into flames in the blazing heat. There was one bus in Serendipity, California, and it operated on no discernible schedule. She could be standing there for another hour.

He pulled to a stop in front of her. "Can I give you a lift?"

"I'm okay. I'll catch the bus."

"Hop on. It's hot as hell out here. No telling when the bus will come along."

"That's nice of you, but I'm staying in the north end of town. Don't you live the other direction?"

They were talking Serendipity here. The entire town could fit on a postage stamp. He could go from one end of Main Street to the other in approximately sixty seconds, and that included having to stop at the one traffic light in the whole town. He unhooked his spare helmet from its perch on the backrest and held it out to her. "Hop on."

She hesitated, but eventually took the helmet from his outstretched hand and strapped it on her head. She slid her leg through the gap between his rear end and the backrest, and settled herself behind him. Abrupt awareness of her hot little crotch nestled against his butt roared through him. *Day-umm.*

Her arms snaked around his waist, which had the effect of mashing her breasts against his back informatively. *Soft. Springy. Resilient.* Well, that answered that. Her female assets were real. Good to know. He'd never been a fan of hard and lumpy implants.

You're about to be her boss. Behave yourself. Nope. His body wasn't listening to reason. His erection swelled until his jeans were uncomfortably tight. Good thing he was sitting on the bike and not trying to walk.

He twisted the throttle and the Harley leaped forward. Ana relaxed behind him and moved easily with the bike. She obviously knew how to stay centered and quiet on top of one. He didn't let many women ride with him because they usually threw off his balance. He could hardly tell she was aboard, though, as their bodies moved in perfect unison. Only that sexy female form clinging to the length of his back reminded him she was there.

The farther inland they went, the hotter the air got. It was official. They were in hell. He followed the directions she gave him through the radio-mike between their helmets, and in a few minutes he pulled into a shabby motel parking lot. A few disreputable-looking surfers were just coming back after a day in the water, but the parking lot was otherwise deserted.

"Need me to walk you up to your room?" he asked. His grandmother was a stickler for the niceties and had raised all the kids to be polite.

Ana stiffened against his back. "No, but thanks for offering." She slid off the bike a little too hastily and he shot out a hand to steady her as she stumbled.

"Dinner, tonight. With me," he stated.

"No, thanks."

"That wasn't a request. Your audition isn't over yet."

If she'd been awkward before, she was board-stiff and epically uncomfortable now. Jeez. Did she think he was going to throw her down and rape her on a casting couch? He said defensively, "I just want to talk more. Get to know you. Find the chemistry between us. I'll pick you up at eight."

"I'll meet you at a restaurant," she countered quickly. "Pick a place."

"Romaletti's." She wanted to have her own ride home, huh? Did she not want to sleep with him or just doubt that he would be interested? Hmm. Intriguing.

She disengaged her arm from his fingers, and he was startled to discover he missed the feel of her skin. He took the helmet she passed him and watched her pull her blond hair out of its ponytail. It swung around her shoulders pertly.

Realizing with a start that he was staring at her, he tore his gaze away from her. For lack of anything else to look at, he eyed the motel. It looked one step up from a crack den. But it was the only low-cost lodging in town. Serendipity was mostly a secret enclave of the rich and famous. It was far enough north of Los Angeles to get out of the rat race, but close enough that a private jet could have a person back in the heart of L.A. in less than an hour.

He and Adrian had chosen the sleepy little town to house their production company precisely because of its laid-back atmosphere and distance from the Hollywood rat race. Not to mention real estate wasn't sold by the square foot up here or for exorbitant prices. That, and his grandmother's home was here. He'd just finished fully renovating the place and adding a few bells and whistles to it. Serendipity was where he'd grown up. His roots ran deep in this town.

"Thanks for the ride, Jackson."

"Anytime, babycakes." Grinning, he revved the throttle and spit gravel at her with his back tire as he peeled out of the parking lot.

He pointed his Harley back toward the coast and let the wind blow away the misgivings trying to creep into his mind. Was he making a mistake casting someone so naive? Her freshness and innocence would play great in the film, but at what price to her? He would hate to hurt Ana. She was a good kid.

He pulled into the driveway of the sprawling Victorian home he'd grown up in. Technically, he owned the place now, but it would always be Gran's house. It was gray-blue with white gingerbread trim and moss-green accents, and looked totally at ease in its rocky seaside environment. The recent renovation and expansion had more than doubled its square footage, but the architect had done a brilliant job of blending the old with the new.

For the past few years, he'd only crashed here between movie gigs. But he was looking forward to living here full-time. The Hollywood grind was getting old. He also thought Minerva liked the company, not that she would ever admit it. The twins had left for college, and he suspected Minerva was empty nesting. Not to mention his grandmother was a flamboyant soul in constant need of an audience.

He parked his Harley in the garage next to the white Cadillac he'd bought her for her birthday last year and headed into the kitchen. Steeling himself to face the baby lecture—again—he sighed.

"Hey, Gran." He paused beside her to drop a fond kiss on her cheek. Still tall and slim at sixtysomething, she was an elegant woman. Beautiful, even now.

"Hello, Jackie. Tea?" She glanced up at him and did a double take. "What happened to your face?"

"Ana—an actress auditioning for a part—clocked me across the face with a club."

"Oh, dear. It looks like you're going to have a hooked nose and a black eye. Won't you make quite the dashing pirate? I assume she didn't get the part?"

"Actually, we're thinking about casting her."

"Well, at least she can defend herself from your advances."

He rolled his eyes. "The crap in the tabloids about me is not true, Gran. I swear."

She waved a "whatever" hand at him and pulled the tea bags out of the pot.

"Can I have some of that tea on ice?" he asked.

"Ruins the flavor, dear."

"Yes, but it's a thousand degrees outside. And the idea of drinking something hot makes my nose hurt."

"There's a nice breeze coming off the ocean. Why don't we take our tea on the veranda?"

He never failed to be amazed at how it could be twenty degrees cooler on the coast than in town. He picked up the tray and followed her outside onto the stone patio. Sure enough, a cool, fresh breeze dried his sweat in a matter of seconds. He sipped at the tall glass of iced tea Minerva poured for him in spite of her objection to chilling her imported Earl Grey.

"Have you thought about what we talked about on the phone?" she asked without preamble.

The memory of Ana's declaration that she could fake out his grandmother flashed through his mind. If only.

He took a long pull at the tea before answering with long-suffering patience, "We've been over this before. I'm not averse to having a family...someday. But right now, I'm traveling and working too much to sustain a relationship, let alone raise kids."

"But now that the production company is up and running, you'll be home more. Have more control of your schedule."

In theory. He had yet to see that play out in practice. He'd been working day and night with Adrian for the past year getting all the financing and business paperwork set up. He was convinced that it was a good business move to invest a large chunk of his accumulated wealth in a long-term venture like this. But it was a big risk. A big project.

"Tell me about this pugilist actress."

"She's a newcomer. Name's Ana Izzolo." He searched for words to describe her accurately. "She's spunky. Fiery. Very un-Hollywood."

Minerva's eyes lit with interest. "How old is she?"

"I don't know. Mid-twenties, maybe."

"Is she pretty?"

"Of course she's pretty. We wouldn't be casting her as a leading lady if she wasn't. Although she's not traditional. She'd be a girl-next-door type if she didn't have…" How to describe the cynical edge he sensed more than saw? He shrugged, and finished lamely, "She has a certain something. She's compelling."

Speaking of which, he only had about an hour until he had to leave for their date. And he needed a shower.

"Going out tonight?" Minerva queried.

"Yup."

"On a date?"

"That's none of your business," he retorted.

"And why not?"

"Because I'm thirty-three years old and don't tell you every detail of my life?"

Her nose went up. "Fine. I'll find out where you went and who with down at the hair salon tomorrow."

He stared at her in chagrin. The hell of it was she would be able to do just that. And that would be the downside of small-town life. "If you must know, it's a working dinner. I'm meeting Ana to talk some more."

His grandmother pursed her lips. "When do I get to meet her?"

"Uh, never."

Minerva glared down her patrician nose at him. "Are you ashamed of me?"

He'd forgotten how effectively she could deliver a guilt trip. "No, Gran. I'm not ashamed. This is just work, not true love ever after."

"Compelling, hmm?" she murmured as he stomped past her toward the house.

Meddling woman. This was getting out of hand. "You don't have the right to run my life, Gran."

"I wouldn't dream of interfering, dear."

Hah. And leopards didn't have spots. Even if the leopard was his grandmother and her heart was in the right place. At least she hadn't played the "I could die at any moment without ever seeing my great-grandchildren" card.

Looking forward to dinner with Ana more than he'd looked forward to a date in a while, he headed upstairs.

Ana couldn't say if she was more excited or scared. Both about her dinner date tonight and the whole idea of landing a major movie role. Either way, she was a bundle of nerves as she primped. She did her best not to mess up Tyrone's awesome makeup job. She wasn't much into the girlie arts and could never duplicate Tyrone's artistry.

She chose a pale pink angora sweater and white jeans to change into. They were basically her only decent clothes left after the vandalism of her other audition clothes at the studio earlier.

She tossed her purse over her shoulder and headed downstairs in the gathering dusk. Tonight, she would burn some of the remaining gasoline in her car to get to Romaletti's and back. If she actually landed this job, money to fill up her car wouldn't be a problem anymore.

She approached her vintage VW Beetle affectionately. The Bug Bomb and she had been through a lot together over the years. Hopefully, times were looking up for the two of them. And it started with this dinner tonight—

Maybe because she was distracted thinking about Jackson Prescott, or maybe because she simply forgot the first rule of self-defense, which was to be aware of her surroundings, but she didn't see the attack coming. One second she was reaching for her car-door handle, and the next she was flat on the ground with a heavy body on top of her.

Ohgod, ohgod, ohgod. Not again. And maybe because this reminded her so much of the last time she was attacked, she panicked a little and forgot the second rule of self-defense, which was to make as much noise as possible and attract help, or at least the attention of passersby.

She pushed in silent panic against the gravelly asphalt, trying to turn over. To get her hands or feet free to defend herself. Something hard and heavy slammed into her right temple, and the world went black for a few seconds. She didn't quite lose consciousness, but she was dazed and had to work to stay conscious, let alone fight back.

Her years of self-defense classes finally caught up with her and one more cardinal rule belatedly registered in her brain: never give up. She struggled weakly beneath her attacker.

"Bitch," a male voice ground out in her ear, dripping with vitriol.

She fought harder. But trapped on her stomach like this, there wasn't much she could do. All her martial arts training was negated by her inability to move. Her purse was gone, the mace container inside it useless. The motel's parking lot had no light in it and was usually deserted, anyway. Fat lot of good noticing all that did her now.

She should have been more aware of her surroundings. But she'd been so caught up in fantasizing about Jackson Prescott that she'd failed to pay the slightest attention to anything around her. She almost deserved whatever happened next.

She didn't want to die, dammit. And that was when the rest of her self-defense training finally, belatedly, came back to her. She opened her mouth and screamed as loudly and bloodcurdlingly as she could.

Her attacker swore as a door opened nearby. A hand reached for her mouth but she bit the salty palm as hard as she could and screamed again.

"Hey! Are you okay, lady?" somebody called.

"Help!" she screamed.

And that was the last thing she remembered before something slammed into the side of her head again, and she did pass out this time.

Chapter 3

Jackson's cell phone rang just as he was heading downstairs. He didn't give many people his private number, so he was surprised when he pulled out the device and didn't recognize the number on the caller ID. Normally, he would ignore it, but he was in a good mood in anticipation of dinner with Ana.

"Hello?"

"Mr. Prescott?"

"Who's this?" he demanded.

"San Placido County Hospital emergency room. Are you familiar with a woman named Anabelle Izzolo?"

"Is she all right?" he burst out in alarm.

"There's been an incident, sir. We couldn't find any emergency contacts for her, but we did find your phone number in her purse."

"I'll be there in five minutes."

Crapcrapcrapcrapcrap. What had happened? He ran for his motorcycle and flung it out of the driveway like a stunt driver. It was more like a ten-minute drive down to the county hospital under normal conditions, but his five-minute estimate turned out to be fairly accurate. He charged through the swinging doors to the emergency room, helmet still on his head.

"Where is Ana Izzolo?" he demanded of the nurse behind the admissions counter. "Is she okay? What happened to her?"

"And you are?" the nurse asked.

"Jackson Prescott. You called me." He tore off his helmet and the nurse gasped in recognition. What the hell good was it being a movie star if he couldn't turn it into preferential treatment now and then?

He leaned forward and murmured low, "I would rather not sit here in the public waiting room until the paparazzi show up. Is there any chance you can take me back to be with Ana and avoid a scene?"

"Of course. Come with me." The woman stepped out from behind the counter to escort him personally.

"Thanks, so much—" he glanced down at her name tag "—Nurse Simpson."

"Oh, it's my pleasure, Mr. Prescott. I loved you in that movie about everyone having to leave Earth."

"Thanks." It had been the success of that movie that had led him and Adrian to produce the space Western they were working on right now.

The nurse led him into a tiny vestibule crammed with machines and a big hospital bed. A young police officer looked up as they entered. Jackson's gaze riveted on Ana, small and pale in the big bed. "How is she?" he demanded. He still had no idea what had happened to her and how serious it was.

The cop answered, "She's just coming around. Maybe she can tell us what happened. I found her in a parking lot, unconscious."

Alarm gripped his chest in a vise so tight he had trouble drawing his next breath. "Was she mugged?" *Or worse?*

"Based on her abrasions, I'd say she was knocked down from behind. A guest at the motel heard her scream and called us. Her purse was still on the ground beside her and her clothes were intact, so it looks like she fought the guy off or scared him away. She's just coming around. Talk to her and see if she'll respond to your voice."

Jackson moved to her side to pick up her hand. "Hey, babycakes. It's me. Jackson. You're late for our date."

Ana groaned. He encouraged her to wake up and talk to him for a few more seconds, and she eventually mumbled, "My head hurts."

The nurse nodded in approval at him and then unceremoniously elbowed him aside, "How many fingers am I holding up, Miss Izzolo?"

Ana squinted and got the number right. That was a good sign, right? Jackson fretted in the corner he'd been relegated to, where he would be out of the way. If only there was something he could do for her. He felt so damned useless. But he didn't have the slightest bit of medical training. Hell, he didn't have training to do anything practical. He could act. That was it. Sure, it had made him a boatload of money, but he figured it was as much a win of the genetic lottery as any real talent he might have. His brothers were soldiers—a helicopter pilot and a Marine officer. Accomplished men with distinguished careers. And he…he was pretty.

Jackson waited impatiently while a doctor came in and peered into Ana's eyes, asked her a bunch questions, poked her some more and declared her basically unharmed. She apparently had a mild concussion that went with the lump on the side of her head over her ear.

A cop came into the room. Good-looking guy—blond, blue-eyed, deep surfer tan, lanky physique to go with it. Introduced himself as Brody Westmore.

Jackson was deeply relieved when she told the cop she'd been mugged but nothing more. She glossed over the details of the attack and finished by describing screaming her head off and then passing out.

Officer Westmore had apparently already interviewed the motel guest who'd called 9-1-1. *Enterprising guy.* Surfer cop concluded that, given the timing of the call to the police and their arrival shortly after the scream, her mugger had fled the scene soon after knocking her out.

The cop asked her to check if anything was missing from her purse. A pitifully small amount of cash in her wallet was apparently intact, but her cell phone had gone missing. She was upset about it, but Jackson intervened quickly. "The studio will replace it for you. We'll need to be able to get in touch with you on short notice." Or more to the point, he would need to be able to get in touch with her on short notice for his own peace of mind.

The police officer asked, "Ma'am, is there someone we can call to let them know you've had an accident? A family member? Spouse?"

Embarrassment flashed through her transparent gaze and she mumbled, "No. No one."

"I'm the significant other," Jackson blurted, leaping

to the rescue of the damsel in distress. Apparently, he had a heretofore untapped knight-in-shining-armor complex. Not to mention a bizarre possessive streak where Ana was concerned.

She looked startled and the cop looked skeptical until Jackson added defensively, "She was on her way to dinner with me when she was attacked." He took satisfaction in the way Surfer Cop's expression fell in disappointment.

The nurse interjected, "Then you'll be with her tonight, Mr. Prescott? We can't release her with a concussion unless she won't be alone."

Ana struggled to sit up, looking freaked at the idea of spending the night in the hospital. Or maybe she was freaked at the idea of spending the night with *him*. He frowned. "Of course. I'll take her home with me. I'll wake her up every two hours or whatever I need to do." He'd been in a movie last year where his female costar had to be woken up periodically after a concussion. It had been a plot point that they made love each time he woke her up. Fun couple days of shooting—

The nurse broke his train of thought. "She won't require anything that extreme. Just keep an eye on her for nausea, vomiting, disorientation, slurring of speech, balance problems, mood changes, restlessness, excessive light or sound sensitivity, or trouble focusing her eyes."

Well, okay then. He followed the nurse out front to deal with the discharge papers, and he wrote a check for the cost of the E.R. visit. He remembered what it had been like to be a struggling young actor couch surfing and living from hand to mouth between jobs.

After all of the paperwork was taken care of, he headed back down the hall to collect Ana. He wasn't thrilled to see the cop still there, perched on the end of her bed chatting her up. She was *his* dinner date, dammit.

"Ready to go home, Ana-banana?"

He caught the glimpse of wistfulness that passed through her expressive eyes before she masked it. It tugged at his heart. An orderly shooed him aside to help Ana into a wheelchair. The cop walked out beside her while Jackson cooled his jets behind the procession. He wasn't used to having competition for women, and he didn't particularly like it.

At least he got to put the hot girl on the back of his bike and peel out of the parking lot while the cop climbed into his piece-of-junk Crown Vic cruiser. There was a little justice in this world, after all.

He murmured over his shoulder, "Hang on tight, baby. I've got you now."

Ana leaned into Jackson's back and wished desperately that his comment could be true. She was so tired of fighting her own fights and looking out for herself. Particularly since she didn't seem to be doing that hot a job of it.

His bike accelerated onto the Coast Highway, and it felt phenomenal to breathe in clean, ocean air as the wind whipped past. It had been a scorching-hot day and warmth still lingered in the evening. She reveled in having survived the attack. In having her arms around this man. Euphoria overtook her at having cheated death for real. In her stunt training, she'd done plenty of risky things, but all of that paled before the danger of real life.

"You okay?" Jackson asked over the comm system between their helmets.

She replied, "Um, yes. Why?"

"You tensed up."

"Oh. Sorry." She consciously relaxed each major muscle group in her body one by one and let herself flow with the movements of the motorcycle and the man confidently maneuvering along the moonlit ribbon of asphalt.

Jackson pulled into the parking lot of her motel. She slid out reluctantly from behind him, startled by how sexy it felt to rub her body across his like that. His gaze snapped to hers, and for a second, his eyes blazed white-hot. *Yowza*.

Embarrassed as all get-out, she made a production of taking off her helmet and passing it to him. He stayed seated on his bike for a few extra seconds, securing first her helmet and then his before climbing off the Harley and following her up the stairs to her second-floor room.

Except as they approached her door, she spied something odd about it. The whole thing looked...crooked. Jackson shoved past her abruptly, hooking an arm around her front and simultaneously pushing her behind him and jumping in front of her. What the heck?

"Get back," he ordered low and hard.

"What's wrong?"

"Your door's busted."

"It was probably like that before—" she started.

"Jamb's broken. Boot print by the doorknob," he interrupted. "Stay out here."

"What?"

He stopped in front of the door and spared her a glare. "You heard me. Don't come in until I tell you it's clear." He used his forearm to push open the sagging door. She frowned until it occurred to her he was intentionally not leaving fingerprints on the doorknob. *Sheesh. Paranoid much?*

He disappeared into the dark interior of her dingy room. Ignoring his instructions, she stepped into the doorway to see what he was doing. She caught sight of him just spinning into her bathroom in a low crouch. Whoa. Where did he learn a move like that?

That was when her eyesight adjusted enough to really see the interior of her place. *What. The. Heck?* It was trashed. As in totaled. As in a tornado had shredded the place. Every piece of furniture was knocked over. Every cushion was gutted, and stuffing was all over the place. Drawers were pulled out and thrown on the floor. The TV was smashed. Curtains yanked down off the rods and sliced into rags.

She jumped as Jackson reappeared in the doorway of her bathroom. "I told you to stay outside." He sounded irritated.

"Is anyone here?" she blurted, her heart pounding.

"No. But if a crook had been in here, you could've put yourself in the line of fire and gotten hurt."

She flipped the switch beside the door that turned on the lamp across the room. Nothing happened. What on earth was going on? It was as if someone was targeting her. But who? The only person on earth who wanted to kill her was in jail.

Jackson moved to her side and reached past her to close the broken door as much as it would go. He pulled out his cell phone and dialed a phone number without answering her question. "Hello, I'd like to report a break-in." He gave her room number and the name of the motel, but he gave the person on the other end of the line *his* cell phone number.

"I understand, Officer. The room is secure, no one's injured and I'm taking the owner to a safe location. I'll have her make a list of stolen property, and when you're ready to come by and have a look, call me."

Jackson called the motel's manager on his cell since the rotary phone in the room was currently in pieces, none of which were still attached to each other or the wall. He pocketed his phone and then asked her, "Did you have anything valuable in the room like jewelry or cash that someone could have taken?"

"No. Nothing like that."

"Can you think of anything someone might toss your place to look for?"

"No."

"You got a torqued-off ex?"

"No!"

"How about an ex you didn't know is pissed?"

"No exes," she admitted reluctantly.

"None at all?" he blurted, sounding surprised.

Well, wasn't this just too embarrassing for words? "I don't date," she mumbled.

"Why the hell not?"

"This from the guy who has no female friends whatsoever?" she replied a shade defensively.

The manager showed up, blessedly ending Jackson's uncomfortable line of questioning. The man confirmed that this had been the only room broken into and commenced shooting her suspicious looks as if this was all her fault.

Jackson must have picked up the guy's hostility because when she started to ask the manager if he had another room she could move into, Jackson cut her off with "I'm taking you to my place to stay until we find out who trashed your room."

"That won't be necessary—" she started.

"Nonetheless, that's what's going to happen. Do you want to grab your toothbrush and some clothes, assuming they aren't destroyed, too?"

She headed for the closet and gasped as she peered inside. It was just like the locker at the studio. Every piece of clothing inside was in tatters. Even her shoes' heels were broken off. The rage behind the attack stole her breath away. "Who would do something like this?" she whispered, tears gathering in her eyes and throat.

"Screw the toothbrush," Jackson said gruffly. "C'mon. Let's get out of here."

A sob rattled up out of her chest and escaped.

With urgency approaching panic, Jackson grabbed her elbow and bodily dragged her out of the motel room. A fog descended over her brain, dulling sound and sensation as he led her back to his Harley and installed her on it. He slid onto the bike in front of her and the engine roared to life.

"There's a hotel at the beach. If you could take me there, I'll grab a room until I head back to Los Angeles," she yelled over the engine.

"Negative. You're coming to my place," he called back.

"I'm not shacking up with you, Jackson."

"I didn't ask for your opinion on the topic. I've got plenty of room." She started to object, but he interrupted. "Someone has to keep an eye on you for a day or two after your concussion."

The doctor at the hospital had given her some sort of industrial-strength painkiller, and she'd actually momentarily forgotten her pounding headache from before.

"Besides," Jackson continued firmly, "I'm worried

about you. Until we figure out who trashed your place, I want you close by where I can protect you."

She subsided, speechless. Other people didn't protect her, particularly big hunky movie stars whom she had giant crushes on. But she had to admit it felt kind of nice to let somebody else worry about things for once. She was wiped out by today's events. And it wasn't like she could actually afford to pay for a decent hotel room. That was why she'd been at the crappy motel outside town in the first place. Still, she'd imposed on him too much. If she wasn't mistaken, he had already paid her hospital bill.

His rich, soothing voice echoed inside the helmet. "Relax, Ana, and let me do the worrying."

She hadn't slowed down enough to get around to worrying about herself until he mentioned it. Who had attacked her? Did it have to do with the attack at the studio, or was it just a terrible coincidence that she had been attacked twice in the same day? What the heck was wrong with her? Did she have a giant *V* for victim on her forehead or something? All of a sudden, mountains of worry crowded in on her, crushing her beneath their weight.

She wrapped her arms around Jackson's waist and huddled against his back, letting him be her bulwark against all of it for a few minutes. His muscular contours felt solid, real, safe. For just a minute, she lost herself in him. She let him be the only real thing in her universe, which had otherwise been knocked completely off its axis.

His next words came to her as if spoken across a long distance. "I've got you, Ana. Everything's going to be all right. I promise."

If only.

Chapter 4

Ana tried to relax as Jackson wasted no time whisking her across all six blocks of downtown Serendipity, but she failed. Had her mugger returned to the motel and trashed her room after the fact? Why go to all that trouble and then not take anything? Sure, she didn't have much, but there'd still been a television and a few personal items the intruder could have stolen.

Jackson guided the Harley north along the coast for a few gloriously beautiful miles. Even the magnificent view of the ocean under the emerging stars couldn't soothe her jangling nerves. Normally she could sit and stare at the waves for hours on end.

The bike slowed and turned off the Coast Highway into a gated drive. Jackson stopped to punch in a security code on a number pad, and the automatic gate slid back to reveal possibly the most gorgeous house she'd ever seen. It was huge and stately. Elegant. Venerable.

"Whoa. You live here?" she asked over the rumble of his bike rolling up the drive.

"It's my grandmother's place. She's lived here since the seventies. I renovated it for her and built on an addition after my first big movie. She had a health scare last year and I moved back in to look after her. I stay here when I'm not on location."

"Talk about a sweet crash pad," she muttered.

He grinned over his shoulder at her as he climbed off the bike in the circular drive in front of the stately double doors. "First time here, you get the grand entrance."

"Please don't fuss over me. It makes me uncomfortable."

The front doors opened and a woman fully as elegant at the house stepped onto the broad porch. "Who've we got here, Jackson?" She sounded surprised. Did he not bring women here often, then?

Ana was startled when he looped his arm over her shoulder to lead her forward. "Ana, this is my grandmother, Minerva Prescott. Gran, this is Ana Izzolo. She's going to be working on the film with me."

Going to? No "maybe" or "probably"? No "after we check out her screen test we might make her an offer"? No explanation to his grandmother that her room had been vandalized and that was the only reason she was here?

Stunned, she barely heard Jackson's grandmother say, "I'm so pleased to meet you, dear." The woman held slender hands out and grasped Ana's hand warmly. "Do come in. It will be lovely to have company. Welcome."

Minerva glanced over at Jackson. "Is this the young lady you were so anxious to go have dinner with?"

Anxious, huh? Jackson's mouth tightened in visible

chagrin, and Ana's mouth twitched in answering amusement. Family had a way of stripping your dignity at the most inconvenient moment.

"Ana was mugged and her place was broken into before she could meet me at the restaurant. She could use some basic toiletries and maybe some clean clothes until she has a chance to go shopping. I'd like her to stay here a few days while we sort out what happened."

His grandmother exclaimed in alarm, "Goodness! Of course, we'll take care of her. Don't you worry about a thing, dear." Her expression lightened and she clapped her hands together. "Actually, it's perfect! It'll give us a chance to get to know each other."

What a warmhearted woman. Her kindness was really infectious. Perhaps this was where Jackson got some of his famous charm. Minerva never let go of her hand as she drew Ana into a front hallway filled with beautiful woodwork—elaborate crown moldings, dark wood door frames, and the stairs— *Oh, my.* The staircases, there were two of them, each had to be twelve feet wide and swept upward in arcs, starting on each side of the foyer, to meet in the middle at the top.

"Wow," Ana breathed. "I'm feeling a little underdressed."

Minerva laughed gaily. "Never fear. We dress casually here at the beach. You're about my size. I'm sure we can find something that will fit you."

Except, of course, that Minerva was a foot taller than she was. Well, half a foot. She was five foot two, and Jackson's grandmother looked at least five foot eight.

Minerva continued gaily, "I run around in a bathing suit and flip-flops half the time."

She had a hard time envisioning the elegant woman

in anything other than a designer dress as tailored and classy as the one she was wearing now.

"Jackson, why don't you show Ana around while I speak with Rosie about making you two something to eat. You both must be hungry after such a stressful day. And you never did get your dinner together, did you?"

"Her solution to every crisis in life is food," Jackson muttered as his grandmother floated gracefully down the central hallway, tsking, to disappear somewhere in the back of the sprawling home.

"Is one the up staircase and the other the down staircase?" Ana asked under her breath.

"Nah. You can go up or down either one. Although, I can say from experience that the left bannister is faster to slide down than the right one."

"You slid on the bannisters as a kid?"

"Still do from time to time. But don't tell Gran. She'd yell at me."

Ana grinned as he led her off the main foyer into a living room with English manor–style cove ceilings and mahogany wainscoting to die for. "This place is stunning, Jackson."

"Pain in the butt to keep up, though. I keep asking Gran to let me sell it, but she refuses. Says we'll have to pry her cold, dead body out of here before she'll go."

"I'm with her. This place is a treasure. Has it been in your family a long time?"

He led her back across the foyer to another set of double doors, which opened to reveal a library. She gasped with pleasure since she'd always loved books. This room was lined, floor to ceiling, with volumes.

"My grandfather was a movie producer. He bought this place for her as a wedding present. It was decrepit, and they restored it to a livable state. It was built in the 1920s by a silent movie star as a getaway back when this stretch of coast was pretty much deserted."

"What happened to him?" she asked.

"He died when my mother was ten. Lung cancer. He was a chain smoker most of his life."

He led her upstairs, and a spacious sitting room stretched toward the back of the house and the ocean beyond. "Gran's rooms are to the left. I'm in the new wing, this way. Let's find you a bedroom."

She could hardly fathom the idea of having to choose between multiple bedrooms. Her upbringing had been modest at best, and rocky during bad times. *Rocky* also described her parents' marriage accurately. She wouldn't go so far as to say she'd had a happy upbringing. It wasn't like she'd been abused or neglected. But love hadn't been particularly abundant. It had been…safe. Adequate.

Jackson stopped in front of a door and chuckled quietly to himself. "In here," he directed her.

The room he led her into was spacious and bright, with huge picture windows looking out over the ocean. The furniture was pickled pine, the fabrics creams and yellows. The view drew her to it and she stared down in awe at the majesty of the ocean and rocky cliffs below. "I can't see a single house from here."

Jackson spoke quietly beside her. "I own the land all the way to that point on the right. I bought all the neighboring properties as they went up for sale and knocked the houses down. Restored the coastal habitat."

Wow. Such wealth was unimaginable to her. First this palatial layout, and now his own movie production company. She was just hoping to get steady work, enough to pay off her student loans and maybe make a modest living in the industry someday, not end up richer than Croesus.

More intimidated than she cared to admit, she asked him, "Is there somewhere I can wash up? And if it's not too big an imposition, can I borrow a clean T-shirt or something? This sweater's pretty trashed after I rolled around on the ground in it."

He looked down at her chest and his pupils dilated noticeably. Alarmed, she glanced down. The sweater was more shredded than she'd realized and her beige camisole, now gray with dust, peeked through in multiple locations.

"Uh, sure. I'll go get some clothes for you." He spun away sharply as if it had just dawned on him he was both staring at and talking to her chest.

Huh. So Jackson had embraced the fact that she was a girl and not just a fight buddy, had he? A foreboding washed through her that his seeing her as a woman would open some doors between them that she didn't know how to handle.

So what if he noticed she was a girl? He was her boss, for crying out loud.

"Bathroom's in here. Towels are in that cabinet."

She stepped into a Victorian bathroom and sighed in delight at the gigantic claw-foot tub sitting in front of the window. Surf crashed into the rocks below, the foam white against the blackness of rocks and sea and night.

"It's one-way glass so no one can see in here from the veranda," he informed her. "If you want to jump in the tub, I'll go get some clean clothes for you."

"Deal."

He hesitated in the doorway and she looked up at him questioningly.

He said low, "I'm glad you're okay, Ana."

"Me, too. Thanks for rescuing me."

"I didn't—"

She cut him off. "Yes. You did. And we both know it."

His gaze skittered away as if he was embarrassed.

She took pity on him and declared, "Scram. I want to go for a swim in that gigantic tub."

"Right." He spun away fast, but not so fast that she didn't spot the stain of color on his cheeks. Jackson Prescott was capable of blushing? Would wonders never cease?

She poked around the bathroom as the tub filled, and found a new toothbrush still in its wrapper, a hair brush, shampoo and conditioner, and even some simple cosmetics. Wow. Talk about the hostess who thought of everything. Minerva must have brought this stuff in here while Jackson had showed her the rest of the house.

Ana lit the half dozen pillar candles clustered beside the tub, poured some of the bath salts she found into the steaming hot water and sighed in pleasure as she stepped into the tub. She sank up to her armpits in the hot embrace and luxuriated in melting bliss. It was wild to think about how, three hours ago, she had been praying for her life, and here she was now, surrounded by this sartorial splendor. The mental whiplash was a little much to take in.

She refreshed the bath with hot water several times and just couldn't seem to drag herself out of this perfect interlude. The rhythmic pounding of waves rolling ashore lulled her into the best semicoma ever. How long she sat there just soaking, she had no idea.

The bathroom door burst open.

She plunged to her neck in the water and it sloshed over the side of the tub. "Jackson!"

"Crap! Sorry. Thought you already went downstairs. Clothes. I've, um, got some. They're Gran's, but she said they would fit you. Sorry. I'll just put them on your bed...."

"Get out, Jackson," she said firmly enough to cut across his babbling.

"Right. Out." But his gaze had riveted on the damned tub. And as tall as he was, he no doubt had a great view of her naked body. Which abruptly felt on fire from pretty much her neck to her toes.

"Go. Now," she ordered him.

"Sorry. Gone." Finally, he tore his gaze away from her and spun. He all but ran out of the bathroom and looked so silly doing it she had to laugh. Guy acted like he'd never seen a naked female before. Who'd have thought a hunk like him would be so self-conscious around women? She wouldn't have guessed it in a million years.

The tranquility of her bath destroyed, she rinsed the last of the soap out of her hair with the detachable showerhead thingie. She stood up to dry off and it felt decadent to stand naked before that huge window with all of nature's glory right outside.

She glanced down onto the broad stone veranda below and started. Jackson was staring up at her, transfixed. The glass was one-way, *wasn't it?* If he'd lied about that, she was going to kill him!

Wrapping a towel around herself fast, she backed away from the window and dried off hastily. Using the blow-dryer she found in the big armoire where the towels and shampoo had been, she dried her hair into its usual shoulder-length frame of her face.

She actually dug into the makeup Minerva had put in the medicine cabinet and applied mascara, blush and lip gloss. Only time she usually wore the stuff was when she had a date, which happened exactly never. Tonight, though, it gave her the confidence boost she needed to go downstairs and face Jackson after he'd accidentally invaded her bath. That *had* been an accident, hadn't it?

Naked, she moved out into the bedroom and smiled at the simple navy knit dress laid out on the bed. Its lines were high-end designer all the way. The lingerie lying beside it made her simultaneously blush and sigh with pleasure. Jackson's grandmother wore silk thongs and see-through lace bras? *Go, granny!*

She'd secretly wished to own stuff like that over the years, but a combination of no one to wear it for and scraping by so she could pay her college tuition meant she'd never indulged the fantasy.

The sexy lingerie was a decent fit. She was more endowed up top than Minerva, which meant her bra cups ranneth over in a rather spectacular display of cleavage. But it was better than crawling back into her dirty, smelly camisole.

She pulled the casual knit dress over her head and the kitten-soft fabric caressed her body like a whisper. It was snug to the hips and then flared into swirls around her legs. The overall effect was to accentuate her curves until she looked like some kind of sexy vamp.

She stared at herself in the mirror. Who knew she could look so good in the right cut of clothing? Jackson's eyeballs were going to fall out his head when he got a load of this plunging neckline and bulging boobage. A sneaking suspicion that Minerva had laid out this dress for that exact reason crept into her mind. So. Granny was machinating to throw the two of them together, huh? Fascinating. Jackson wasn't lying when he'd said his grandmother was pushing him to settle down and start a family.

She wished the woman luck but held out no real hope of Minerva succeeding. After all, Jackson had been a superstar for nearly five years and could have had pretty much any woman on the planet in that time. But he'd never shown the slightest inclination to get married. There was no reason to think things would change at this late date.

Still, she gave the neckline one last downward tug before heading downstairs. Next to the library was a music room with a grand piano dominating the space. On a shelf behind it, she spotted…

Oh, my God. Is that an Oscar? She moved into the room and stopped before the famous statue on the mantle over a huge fireplace.

"I won that for being a coproducer on a documentary last year. I'd like to win another one with the new production company," a male voice said from behind her.

She whipped around to face Jackson, the skirt swirling around her hips.

His eyes went wide as he stared at her. "Ana, what happened to you?"

Alarm slammed through her. She reached for her hair, her face. "What? What's wrong?" She hadn't seen any major bruising when she'd checked herself in the mirror before she came downstairs. Most of her scrapes and scratches were on her arms and hands. Amazing really, considering what she'd been through.

"You've got—" He broke off. "You're—"

Her alarm escalated to panic. "What the hell's wrong, Jackson? I've got what?"

"Uh. Breasts."

She stared back at him. "I know. But what's wrong?"

"Nothing," he mumbled. "You just look…"

She strode over to him and stared up at him. "You're scaring me. Tell me what's going on, right now."

"Jesus, Ana. Nothing's wrong. You just look like…a… a woman. A hot one. With great…well…cleavage. That dress… You in it… Christ…" he mumbled.

Oh. She stood down from threat mode, letting out the breath she'd been holding. He'd scared the hell out her for a minute there. A little irked, she said, "I've been a woman all day, you know."

"Well, yeah. But you weren't wearing stuff like that when we were fighting."

"The operative word being *fighting,*" she retorted. "Kinda hard to do that in heels and a French manicure."

He cleared his throat and finally managed to tear his gaze away from her chest. She owed Minerva a big thanks later. At least the guy had finally figured out she was not only a girl, but a marginally attractive one. For him, that was apparently a big breakthrough.

"How about that tour of the rest of the house now?" she asked.

"Uh, yeah. Sure."

He guided her through the mansion. It was a fairly simple layout, actually. A series of spacious rooms opened off the original central hall that ran from front to back. She gathered a kitchen was beyond the dining room he showed her and servant quarters were off in another direction. The entire back of the house was new and boasted big picture windows looking out on the ocean. The blend of old and modern was seamless and comfortable.

"There's Gran on the veranda. Looks like Rosie's got dinner ready."

"Rosie?"

"Gran's housekeeper, cook, companion and second-in-command around here. Be warned, she runs a tight ship. Don't cross her."

A tiny, gray-haired woman stepped into the family room just then. "Jackson Prescott. What lies are you telling your lady friend about me?"

"Rosie, this is Ana. And this is the infamous Rosie McKay."

Wow. She was used to being the shortest person in a room, but Rosie barely reached her nose. The woman must not top four foot ten. But her eyes sparkled brighter than a sparrow's and she looked ready to take on the world.

"Don't listen to a thing that boy says about me," Rosie declared. "Lies. All of it."

Ana grinned. "I won't listen to what he says about you if you won't listen to what he says about me."

"Agreed. Now head on outside. Supper's served, and don't you dare let my famous fried chicken get cold."

She shooed them out through the French doors. Ana sank into the wrought-iron chair Jackson held for her, acutely aware that from his vantage point he was getting a great look down the front of her dress. She hoped he liked what he saw.

The moon rose as they dug into the platter of chicken and fruit salad. The simple meal settled her stomach and made her feel better. There was just something comforting about home cooking. There hadn't been a lot of it in her house growing up. She'd mostly fended for herself by the time she was in school full days.

A chill crept into the air, and Ana was chagrined to feel her nipples puckering beneath the thin fabric of the dress and the thinner lace of the bra. God, did she have to go and starting nipping now?

Darned if Jackson hadn't noticed it, too. He took in the view unabashedly, and darned if Minerva didn't take in him taking it in, as well. Ana couldn't be sure, but she thought she caught a hint of a smirk in the older woman's expression. *Schemer.*

"So, dear. Do you feel like talking about today or would you rather not?"

She shrugged at Minerva. "There's not much to tell. I walked out to my car to meet Jackson for dinner and some guy jumped me from behind. I didn't see his face. I fought and screamed, but he hit me in the side of the head and apparently knocked me out. Someone called the police and... I was lucky. Then Jackson came and rescued me from all those medical people and their needles in the emergency room."

"I did not—"

She threw him a withering look. "We've already been over this. You rescued me. I'm grateful, and you can just get over it."

Minerva chuckled in delight. "Oh, I like her, Jackson."

He rolled his eyes.

"Stay here as long as you'd like, dear. It's entirely too much house for one person to rattle around in."

"What about me?" Jackson complained.

"You're always haring off to who knows where, and when you're home you practically live over at that studio of yours. You're gone more than you're here."

Ana grinned. Salty, the woman was. She officially liked Minerva back. They finished the meal with Jackson glaring at his grandmother, Minerva smiling smugly and Ana privately enjoying his discomfort. He struck her as the type who was used to always being in control, always in charge, always self-contained. It was refreshing to know he was a real man with real feelings and not some kind of robot under all that movie-star perfection.

Rosie came out to clear the dishes and Jackson jumped up to help her. He hauled in the heavy stuff while Minerva topped off Ana's water and refilled her own wineglass.

As Jackson disappeared inside the house, Minerva asked, "How long have you and Jackson been together?"

"Uh, we're not together. We just met today at an audition."

Minerva looked visibly startled. Not his style to bring home his casual conquests, huh? Ana added by way of explanation, and in defense of her own morals, "I don't think he even noticed that I'm a girl until he saw me in this awesome dress."

"Oh, I noticed," Jackson groused from the doorway. "Just because I was too professional to make a pass at you when I was lying on top of you in your audition doesn't mean I didn't notice."

Ana gulped as Minerva smiled archly. "She does wear that dress rather well, doesn't she?"

"Yes. She does." Jackson's voice was low and deep. Sexy. Slid across her skin like velvet. "Would you like to see the beach, Ana?"

"There's a beach around here?"

"I blasted one out of the rocks a while back." He

moved over beside her chair and held a hand down to her. "Let me show you."

He held out his hand to help her to her feet. She laid her palm in his and started at the heat of him. It permeated her flesh and drew her to him like a moth to a flame.

"Have fun, you two," Minerva said behind them, her words floating away on the muted roar of the ocean.

"Interfering busybody," Jackson muttered as he led her to a wooden staircase.

"She means well."

"She just loves to meddle."

"She loves you."

Jackson snorted, but Ana would bet he knew she was right. Narrow steps wound down the cliff steeply. To a normal person, the descent would probably be a little alarming. But after her stunt classes, it was kind of fun to navigate.

They got to the bottom and stepped onto a tiny, secluded beach surrounded on three sides by towering cliffs and on the fourth by the ocean. White sand the consistency of sugar buried her toes. The whole beach probably wasn't more than fifty feet wide and maybe half that deep.

"It's perfect," she breathed.

Jackson looked over at her in the moonlight. "Yup. Perfect."

She got the feeling he wasn't talking about the beach. She spoke over the ocean soundtrack. "Your grandmother seemed to think we were a couple. Do you need me to pretend that we are for a while to get her off your back?"

"You'd do that for me?" he blurted.

"Why not? She's a lovely woman and it would make

her happy. I'd love to repay her in some way for her hospitality."

Jackson frowned doubtfully. "You don't know her. This could backfire on both of us."

"How?"

"No idea. But I know my grandmother. If there's a way to make a fake girlfriend bite me in the butt, she'll find it."

Ana grinned. "It's a good thing I'm not going to take that remark out of context, Mr. Prescott."

Jackson laughed and snagged her around the waist, pulling her up against his delicious body laughingly. She tensed against him, and he turned her loose instantaneously.

He spun away, shoving a hand through his hair. "God, I'm sorry," he mumbled over his shoulder. "You were just attacked. Of course you wouldn't want some guy to grab you...."

"It's not that," she responded quickly. It was just that he was so darned gorgeous. So out of her league. So...perfect. And she was so...not. How to put that into words that wouldn't make her sound like a total dork? She opened her mouth, mumbled incoherently and shut it again.

"What can I do to help?" he asked, steamrolling right over her attempt at an explanation. "Anything. Just tell me what to do. I want to help."

"I'm fine," she insisted.

"No, you're not. You freaked out when I touched you."

It wasn't quite that dramatic, but he didn't seem interested in listening to her protests. If she were more of a shark, she would play on his sympathy and get him to woo her romantically. But lies weren't her style. "I swear,

Jackson, I'm okay. Go ahead. Put your arms around me again and let me prove it to you."

Very carefully, he stepped close to her.

"How tall are you?" she muttered, craning her head back to stare up at him in the dark.

"Six foot three."

"Isn't that huge for a movie star?"

He shrugged and rested his hands cautiously on her waist. "I guess it's tall. I never have to worry about my female leads being taller than me."

She smiled a little and reciprocated by putting her hands on his waist. "See? I'm fine."

"So it wouldn't bother you if I moved one of my hands up your back like this?" he murmured.

"Uh, no." Shivers were spreading outward from the slow glide of his fingers, threatening to shatter her into a million pieces. But other than that, everything was hunky-dory.

"Can I cup the back of your neck like this? Your hair feels like warm silk on the back of my hand."

"Yeah. Sure. That's, um, great."

"Do you mind me moving a little closer to you?"

A *little* closer? His clothes brushed against her dress from her shoulders to her knees. Something akin to a magnetic field emanated from him and enshrouded her, energizing her from head to toe. Dang. What was that? Charisma? Raw, animal sex appeal? Whatever it was, she could see why he had become a movie star.

He stared down at her, his eyes black pools in the shadows of his face. Even wreathed in darkness like this, he was beautiful. It just wasn't fair. His mouth was less than a foot from hers, and she could taste the fine wine on his breath. She hadn't been able to drink any of it because of the painkillers she'd been given, but she savored the hint of it, anyway.

The—whatever it was—zinging between them built until she thought she was going to explode. His eyes actually glowed a little as he stared down at her.

"Say something," she whispered. "You're making me nervous." Not nervous in the way he was going to think she meant, but what he didn't know wouldn't hurt him.

"My grandmother likes you."

"I like her, too. I'll bet you I could convince her we're dating."

He exhaled a gust of silent laugher. "You could convince me without too much trouble."

Ana blinked up at him in shock. Her? Him? Her and a movie star?

"Talk to me, Ana."

Her mind was completely blank. The notion of the two of them as a couple knocked words completely out of her brain.

She blurted the first thing that came to mind. "Kiss me."

Oh, no. Where on earth had *that* come from?

His head bent down toward hers. "If you're sure, I won't say no." He was actually going to kiss her!

Her stomach leaped and twisted while she tried to think of something clever and casual to say back to him that wouldn't make her sound like a moron.

His mouth touched hers very lightly. It wasn't tentative in the least, merely very tightly controlled. Careful. Intentionally gentle. Ana shocked herself by surging up into him like one of the waves pounding the rocks behind her. His lips were as hot as the rest of him, scorching her mouth as they moved restlessly, obviously interested in deepening the kiss, but unwilling to do more.

She opened her mouth hungrily, and when he didn't act on the invitation, she caught his lower lip between her teeth and bit down on it enough to get his attention.

"Well, then," he breathed. And then his tongue plunged carnally past her lips. She met his tongue with her own, and they swirled together, wet and hungry.

Her arms looped around his neck, and one of his hands simultaneously slid down her back to the indent of her waist. He dragged her up against him until her toes barely touched the sand. Another kind of heat pressed against her belly, hard and demanding through the zipper of his jeans. He turned to the side, taking her with him, and pressed her back against a wall of cold, hard rock. "You okay?" he asked roughly.

Her entire body strained toward him, toward the fire of his hard body surrounding her. Oh, yes. She was more than okay. Her hands slid down his chest, down to his waist. Tugged at his shirt. *Ahh, skin.* Her palms flattened against his ribs, sliding around to the slabs of muscle that defined his back. The same muscles that had surrounded her in safety earlier.

He tasted of the wine he'd sipped at the end of the meal, sharp and heady and masculine. His mouth lifted away from hers, then kissed its way across her cheekbone. Across her jaw, her neck. Her shoulder. And then his kisses trailed across her collarbone toward the low neckline of her dress. He nipped at the higher curves of her breasts. And heaven help her, she ran her hands into his hair and pulled his head down to her breasts more tightly.

"I wanted to do this all the way through dinner," he muttered.

"And I wanted you to do it."

"The way your nipples puckered up made me crazy...." His teeth closed on one of the offending body parts through her dress, and she gasped at the pinch, her breast arching up into his mouth hungrily.

His hand closed on her rear end, pulling her hips up against his erection snugly. She didn't recognize the wanton woman she'd turned into all of a sudden. Her right leg wrapped around his hips and he ground his hard-on lightly against her core through that thin little thong that did nothing to dull the delicious sensations exploding through her.

"What are you doing to me?" she gasped under the roar of the surf.

He made an incoherent sound in the back of his throat that managed to convey both laughter and possessiveness. Apparently, whatever it was, she was doing the same thing to him, too.

"You'd better tell me to stop right now, Ana. Or this is going to turn into something more pretty damned fast."

"Don't stop, Jackson."

Chapter 5

But, to Ana's vast chagrin, he did stop. He pressed his forehead against hers, and she was gratified to feel his chest rising and falling heavily.

"I was afraid you'd say that," he groaned.

She pulled back from him, staring hard. "Why does that make you afraid?" she demanded.

"Because it means I've got to be strong for both of us." Slowly and deliberately, he took a tiny step back from her. Unwrapped her foot from around his waist and set it down in the cold sand. Grasped her wrists and unwound her hungry fingers from around his neck.

Disappointment—and embarrassment, dammit—rolled through her. "You don't want me?" she asked in a small voice.

"Ana, I want you so bad I can barely stand up. But you've had a hell of a day, and I'm not a big enough schmuck to take advantage of you in your vulnerable emotional state."

"I'm not in a vulnerable emotional state!" she exclaimed.

"Yes, you are. You're just in too much shock to realize it. But you would never throw yourself at me like this if you were yourself. It's okay. I'm not angry. I get that you could have died today, and you've decided you owe me for rescuing you in part."

She stared at him, aghast. Is *that* why he thought she'd thrown herself at him? "Is that the only reason you kissed me? Because you thought I was needy?"

"Well, uh, no—"

"You son of a bitch! Don't you ever pity kiss me again. You understand? Never. I don't need anyone's pity, and I certainly don't need yours!" She whirled away from him and stormed up the stairs. About halfway up, she ran out of breath, and she had to huff hard to keep her quick pace all the way to the top.

Those were not tears in her eyes, and even if they were, it was only the salt spray and the night breeze making her eyes water. She rushed into the house and headed straight for her bedroom. Out of respect for her hostess, she didn't slam the door behind her, but boy, did she ever want to.

She flopped across the bed and burst out in tears into her pillow. She sobbed for about five minutes, until it occurred to her that she was actually throwing a hissy fit.

Weird. She never did hissy fits. It wasn't that she had a thing against them. Lord knew she wanted to cry and scream and indulge in drama sometimes. She'd just learned over the years that they didn't accomplish anything. Life was hard enough without giving herself a runny nose and red eyes on top of everything else.

But she'd truly had a close call with danger today—three close calls if she counted whoever had shredded her clothes at the studio. Her first impulse was to tell Jackson about the petty vandalism, but it was undoubtedly just one of the jealous Barbies getting even with Ana for getting to audition with Jackson, not to mention she didn't want to come off as a whiner to him.

Her mugger hadn't taken her purse with her wallet in it, so she had access to her financial resources, as meager as they were. With the pittance in her bank account, she needed to replace everything that had been destroyed in the motel room. Unfortunately, Serendipity didn't strike her as the kind of place that would have a thrift store. She sighed at the prospect of emptying her bank account over toothbrushes and cheap granny panties. It just wasn't fair. Maybe she could call the bank and skip a student-loan payment....

The cost of all the things that had to be replaced threatened to overwhelm her. Tomorrow. She'd deal with it tomorrow. She would make a bunch of lists, prioritize them and then purchase what she could afford. Nice and orderly, one step at a time. And eventually, her life would come back under control. Jackson Prescott would move on with his movie and go back to ignoring her, and she would get on with her life. Alone.

Jackson was never going to get to sleep. He couldn't for the life of him get the feel of Ana's curvaceous body nor the sweet-tart cherry taste of her mouth out of his head. It didn't help that she was in bed not twenty feet away from him, just on the other side of the door adjoining their two rooms. He'd figured giving Ana that room would cause Minerva no end of delighted speculation about who this girl was to him. But now, he was having serious second thoughts about his decision.

Even the easy rhythm of the ocean outside failed to lull him to sleep tonight. Hell, it always knocked him out. It was part of why he'd moved up here, away from the hustle and bustle of L.A. He couldn't get enough of the sound and smell of the ocean.

A cry from Ana's room brought him bolt upright and out of bed in a single bound. He tore through the door, ready and willing to kill whoever was hurting her.

Her bed, a four-poster affair with a wrought-iron frame supported by the pickled-pine bedposts and white gauze draped romantically over it, was wreathed in shadows. Another cry came from the bed. *Ana. In distress.*

He moved over to the bed silently, on the balls of his feet, hands outstretched. His brothers were the trained killers in the family, but he'd learned a thing or two shooting fight scenes in movies, and he was big and strong. He'd break the bastard—

"Nooo…" Ana moaned. "Lemme go…" Her head tossed back and forth on the pillow like she was struggling to escape an invisible attacker. She was alone in the bed. He released the breath he'd been holding.

"Ana," he said gently. "Wake up."

"Nooooo…" Her entire body got into the act, thrashing back and forth, tossing off blankets and sheets like they were ropes tying her down. Well, hell. He put a knee on the edge of her bed and leaned over to touch her shoulder. "Wake up, Ana. You're having a nightmare."

Her fist flew up at him from the tangle of sheets. He threw a hand up and barely managed to catch her wrist before she clocked him in his already swollen nose. Damn, she was fast.

And apparently, she didn't appreciate having her arm restrained. She struggled wildly, one of her knees grazing his groin, and her other fist swinging up at him. Out of hands he could use to keep her from killing him, he resorted to stretching out half on top of her to hold her down…and remove his crotch as a target for her flailing limbs.

"Ana," he grunted. "Wake. Up."

She lurched up against him hard, her breasts smashing against his chest. Jeez, she felt so sexual writhing against him like this it was damned near impossible to keep his mind on waking her from her nightmare.

"Get off me—" she shouted. "Oh." She subsided beneath him as quickly as she'd erupted before. "Jackson?" she mumbled groggily. "What on earth are you doing here?"

"I was trying to wake you from a nightmare."

"Then why are you on top of me?"

"You tried to hit me. I was trying to defend myself without hurting you," he ground out. He was vividly aware of her body beneath his, molding to him sensuously and cupping him in all the right spots.

"Um, Jackson? What are you wearing?"

Shock blasted across his brain. He mumbled in massive chagrin, "Uh, that would be nothing." And furthermore, she was wearing a T-shirt and not much more if the miles of sleek legs entwined with his were any indication.

"Well, okay, then," she breathed.

She sounded intrigued by his nudity. If he stood up right now, he was going to display just how turned on he was by their little wrestling match, and embarrass them both quite a bit more than they already were.

He cleared his throat uncomfortably. "What were you dreaming about?"

"Nothing," she mumbled evasively.

And truth be told, it really wasn't any of his business. He was just worried about her after her day from hell. He rolled off her and propped himself up on one elbow beside her. But he kept an arm and his knee thrown lightly across her to hide his…reaction…to her.

"How are you really doing, Ana?" he asked quietly.

She sighed. "I don't know. I can't figure out who would mug me and trash my room like that. And there was this little thing at your studio…" Her voice trailed off uncertainly.

"What thing?" he asked in a deep, soothing voice.

"It's probably nothing."

"If it's giving you nightmares, it's not nothing. Tell me about it."

"After my audition with you, I went to the locker room to clean up and someone had trashed my clothes."

"Like thrown them around?"

"No. Like sliced them to ribbons."

"Any idea who did it?"

She shook her head in the negative, her silky hair rubbing against his cheek. It smelled like vanilla. "I wouldn't want to make any unfair accusations. But one of the blondes was mad that I got to audition with you and was pretty bitchy about it afterward."

He asked soberly, "Would you recognize her if you saw her again? We've got head shots of everyone who auditioned."

"It might not even be that girl. It could have been anyone."

"Not on my crew. Adrian and I have handpicked all the key personnel."

"It was probably meant as a joke."

He reached up with his free hand to push her hair off her face. "I'll take care of it. Don't you worry about it." Of course, finding and firing whoever had cut up her clothes might have nothing to do with whoever had jumped her at the motel. He would find that bastard, too. And he would do considerably worse to that guy than getting him fired from his job.

"Don't fire anyone on my account," she declared in alarm. "But it's nice of you to offer."

"Neither Adrian nor I will tolerate stuff like that on our set. It's a done deal."

She sighed. He couldn't tell if it was in relief or exasperation. He went with relief. Silence fell between them. Did someone really have it in for her? Whoever had trashed her motel room had been seriously pissed off. Pissed off enough to try again? She'd already claimed to have no enemies that she knew of. Who, then?

He realized with a start that his free hand was absently stroking her hair. "Think you can go back to sleep now?" he asked.

"Yes."

"Okay, then. Sweet dreams."

He rolled out of bed and strode from her room quickly, his rear end burning with embarrassment as he flashed it at her in all its naked glory. Please God, let her not be looking at it. Or if she was, please let her like what she saw.

Chapter 6

When morning came and Ana woke, she stretched deliciously. There was a reason she felt so wonderful this morning—

Oh. Right. Jackson had come into her room, *naked,* to wake her up from a nightmare. *Aye Chihuahua.* He'd even been gentlemanly enough to stick around and talk her down off the emotional ledge of her dream after she'd woken up.

Not that he had to coax the topic of the nightmare out of her subconscious. She remembered it perfectly well. It was the same nightmare that had haunted her for two years. A toxic combination of terror and hatred surged in her gut, and she took a huge breath, held it for a count of five and let it out slowly.

Exhale the fear. Release the anger. It's over. Past. Holding on to old emotions does no good in the pres-

ent. She went through the well-worn litany by rote. She might have consciously conquered the trauma, but her subconscious stubbornly refused to get with the program.

Crap. She had a ton of stuff to do today. She didn't need to be paralyzed by flashbacks all darned day. She threw back the covers and jumped out of bed energetically. The air was cool, and the morning sun shone brilliantly off the calm ocean outside. Lord, she could wake up to that sight every day for the rest of her life. No wonder Minerva refused to sell the place.

She headed for the restroom and was not surprised to spy another pile of clothes folded and waiting on the edge of the bathtub. Her hostess did not miss a trick.

This time Minerva had left her a strapless sundress with a smocked top that hugged the curves of her breasts, possibly more revealingly than the dress from the night before. She was going to wear two dresses in under twenty-four hours? Yup, the world had officially come to an end.

Ana pulled on the sundress and had to admit it looked great on her. The bright cobalt-blue background of the tropical print picked up the color of her eyes, making them look even bigger and bluer than usual. They were her best feature. Those and her cheekbones. She did like her nose, too, but as she got older, its general cuteness and pertness were starting to get on her nerves.

She was twenty-five years old, but she still routinely got carded at bars as if she wasn't even twenty-flipping-one. In another dozen years, she probably wouldn't mind being taken for younger than she was. But right now, it sucked.

Jackson was nowhere to be seen as she wandered

through the mansion and into the kitchen. Rosie was there, though, kneading a big ball of dough.

"May I help?" she asked.

"Not unless you've got a mighty pile of emotion to work out of you," Rosie replied.

If Ana wasn't mistaken, that was just a hint of an Irish brogue in the woman's voice. "I've got enough stored up for that dough," she retorted.

"Sit. Tell me what makes you emotional on a pretty day like this."

"In a word, *Jackson*."

"Ah, well. There's not enough bread dough in California to deal with that boy."

"Have you known him a long time?"

"I used to chase him out of my kitchen with a rolling pin when he stole cookies as a boy. I've been with Miss Minerva for going on thirty years."

"What was he like as a kid?" Ana asked as she perched on a bar stool by the counter and commenced snacking on the bowl of red grapes in front of her.

"About what you'd expect. All boy. But a good heart. Excellent student. Star athlete. Never gave his grandmother a minute's trouble."

Ana frowned. "Minerva raised him, then?"

"Aye, she raised all her grandkids. Linda, his ma, wanted to be an actress bad. Chased her dream until it killed her."

Ana stared, shocked.

"She got mixed up with the wrong crowd. Got into partying. Drugs. She OD'd when Jackie was fourteen. Took it hard when she died, he did. I always thought he became an actor to give her dream a happy ending."

"Did he move in with Minerva, after his mother died?"

"All the kids had been living here on and off for years already. Linda never was very good at organizing a house with five little ones in it. Her husband died when the twins were babies, so that would have made Jackie about four. Didn't change his life that much when his da died. But when he lost his ma, that hurt his heart bad. You could see it in his eyes. He grew up all at once when she passed."

"How did his father die?"

Rosie shrugged. "Soldier. Killed in action overseas and widowed Linda with all those babies. That's when she got it in her head she'd become a movie star."

"How many kids are there? And where does Jackson fall in the bunch?"

"He's the middle child. Has two older brothers and two younger sisters who are twins."

Wow. She'd had no idea....

"What lies is Rosie telling you about me?" Jackson asked from a doorway he proceeded to barge through. Ana glimpsed a garage over his shoulder. "Here are the groceries you asked for, Rosie." He set several plastic grocery bags down on the counter.

"Thanks, Jackie. I've laid out coffee and bagels from Wollenberg's in the breakfast room. Take your young lady in there and feed her for me, will you?"

"You haven't eaten?" he asked her.

"I had some grapes. I'll be fine."

"Not in this house, you won't. They live for food around here. Why do you think I have to work out so much?"

Gee. She'd thought he was just staying in shape to do his job. She pursed her lips and followed him to this alleged breakfast room. It turned out to be a sunny, hexagonal nook in the corner tower. Window boxes full of bright flowers under each window lent even more cheer to the space.

As soon as they were alone in the cozy room, he turned to face her. "Are you all right?"

"Yes. Fine," she answered automatically.

"Seriously. Are you okay?"

She turned away, mumbling, "I don't usually have nightmares like that. One-time anomaly…"

A big hand landed lightly on her shoulder. "Hey. You were authorized to have nightmares after the day you had yesterday."

"Just so you know, I don't do girly emotional outbursts as a rule."

He stepped so close behind her she could feel the heat radiating off his big body and said, low and sexy, "In case you forgot, I can handle occasional outbursts. I work with actresses for a living, remember?"

And apparently, she was about to be one of those actresses. Although frankly she was in total denial about landing the lead role in his next film.

Blessedly, he changed the subject and commented, "You might as well eat. Minerva and Rosie will bedevil you until you do."

She took a cinnamon-raisin bagel and commenced nibbling at it pensively. Jackson remained standing, staring out at the ocean, arms crossed. He looked lonely. It was probably just learning about his past that made her think such things.

"I'm sorry about the beach last night," he said solemnly, his back turned to her. "And, the, um, naked thing. It won't happen again."

Seriously? He was going to go all noble and formal on

her after he'd had his tongue down her throat and practically had hot sex with her? She responded tartly, "And why won't it happen again?"

He whipped around to stare at her. "I beg your pardon?"

"You heard me. Why won't it happen again?"

"Because…because…we work together. I'm your boss, for crying out loud."

Dammit. He was right. He was off-limits. Not to mention he was also completely out of her league. Heck, they didn't even play the same sport. He was a glamorous, sexy movie star with all the polish and packaging of a megastar. And she was a struggling extra wannabe with a pile of debt and a mountain of doubt.

"Is your grandmother okay with me having a room that adjoins yours? She strikes me as pretty old-school. And she's also an intelligent and observant woman."

"I'm an adult, and I haven't asked her permission to date anyone since I was about fifteen. I'm keeping you close by where I can keep an eye on you." He glared at her a little for good measure.

She couldn't resist asking in disappointment, "So you think we shouldn't make out again?"

"We'll do plenty of making out during filming. The hero and heroine fall in love over the course of the movie."

She had to shake her head. "And you're sure you want me for this role? I mean, far be it from me to talk you out of hiring me, but I don't want to wreck your studio's first film."

"I'm sure," he replied quickly. "I want you."

She stared as he spun away, his cheeks suspiciously colored. God. If only he meant that in more than just a professional way. She could fall hard for him if he ever said something like that to her for real.

"If you're uncomfortable touching me or kissing me, we can rehearse that. You will have to get over being hinky before we start filming," he said a shade awkwardly. "Do you want to make out now, or do you have somewhere else to be?"

She laughed in spite of herself. "Sheesh. You make it sound worse than a root canal. I didn't think it was *that* bad last night."

"Are you kidding?" he blurted. "It was epic."

Warmth flooded through her. *Really?* She'd thought so, too. She said equally awkwardly, "I need to go shopping this morning. Get a few basic supplies, maybe some clothes."

"Gran's got closets and closets full. She was saying earlier how glad she is to pass on some of the stuff that's too young for her."

Ana cleared her throat and said uncomfortably, "I need bras that fit."

"I dunno. I liked the results of a tight bra last night." He shoved a hand through his sun-kissed hair. "Christ, I'm sorry. That was out of line."

"We're about to make out all the time professionally, remember? It's not out of line for lovers to say something like that to one another."

"Lov—" He broke off, swearing under his breath.

"Pretend lovers," she corrected hastily. Oh, God. Beyond awkward. She changed subjects and didn't even try to disguise the awkwardness. "If I'm going to be staying here for a few days, I need to pick up my car. Could I beg a ride over to the motel to pick it up?"

"Of course. Let me know when you'd like to go, and I'll arrange my schedule to drive you over."

"I'm turning into a giant imposition here."

"You're not imposing on anyone. Get over it, and let me help you."

Ana frowned until he added, "If it'll make you feel better, think of it as a business arrangement. A trade, if you will. You work on my film; I help you get your affairs straightened out."

That, she could do. Business. A fair trade. She nodded her agreement.

He said casually, "I've got a meeting with Adrian Turnow today. But tonight, we can start rehearsing if you'd like."

Gulp. Rehearsing as in making out and putting their hands all over each other. And there went her ability to concentrate on a blessed thing today. He patted her shoulder awkwardly and all but ran from the breakfast room.

Tonight, huh? More making out, huh? What if he didn't have the strength to stop this time?

Chapter 7

Ana spent most of the morning wrangling with her insurance company. There was confusion over the fact that a full criminal investigation had yet to be filed, but they eventually agreed to send her a preliminary check based on the initial police report. It should be enough to cover a new toothbrush and some new clothes.

It was shocking how getting a few basic items turned into more or less a shopping spree. She blamed Jackson for it. He'd made her nervous about "rehearsing" tonight, and she'd shopped to distract herself from thinking about making out with him…or more.

It had been one thing to be fresh off a bad scare and kissing the guy in sheer relief at being alive. It was even manageable to have woken up disoriented with his delicious body draped all over hers and to have kissed him. But to intentionally set out to snog the guy…that was just weird. She was particularly worried that it was going to be monstrously weird to make out with her boss as an ongoing part of their working relationship.

In celebration of the apparent big movie role she'd supposedly landed, she indulged herself with a few lacy bras and skimpy bikini panties. They made her feel naughty. And feminine. And wanton.

It felt a little like Christmas being surrounded by a bunch of shopping bags and wrapping paper as she sat on the floor of her beautiful room in Jackson's home. If yesterday's disasters had accomplished nothing else, they'd been a sharp reminder that the most important things in life weren't things. But still. It was nice to have a few items to call her own.

A knock on the connecting door between her room and Jackson's made her look up guiltily. "Come in."

Jackson poked his head in and looked around at the chaos. He broke out in a big grin. "Merry Christmas." He held out a small bag to her. She peeked in it and was startled to see a cell phone. Latest model, waterproof case, car charger, and top-of-the-line earbuds.

"You shouldn't have!"

"I said the studio would get you one so we can always get in touch with you. It's a tax-deductible business expense for us, so don't get worked up over it."

"Thanks." She ducked her head, ashamed of him having spent so much money on her.

"In all of yesterday's excitement, I forgot to ask who your film agent is. We need to get going on the contract for you."

She snorted. "Are you kidding? I'm a nobody. I don't have an agent."

He momentarily looked startled but recovered smoothly.

"I can recommend a couple of the top folks in the business to you. And I swear I won't recommend any lightweights whom I can push around. I'll take care of you."

He rattled off several names she recognized from the trade papers. Then he looked at her expectantly. "Any preference?"

"Um, not really."

He hit the speed dial on his phone and murmured as he listened, "Aaron Steinburg is the best. He's been waiting for my agent to die for years. If she ever does, he's the guy I'd go to."

Ana stared as Jackson spoke casually. "Hey, Aaron, It's Jackson Prescott. I've just signed an unknown actress to be the lead in a movie I'm producing. Yes, the one with Adrian Turnow. She needs an agent. You up for taking on a hot new up-and-comer? Great. I'll have her call you. Her name's Ana Izzolo. And my lawyer will call you in the morning with the offer."

Her eyeballs about fell out of her head as Jackson glanced up at her even more casually. "Okay. That's taken care of. You've got an agent. I'll have my lawyer contact Aaron first thing tomorrow to get the negotiations moving."

"You do realize I'd take this job in return for room and board—and maybe enough to pay off my student loans—don't you?"

Jackson grinned. "Rule number one, don't ever give away that kind of information to the studio executives. They're sharks. And unless your debt runs into the hundreds of thousands of dollars, we'll be paying you quite a bit more than your student loans." His famous dimples flashed as he added, "Take my advice. Insist on a back-end percentage of the box-office income rather than cash up front."

She winced and confessed, "Actually, I could use some cash up front pretty desperately."

"Hey, if you get in a cash flow bind what with having to replace your stuff, let me know, okay?"

"Thanks. So far, I'm good." She'd promised herself this afternoon that she wouldn't blast through the entire insurance check, but would save enough of it to cover her next student loan payment. She'd kept her promise to herself, barely.

"Enough talk of money. Rosie wanted me to tell you dinner will be ready at seven. And Gran wanted me to tell you she's going out tonight. It'll be just the two of us this evening."

Just the two of— Uh-oh. She wasn't going to be able to rely on Minerva's nearness to end that scheduled make-out rehearsal.

"Got any trash I can haul downstairs for you?" Jackson offered.

"I guess so. Those bags over there." Belatedly, she remembered to ask, "How'd the meeting with Adrian Turnow go? Did he like how my screen test went? At least up until I tried to break your nose?"

"Actually, he loved the part where you clocked me. Cracked him up." Jackson scooped up the empty bags. "Until dinner, then."

Dang it. Why did he have to sound so blasted suave and debonair? She could never match all that raging charm and raw sex appeal on-screen. Acting opposite a powerhouse like him was going to be a disaster. Before this crazy train got too far down the tracks, she had to pull the emergency brakes.

Aaron Steinburg her agent? Directed by Adrian Turnow? Leading lady to Jackson Prescott? Oh, yeah. This was sheer madness. Dinner. She'd tell Jackson at dinner that she couldn't do this film of his.

At about six o'clock, she started primping for dinner at seven. Which was totally unlike her. She went looking for moral support in a tube of mascara and, shockingly, found a little bit.

If only they weren't going to be alone. Minerva's presence would have deflected Jackson's reaction to her pulling out of the film. He might be a dreamer, but she was not. Her entire life was based on pragmatic, hardheaded practicality. It was the only way she'd survived a dysfunctional family and dismal home life. It was how she'd recovered from nearly being murdered two years ago, and it was how she'd picked up the pieces of her life and gotten an education. A trade. A shot at a stable living.

She stopped putting on eyeliner and stared at herself in the mirror. Who was she trying to kid? She was backing out of this miraculous opportunity because she was scared out of her mind of failing. Spectacularly. And then there was her fear of Jackson himself. Heck, she hadn't even had a date since the attack. The whole business of making small talk with strangers and praying the cute ones weren't creepy stalkers made her more nervous than she could stomach.

She'd gotten it so very wrong the last time she actually got involved with a guy. It had landed her in the hospital and sent her into the martial arts training that had ultimately led to her attempt at a stunt career. Yup, that was her, the ole lemonade-out-of-lemons girl.

It had been great to fantasize about Jackson Prescott. But the reality of actually working and living with him…

not so much. She couldn't do this. The guy had shown up naked in her room last night for God's sake, and she'd done her best to knock his head off before he'd finally subdued her.

Heck, she just hoped he didn't go crazy when she broke the news to him that she couldn't do this—no, wait. Tonight would be okay. Jackson was a dependable, safe, charge-to-the-rescue guy. He'd been nothing but kind to her so far. He was famous, for crying out loud. If he had creepy tendencies, the paparazzi would have caught him and outed him long before now, right? There would be a tell-all book or an exclusive interview on prime-time TV. Besides, he was strictly off-limits. He was the boss.

A thunderous realization struck her. Maybe that was why she was so stuck on him. He was safe to like. No way could there ever be anything between them. He was a movie star who blasted through women like rocket fuel—women totally different from her. And, he was apparently an honorable and conscientious boss. Yup, a nonstarter as a love interest.

More nervous than she could believe at having to quit this job, she randomly picked one of the half dozen dresses that had appeared like magic in her armoire while she was out today. Minerva really was quite the schemer, loading her up on feminine, sexy clothes like this. Too bad it was all for naught.

The dress Ana chose was short and sassy, its wispy, floaty material skimming the tops of her thighs. It was more girly than anything she'd ever worn before. By a lot.

It was pale silver-gray that made her caramel tan and blue eyes pop like crazy. Her hair even looked more blond in contrast. It was as if the garment had been made for her. She had a hard time believing Minerva had bought this hot little number for herself. One of the spaghetti straps slipped off her shoulder, and she pushed it back up nervously. This dress was too much. She should default to the jeans she'd bought today and one of the simple T-shirts she'd picked up.

She glanced at her cell phone and gaped at the time. Crud. Five till seven. No time to change. She would just have to brazen it out in this outfit.

Her feet dragged as she descended one of the grand staircases. She hated to disappoint Jackson and she dreaded his reaction to her announcement. Her father tended to react first with his fists. She prayed Jackson wasn't the same.

When she rounded the corner into the family room, she stopped in her tracks. Jackson was wearing tailored slacks and a polo shirt that clung to every powerful muscle in his back. He looked every inch the movie star that he was. His hands were jammed in his pockets and he stared out at the sea, which was a brilliant orange as the sun, low in the west, bled across its glassy surface.

He must have caught her reflection in the window because he turned around as she stepped fully into the room. "Wow. You look great, Ana."

"Thanks. You don't clean up too bad, yourself. You know," she commented lightly, "you might make a half-decent leading man."

He smiled wryly in response. The swelling in his eye had come down and only a little purple around it announced that she'd clobbered him yesterday. His nose was still swollen, but he wore the hawk-nosed look better than any man had a right to.

He asked, "Would you like to eat inside or out? Rosie set both the dining room table and the one on the veranda. She wants to serve dinner before she leaves and needs to know where to take the food."

"Outside if you don't mind." Frankly, she was feeling a little claustrophobic around him and all his flesh impact. No need to close herself indoors if she didn't have to.

He nodded and stepped into the kitchen. While he was gone, Ana used the time to breathe deeply and slowly. Not that it helped her nerves one tiny little bit. She could do this. It was just dinner. A business discussion. And then he'd throw her out on her can. As unappealing as that was, it was better than the alternative. Yup, staying here and making out with a famous celebrity hunk would suck....

Hoo baby. Her breathing accelerated and her pulse jumped like crazy as he stepped back into the family room. She spun on the platform sandals Minerva had left for her and, on cue, tripped. He made a quick grab for her that kept her from face-planting on the floor at his feet.

Her face hot, she mumbled, "Great reflexes you've got there."

He chuckled. "Walk much, Grace?"

"Yup, and I hope to jump off tall buildings and play with explosives for fun someday," she retorted.

His smile lingered as he offered her his forearm. "Shall we?"

She stared down at his arm's muscular sculpting and light covering of sun-bleached hair. Oh. Right. The girl was supposed to take the guy's arm. She wasn't accustomed to chivalrous male behavior, and certainly not from her boss. Who looked totally hot.

She laid her palm on his arm and was chagrined to feel her hand trembling. Please, please, please let him not notice it.

"You okay?" he murmured low.

He noticed, dammit. Too flummoxed to think up a lie, she admitted, "You make me nervous."

"Good nervous or bad nervous?"

"Both."

He held her chair for her and pushed it in as she sank into it. "Why bad nervous?" he asked as he sat down in the chair beside hers.

"Long story."

"We've got all night."

He poured her a generous glass of wine and she took a big gulp to fortify herself. "I haven't had great luck with men over the years."

"Hard to fathom that."

"It's true. I went out with a guy a few years ago who tried to kill me."

"What?" Jackson lurched forward in his seat. "Jeez. And I thought women constantly trying to trap me into marrying them was rough."

She shrugged. "He didn't rape me or anything. He just tried to strangle me. His buddy was driving and we were in the back of a pick-up truck. I managed to get loose long enough to fall out onto the road. Hit my head. Knocked me out. Luckily, a car stopped to help before he could stuff me back in the truck and finish the job."

"Christ." He took a big gulp of wine. "How did you end up in the movie business?"

She shrugged. "After the attack, I went looking for training in how to defend myself and how to get out of a moving car safely. It led me to some stunt classes, and here I am, a wannabe stuntwoman."

"So you really weren't interested in landing an acting role when you auditioned yesterday?"

"Well, a girl can always dream. But I'm totally un-quali—

He cut her off briskly. "Let's not talk business. Rosie's enchiladas are best eaten hot." He served her a plateful of chicken enchiladas smothered in a cream sauce to die for. If she was not mistaken, he'd sensed where she was going with that last remark and had derailed the conversation intentionally. What was up with that?

"How are you not the size of a house with food like this to eat?" she demanded a little while later.

"Lots and lots of exercise," he replied, grinning.

The sun blinked below the horizon, and the glow of the pillar candle in its glass globe on the table took over lighting their meal. The ocean murmured and chuckled quietly below and the setting was so romantic she could hardly bear it.

Jackson pushed his plate back and took an appreciative sip of his wine. "So, I met with Adrian today."

"And?"

"He loved your screen test. He's fully on board with bringing you in as the female lead."

"Seriously?" she blurted, startled.

Jackson frowned. "Is it so far-fetched to believe that you might have talent and that he and I might have spotted it?"

She had no idea what to say to that. Silence fell between them, filled only by the rhythmic wash of the ocean.

"I'll admit it's a calculated risk to hire an inexperienced unknown for a major movie. But I want to make a movie that's never been seen before. That means faces that have never been seen before."

"I have no idea what I'm doing."

"Your instincts during your audition and screen test were spot on. Trust them."

Trust her instincts? The same instincts that led her to go out with a murderous psychopath? The instincts that led her to panic when Jackson had put his hands around her neck? That wasn't acting. That was real.

"Jackson, I can't act. I don't know how to put it any more clearly than that."

"Want in on a little trade secret? Very few actors can act."

"But—"

He waved off her protest. "I don't act. I find truth—a piece of myself—in every character I portray. Then, I'm just that part of myself on-screen."

He wasn't listening to her. It wasn't just about the acting. It was about fear. Insecurity. Complete lack of faith in her instincts. Frustrated, she tried, "What does Adrian think of having a rank amateur forced upon him?"

Jackson grinned. "He says he can teach a chimpanzee to act if it will do what he tells it to. He's pretty adamant about wanting you. He saw something in you, and he wants to start shooting immediately. We can go into full-blown production as early as next week."

"What kind of acting will this role entail?"

"Dialogue. A few love scenes. Several fight scenes. A fair bit of green-screen work. Adrian's gonna do CGI enhancements in postproduction to make us look alien instead of messing around with a lot of prosthetics and makeup."

That was a relief. She'd heard horror tales of actors spending hour upon grueling hour in the makeup chair for a few seconds of camera time. It dawned on her abruptly that she was actually considering going through with this insanity. How had he managed to deflect all her arguments?

"I don't want to let you down," she tried. "I can't have a huge movie depending on me. You can't depend on me."

He was out of his chair and kneeling beside her before she could blink. "You won't be alone. I'll be with you. And Adrian is the best in the business. He will teach you what you need to know, and he'll get the performance out of you that he needs. I promise. Just trust him. Trust me."

"I suck at trust."

"You've got good cause. But I'm not homicidal."

She stared at his face, so open, so earnest. So...real. Was he acting? Or was this the real man giving her actual honesty? God. If only she could tell. She whispered, "How do I start to trust you?"

"In acting classes, we do trust exercises. Maybe we could try a few of those."

"Do I have to fall backward into your arms and let you catch me?" she asked skeptically.

He smiled. "Well, that's a classic, but no. You don't have to fall into my arms."

"It might help if we knew more about each other," she suggested.

"You mean like those 'your lover's favorite things' quizzes in magazines?"

Her lips twitched humorously. "You read women's magazines?"

He snorted. "No. I get interviewed for them. And I check out my articles when they're published."

Her lips broke over into a full-blown smile. "That's your story and you're sticking to it, I gather."

"Darn tootin', I am."

"So how does this work? Should we come up with a

list of questions? Stuff we'd want to know about each other if we were dating?"

"Sure."

Silence fell between them as her mind went completely, totally, blue-screen-of-doom blank. What on earth would she ask him if she was dating him? She'd read the women's magazine articles about him already. *When's your birthday, Jackson?* Oh, wait, she knew that one. *July 4th.* How could anyone forget that? *What's your favorite color?* Nope, she knew that one, too. Same as hers. *Green. What's your favorite food? Barbecue chicken pizza and a cold beer. Hobbies? Working on and riding his Harley.*

How about, *what on earth do you see in me as a woman?* That one would send him screaming for the hills.

Freaking out, she changed subjects in barely contained panic. "Is there a script for this movie of yours?"

"I can have Adrian send over the working draft for you to read tomorrow."

"Is it good?"

Her gaze snapped to his. His hazel eyes were grim. Determined. "It had better be. The future of our company depends on it."

Gee. No pressure there. All her doubts came flooding back, threatening to drown her.

"Don't make that face," Jackson warned. "You're doing this movie, and that's that. End of discussion."

"But *why?*"

"Because Adrian and I agree you're the best person for the job. And we both know what we're doing."

"So I'm gonna be in the movies, huh?" she muttered.

Relief relaxed his features into the handsome face

women the world over knew and loved. "Looks that way, kid."

Wow. "Now what?"

"Now I take you inside because I can see the goose bumps on your arms from over here, and then we practice making out and building some trust."

Dammit, did he have to be so blasted single-minded? He was already back to the making-out thing. She looked back at the house in alarm. "What about Rosie?"

"She left right after she brought out the flan. Went to see a movie with her sister. Won't be back for hours."

"I'd accuse those two women of throwing us together if they were here."

He rolled his eyes. "You would not be wrong."

"I'd be scared silly of going inside with you if this weren't just business," she confessed with a shaky laugh.

An expression of…surprise, maybe, or perhaps that was determination…crossed his face. He stood up and held his hand out to her. "C'mon. This won't be so bad. I promise I won't try to strangle you."

"Gee. Thanks." Then why did she feel like he was leading her to her freaking doom?

Her knees all but knocked together as she stood up. He was a trim man, but he was also strong, athletic and a lot bigger than her. If this making-out thing went psycho, there was no way she could fight him off. Had their fight scene two days ago been real, he'd have killed her. Easily.

The house's warmth was comforting. Like a badly needed hug. He picked up a remote control, and quiet music floated out of unseen speakers, as tranquil as the ocean below. He came to stand behind her as she stared unseeing out the big windows, and ran his palms lightly up and down her arms.

"I know I'm asking a lot of you. Doing this film with me is going to push you way outside your comfort zone. Especially after you told me about that attack. But the film needs you. I need you."

She was already way outside her comfort zone, but not in the scared way he meant. She'd had no idea she could be this attracted to any man. Not even a hunk like Jackson Prescott. All these girly feelings roiling around in her gut were totally foreign to her. "I got over the attack a long time ago." *If you could call walking away from all men and never looking back being over it.* "My attacker has been in a mental institution for years and won't get out for a very long time, if ever."

"Still. If you ever need protection or don't want to be alone late at night when the boogeyman comes calling, you call me. Anytime, day or night."

"That's very sweet of you."

"I've got your back. Understood?"

She smiled gratefully at his reflection in the glass. "Thanks. Really."

His reflection smiled back at her, and something melted inside her. Was he as heroic as the characters he played in the movies? Her own smile faded as it dawned on her that maybe she was projecting pretend characters onto the real man. How was she supposed to separate the two?

As she stared at his transparent reflection, a frown of concentration took over his forehead. He announced, "After what you told me about being attacked, I think you should take the lead tonight. I don't want to scare you."

"I don't know exactly what I'm supposed to do here," she mumbled, flummoxed.

"Well, you can start by giving me a hug."

That sounded innocuous enough. Okay. She could do that. A little in disbelief that she was hugging a movie star, she looped her arms around his waist. His arms came around her in a loose circle, and her head naturally came to rest on his chest. His heart thudded slow and steady beneath her ear. Gently, he tightened the embrace until she was plastered against his muscular chest.

"This is nice," she admitted.

"Yes. It is."

She gulped against his soft shirt. "Now what?"

"Tilt your chin up. Smile a little at me. And, when you're ready, invite me to kiss you."

She glanced up at him sidelong, shy. "Like this?"

"The woman is a born flirt. You sure you haven't had acting lessons?"

It wasn't hard to act like she wanted him to kiss her when she'd been secretly fantasizing about it for years. She shrugged and let a little more heat creep into her come-hither gaze.

He crooked a finger lightly under her chin and lifted her mouth to his. He leaned down and brushed his lips across hers once, twice. His mouth touched hers lightly, and it was as if he paused, waiting for her to signal that it was okay to continue. Her nervousness sloughed away. This was Jackson. Sweet, safe, responsible Jackson who'd been frantic at the hospital and had kissed her last night like he really gave a damn about her. The same Jackson who bolted into her bedroom naked to save her from a nightmare.

She kissed his delicious mouth experimentally, savoring its warmth and firmness while he stood still and let her do whatever she wanted to it. Eventually, though, something restless unfolded inside her.

"Kiss me back," she finally muttered.

His mouth surged against hers, taking over the kiss in an instant. She'd had no idea how tightly he'd been holding himself back until he loosed the reins of his control. His arms tightened around her, lifting her against his strength and size. She stood on tiptoe as her arms crept up and slid around his neck. He felt good against her, all hard and protective and sexy hot.

Something crackled abruptly between them. Not heat. Not electricity. Something sharper. A driving need that vibrated all the way to her core. She reveled in the hardness of him against her belly. The way he pressed her hips more closely against him. The way his hands roamed her back in search of…something.

One of her spaghetti straps slipped off her shoulder. And then the other one. It dawned on her belatedly that neither had been accidents, but rather his fingers pushing them down. The thin elastic strip at the top of the dress stretched as something—someone—tugged her dress down inch by inch over her breasts.

"Jackson," she gasped.

"Need me to stop?" he responded immediately, her dress stopping in its tracks.

She weighed her reactions to him. Nope. No panic anywhere. She shook her head, her hair flipping around her face.

"You're going to have to say it aloud, baby. I don't want there to be any miscommunications between us."

"Don't stop," she managed to whisper hoarsely.

"What do you want me to do?"

Dammit, this was embarrassing. But then his mouth kissed a path of destruction across her temple, down her cheek and back to her mouth, where his tongue did all kinds of wonderful things to hers. Who knew one tongue could stroke another like that? Or that it would feel so slippery and rough and damned sexy?

"Keep taking off my dress," she breathed.

"Roger that." The fabric resumed its achingly slow descent down her body. Her strapless bra came into sight, and then the dress's elastic popped against her waist as it slid free of her chest all of a sudden.

His fingers followed the strapless bra around her ribs and paused on the hooks at her back. "Mind if I get rid of this?" he murmured against the tender flesh just below her ear.

"Um, no," she managed. He wasn't speeding up their trust exercises. He was obliterating them! But she was so delirious at the prospect of Jackson Prescott living up to a few of her fantasies that she could burst.

The hooks popped free easily. Scant lot of protection they'd provided. The bra fell to the floor between them. Thankfully, Jackson kept his mouth on her neck and didn't lift his head right away to take a look. But his hand did creep forward under her arm. His knuckles grazed the swell at the side of her breast, and she groaned at how good it felt. His other hand did the same to her other breast.

"Now what?" he asked against her lips.

"Your shirt. I think you need to take it off if we're going to have mutual trust here."

"Mmm. I like the way the lady thinks."

She reached for the hem of the soft cotton and lifted the shirt over his head, reveling in the slabs of muscle uncovered as she went. "My, my. You are pretty, Mr. Prescott." She indulged herself and leaned forward to kiss the sprinkling of dark hair over muscles that flexed abruptly beneath her mouth.

"You're pretty damned hot, yourself, Miss Izzolo."

He did step back then, and his gaze slid down her entire body with aching slowness and back up again. She trembled before him in nothing more than a skimpy pair of lace panties and a pair of high-heeled strappy sandals. "Beautiful." He sighed.

"You're not going to fire me?" she asked in a small voice.

"No producer on earth would fire a woman who looks like you from his movie. He might invite you into his bed. But fire you? Absolutely not." He took a small step forward, and for the first time, their naked chests came into contact with one another. She inhaled sharply and Jackson froze against her. "You okay?" he murmured.

"Well, yeah."

"You feel incredible, Ana. I could stand here forever."

He didn't feel half-bad himself. Her thoughts were leaping ahead to all kinds of X-rated possibilities that involved him losing the rest of his clothes and her losing what little remained of hers.

"How intimately do you think we should get to know each other?" he asked.

If she wasn't mistaken, he sounded a bit out of breath. "I have no idea."

"Should I do this?" His hands wandered down her back to cup her mostly bare behind rather more intimately than any man had in a very long time. She'd tried to date after the attack. She'd even had sex a few times. But she'd never been able to get past her basic distrust of men to let herself get into a real relationship. Her shrink would have a ball analyzing this trust game between her and Jackson.

He murmured, "You fill my hands perfectly." He traced the line of her thong, his fingertips pressing into the crevasse between her cheeks, and making her gasp with shock. A surge of lust and liquid heat between her legs all but made her knees collapse, and she clung to him more tightly.

"You like that?"

"Mmm-hmm," she answered shyly.

"Me, too." His palms rubbed her behind lightly, tantalizingly. "What else do you like?"

"I don't know."

"Why not? You've had sex before, right?"

"Well, yes. But that doesn't mean I know what I'll enjoy with you. Maybe you've thought of things to try that I haven't."

"So you've had *bad* sex before," he declared. "We should fix that."

"But...just rehearsing...trust exercise..." she mumbled, alarmed. It was one thing to have secret dreams of bedding a man like him. It was another thing entirely to be mostly naked in his arms and have the man propositioning her for real. Aw, heck. She was such a poser. All talk and no action. A wimp. A *chicken*.

Jackson drew a gratifyingly shaky breath. "Right. Rehearsal. Damn." His hands retreated to the safety of her waist.

Make that a moronic chicken.

"Here's the thing, Ana. If you and I are going to have to do a bunch of fight scenes and love scenes together, we're going to have to put our hands all over each other before it's said and done. We may as well get used to it now, right?"

The logic seemed perfectly sound to her. She stepped back a little to place her palms on his chest, right over his sternum. She moved her hands in ever-widening circles across his skin, reveling in the way his copious muscles jumped under her touch.

"You have a beautiful body, Jackson."

"Thanks."

She caught the frown that flickered across his brow and lifted her hands away from him immediately. "What's wrong?"

"Nothing. Old memory."

"Of what?"

The frown came back, heavier this time. He physically shook his head to get rid of it. "Sorry, Ana. Not you."

Whatever he was remembering flipped him out more than he wanted to admit, though, because he spun away from her and jammed a hand through his hair. She'd noticed he did that when he was frustrated or worried about something. She picked up her dress and shimmied back into it behind him. Note to self: telling Jackson he was beautiful was the mother of all mood killers with him.

She was relieved that the hot tension of the moment had been effectively crushed. Right? Yes, darn it. She was relieved. *Not.*

Crap. He was her boss and was just teaching her the ropes so he could coax a good performance out of her. For him, it was just business. It. Was. Not. Real.

She picked his shirt up and paused on her way past to hold it out to him. "I'm sorry I dredged up bad memories for you."

"Dammit, I'm the one who should be apologizing. I swear it's not you."

No, but she would bet the contents of her measly checking account that it was some woman. Who was she and what on earth had she done to him?

Chapter 8

Jackson looked around the conference room trying to find Ana in the cast-and-crew meeting. When she'd thrown him that take-me look out of the corner of her eye last night, he'd about thrown her down and had his way with her on the spot. Only by the barest of margins had the memory that he was her boss and responsible for her safety prevented him from doing it. He was an idiot. And a horny bastard.

If long years in this industry hadn't taught him to be cautious of rising starlets, surely his mother's cautionary tale of addiction and self-destruction had. She'd thrown herself on every casting couch in Hollywood in search of the fame that ultimately eluded her.

He owed Ana an apology. But what the hell was he supposed to apologize for? For kissing her back when she kissed him? For thinking dirty thoughts while he took off her clothes? For dreaming last night of her naked and writhing beneath him and waking up with the mother of all hard-ons this morning?

He glanced at his watch. Time to start the meeting. His crew contained a high percentage of ex-military types— Adrian liked working with them, and they came out of the service with a lot of the technical skills needed around a movie set. Punctuality was a sign of self-discipline to them as a group. He picked up the remote control for his laptop and the spreadsheet of the next week's schedule flashed up on the wall.

The door opened just as someone turned out the lights and he recognized the petite, curvy silhouette briefly outlined in the door. Ana slipped into a seat in the back of the room. *Was she avoiding him?*

Distracted, he forced himself to go over the various projects on the schedule and divvied them out to his crew to work on. Experienced pros one and all, none of his people needed much more direction than that, and he dismissed them all to get to work.

He and Adrian had handpicked their crew from all the previous films they'd worked on, offering top dollar to lure away the best in the business to help them get this new studio rolling. They'd come together beautifully as a team over the past few months.

The lights came on and a bunch of the crew clustered around Ana, ostensibly welcoming her aboard. More like checking out the new talent. She seemed a little over-whelmed at all the attention.

An urge to shove his way to her side and shelter her from the crowd startled him. He eyed the way the crew was circling her with an entirely new perspective today. Were those hungry looks being thrown at her? Did someone just steal a look down her shirt? Something tight and angry jumped in his belly, and Jackson was shocked to identify it as possessiveness. Since when was she his exclusive territory?

Since he'd heard about her rough past and seen how nervous she was about this whole movie thing. He politely but firmly chased everyone else out of the room with a brisk comment that he wasn't paying any of them to stand around chitchatting.

"Sorry I was late," Ana said guiltily. "My locker in the ladies' locker room was broken into. Nothing was taken. Just some shampoo and body lotion. I don't know why anyone bothered."

"Lemme see."

Frowning, she led him to the locker room and shouted in to make sure no women were inside before leading him in.

"God, the estrogen's so thick in here I could cut it with a knife," he muttered. Jackson examined her busted locker door closely. "Jimmied with some sort of tool. Maybe a small crowbar."

The locks were flimsy in here. Hers appeared to be the only locker that had been robbed, which was raising all kinds of red flags in his head. What the hell was going on with her? Why was some bastard targeting her specifically? He supposed it was possible that a thief had been startled after breaking into just one locker, but why hers? Ana's locker wasn't on the end or on the more easily accessible top row, for that matter. He didn't like this. Any of this.

Jackson's frown deepened. "And you're sure no one could be targeting you specifically?"

"Positive. I'm just that boring, I promise."

He seriously doubted that. But he also didn't want to alarm her any more than necessary. She'd already been through enough. If anything, a little distraction was called for. "Use my office for now to store your things, change and shower. It has a private bathroom. I'll get you your own trailer and a security guard once shooting starts."

"You don't have to—"

"I want to," he cut off her protest briskly. To distract her, he asked, "Feel like fighting with me?"

Her gaze, wide and blue, snapped up to his, sparkling. "Sure."

"You think you can take me, squirt?"

"Bring it on, buddy."

Joking and insulting each other, the two of them headed for the cavernous soundstage and stepped onto a huge, green padded floor the size of a basketball court where a pair of stuntmen were working out a fight choreography. She commenced stretching and warming up. He enjoyed the view while he did the same.

Well, now, she was quite the pretzel. Some of the poses she was taking made him think downright pornographic thoughts about what they could do in the bedroom with all that flexibility of hers.

"You okay?" she murmured.

"Why do you ask?"

"That's a strange look you've got on your face. What are you thinking about?"

"The Kama Sutra."

She straightened abruptly to stare at him.

He added hastily, "Some of the contortions in it remind me of aliens. I think we could lift some of the poses and incorporate them in a fight sequence. It would be sexy as well as cool."

"Sorry. I've never studied it in detail," she mumbled. Her face was beet-red.

He gave himself a mental kick in the head for embarrassing her. He was used to working with experienced actresses who had little by way of inhibitions. Distracting her yet again, he said, "I was thinking about what you said the other day before you walloped me about how you're fast and small. I think we could exaggerate that more...."

They'd been working on choreography hard for a couple of hours and had paused to catch their breaths after a strenuous sequence when Jackson heard a strange popping sound. Like tiny little shaped charges firing in a daisy chain.

Pop-pop-pop-pop-pop.

Frowning, he looked up into the rafters where it sounded like the noise had come from. He was just in time to spot a huge steel track that stage lights slid back and forth on come swinging down out of the rafters.

Right at Ana.

He dived forward, crashing into her and knocking her to the ground, hard. He managed to get his hands down on either side of her head and break a little of his fall from crushing her. The wind of the broken light track's passage lifted his shirt off his back.

He grabbed Ana and rolled away as an explosion of sparks showered them, stinging his skin sharply. The studio went pitch-black. Power outage. He came to a full stop back on top of Ana as male voices erupted around them.

"What was that?" she gasped.

"Are you okay?" he bit out.

"No. You're smashing me. And that tackle hurt."

"Sorry. Lighting rig was coming down at you. No time to warn you. Just had to knock you out of the way."

"Oh." A pause. "Oh!"

The dark was velvet and warm around them, and relief flooded him with heat. She was alive. Unhurt. *Thank God.* He tilted his head down and found her mouth with his. He kissed her voraciously…and she kissed him back like she bloody well meant it.

"Jackson? Ana? You guys okay?" someone shouted, going down through the roster of crew who'd been on the stage when it went dark.

Reluctantly, he tore his mouth away from hers. "We're good!" he called back. Lower, he muttered, "I gotta go do the producer thing. Hold that thought." He kissed her hard and fast and then pressed up and away from her luscious body. Lord, that woman was made for sin.

He'd no sooner gained his feet when dim lights flickered on in each of the corners of the room. They were big halogen spots, illuminating slowly. Emergency lights. They would get brighter over the next five minutes or so as they warmed up.

Ana was sprawled on the floor at his feet, her fingers on her lips and a blissful look on her face. She blinked up at him for a moment and the look fled, replaced by something that looked a lot like chagrin. She liked kissing him, huh? Good to know.

He held a hand down to her and pulled her briskly to her feet. He spared her a brief, private smile and then spun away, shouting, "I need whoever's the best explosives guy on set over here, now. And nobody touch that lighting rig!"

* * *

Ana sighed in delight as the shower's hot water pummeled her sore muscles. Jackson had tasked one of his security guys—a beefy ex-commando of some kind—to drive her back to his beach house. The guy was still outside, prowling around the property doing some sort of security sweep.

That tackle Jackson had laid on her hadn't been a stunt tackle where he caught most of his body weight on his hands and didn't crush her. Nope, he'd hit her with his full body weight and clobbered her good.

Thankfully. That lighting rig had weighed a couple of tons and had crashed right through where she'd been standing an instant before. Jackson had ordered her off the set while he and a couple of his guys took a close look at the big steel track and figured out what had brought it down.

A horrible suspicion that it hadn't been an accident niggled at the corners of her mind, but so far, she'd managed to hold it at bay. She was safe. She was alive. And no doubt being totally paranoid. Stuff like that happened on movie sets.

But not on Adrian Turnow's, the little voice in her head whispered. He was as conscientious as directors came.

Someone was targeting her, and there was no way around it. And like it or not, she had to let Jackson and Adrian know. As her producer and the director of the movie, she owed it to them to give them a chance to remove her from the work environment they were responsible for keeping safe. But to leave Jackson? Out of sight, out of mind, right? Her heart hurt at the notion of him forgetting her with ease.

She pulled on the gauzy beach pants that had appeared

in her armoire and one of her new camisoles, a mint-green one that looked awesome with her fair coloring. Minerva really had to quit buying her clothes. She already had more than she'd owned before the earthquake. She made a mental note to thank her hostess profusely and beg her to stop her largesse.

And then she made the mistake of stretching out on her bed for just a minute. She'd slept for crap last night. She kept waking up all hot and bothered after dreaming of that smoking-hot kiss she and Jackson had shared.

That shower had really relaxed her. Not to mention she was dreading talking with Jackson about today's accident. She closed her eyes. She would rest for just a minute....

Hands kneading her shoulders into jelly roused her slowly from her unconscious state. It was dark outside. She lurched, or would have if the hands on her back hadn't held her down.

"How long was I asleep?" she mumbled.

Jackson answered, low and soothing, "A while. I figured you needed the rest or else you wouldn't have crashed like that."

"I'll never sleep tonight."

"I can think of other things you can do all night."

She smiled reluctantly. "I'm sure you can."

He shocked her by tossing a leg across her hips and straddling her backside to continue her back massage. She'd be alarmed if she couldn't chalk it up to the "getting comfortable touching each other" conversation from yesterday. As it was, she was too sleepy to think of a reason why he shouldn't give her a back rub and too bonelessly mellow to care. It felt great to let his big strong hands work out the kinks in her shoulders.

"To what do I owe this special treatment?" she eventually murmured when her body had melted into a boneless puddle.

"No reason. You just looked like you could use it."

"Mmm. I'm in heaven."

Silence fell between them as she drifted between sleep and waking, luxuriating beneath his magical hands. But gradually, consciousness returned. And with it, memory of this afternoon.

"What did you find out about why that lighting rig came down?"

His hands tensed. Stilled on the small of her back. He resumed massaging her, but the magic was gone from his hands.

"Jackson?"

He exhaled audibly. "Sabotage."

She partially rolled over between his thighs to stare up at him. She'd suspected that was the case, but hearing him say it seemed so much more real. Someone was definitely out to harm her. A cold chill chattered across her skin.

"How?" she asked reluctantly.

"A series of small cutting charges were set to blow out the key bolts holding the thing to the ceiling," he explained grimly.

"Any hints at who did it?" she mumbled.

"Maybe someone's got it in for me or Adrian, or for our studio in general," Jackson muttered.

"That's nice of you to say, but what if that lighting rig was aimed at me?" She failed to keep a tremor out of her voice when she stated the obvious. "I'll totally understand if you and Adrian want to take me off this movie for the safety of the rest of the crew." She took a deep breath and then added in a frustrated rush, "I just can't figure out who'd want to hurt me."

"You're not exactly the kind of person who attracts crazy stalkers."

She snorted. "I'd have to have a social life to do that."

"After dinner, I'd like to sit down with you and talk about your life in detail. See if we can come up with any ideas of who might be out to hurt you."

She nodded, staring up at him, and he stared back down at her. Gradually, it dawned on her that they were lying crotch-to-crotch in an extremely suggestive fashion. It was so easy to imagine him naked like last night, straddling her body. Taking her. Making her his...

He pushed away from her and stood abruptly, clearing his throat uncomfortably. Dang it. Had he seen what she was fantasizing? Her face heating up fast, she mumbled, "Where'd you learn how to give such a great back rub?"

"Dated a masseuse once," he bit out. He turned away from her and, sure enough, shoved a hand through his hair. He left her room without even a backward glance. The door thunked shut solidly behind him.

Seriously? He massaged her into a horny mess and then just walked out on her? Was he that massively disciplined, or was he sending her mixed signals? She was inclined to open that door, pick up the nearest heavy object and chuck it at his head.

Almost as curious as she was hot to trot and irritated, she rolled out of bed and powered up her laptop, which had thankfully been in her car when her motel room was trashed. She typed Jackson's name into a search engine and sorted the results from oldest to newest. She browsed through newspaper articles about his sports accomplishments in high school and early acting accomplishments.

She hadn't realized he'd been acting since he was sixteen. She thought he had burst onto the scene all at once a few years ago with his first big action-adventure movie.

But then a hit popped up that shocked her. An engagement announcement from about five years ago in a Florida newspaper. His fiancée, Vanessa something, was blonde and beautiful…and petite. *Crap.* Did *she* remind him of Vanessa? Although Vanessa was stunningly beautiful whereas she tended toward wholesome or even cute.

Ana typed the fiancée's full name—Vanessa van Buren—into a search engine. Hits started scrolling down her computer screen almost faster than she could scan them. She was from a rich East Coast family. No surprise, Vanessa van Buren had attended a snooty women's college. Wow. Not once had she ever heard of Jackson being married. The divorce must have been kept really quiet.

She kept scrolling. A YouTube video popped up. Of Vanessa's *wedding.* It was as grand and over-the-top as Ana would have expected. She watched reluctantly as the camera panned across the wedding party.

Whoa. Rewind. Who was the guy in the tux grinning like an idiot? The groom was *not* Jackson. What the heck? Who had Vanessa ended up marrying? The video title called him Dr. George Bostick. What had happened to Vanessa and Jackson?

Ana checked the time-date stamp in the corner of the wedding video and frowned. Based on what she'd gleaned about his film career, Jackson would have been on location at that time shooting the movie that would go on later to make him famous—

Oh. That. Bitch.

Vanessa must have dumped Jackson, or at least started

cheating on him, as soon as he'd left to shoot his movie. She'd snagged herself a doctor and gotten him down the aisle as fast as her Jimmy Choos would haul her greedy, disloyal ass.

No wonder Jackson was a confirmed bachelor who didn't take relationships with women seriously. She moved over to the adjoining door and knocked on it. "May I come in?"

"It's open."

She stepped through and into a bedroom similar to hers except for darker, more masculine décor and the big armchair and ottoman facing the ocean. Jackson sprawled in it, feet up, beer dangling from his fingers. A six-pack stood on the floor beside him, mostly empty. Had her mention of the woman who'd taught him to give massages driven him to drink away the memories?

"How did Vanessa dump you? Dear John letter? Email? Phone call?"

Jackson scowled in her general direction and took a long pull from his beer. "None of the above."

"How then?" Ana stepped farther into the room so she could look him fully in the face.

"Didn't dump me at all."

"But I saw the wedding video. You were overseas shooting a film."

"I saw it, too," he snapped.

"I don't follow—"

He surged to his feet in front of her, fury abruptly rolling off him. "She never broke up with me. I happened to get onto the internet in some downtime—with the intent of writing my fiancée a love letter—and I found the video of her wedding."

Ana's jaw dropped in shock.

He added lightly, bitterly, "Imagine my surprise. That's how I found out she and I were no longer engaged."

"Ohmigod, Jackson. I'm so sorry. Do you need me to go to Florida and kill her for you?"

He gripped her shoulders almost painfully tight. "I need you to stay the hell out of my private life," he ground out. "Don't dredge up crap you're not willing to deal with."

"Who says I'm not willing to deal with it?" she retorted.

"You *like* inheriting other women's crap? She made a head case out of me. Run screaming while you can, Ana."

"I'm still standing here."

"I'm serious. I've got issues regarding women."

"You've been nothing but decent and kind to me."

"We're not in a relationship," he snapped.

Okay, that hurt. But she was the one who'd poked into his past and put it out there between them. "Just because Vanessa was a liar and a cheat doesn't mean all women are. Take me, for example. Once I give my affections to someone, I'm committed all the way. Loyal to the end."

"I thought you don't date at all. And why is that, exactly?"

"We're talking about your hang-ups, here."

"Sucks when the shoe's on the other foot, huh? Why do I have to talk about my crap if you don't have to talk about yours? Tell me the truth, Ana. Why don't you date? Ever? It's more than just that one attack."

The truth exploded across her brain as he stood there glaring daggers at her and she glared back. *He's right. I've had issues with men since before the attack. Since my father was cold and unloving my entire childhood.*

Stunned, she managed a shrug. "This isn't about my issues. This is about yours."

He snorted. "You can't handle mine. Or me, for that matter."

"How do you know that?" she demanded. "You won't engage with me enough to tell. Every time things get interesting between us, you walk away."

"What the hell are you talking about?" he demanded.

"At the beach two nights ago. I told you not to stop. But you did, anyway. Last night, I freaking told you to take off my clothes and got more naked than not, and you *still* walked away from me. I don't think you've got anger issues toward some chick who dumped you *years* ago. I think you're scared of women."

"Am not."

"Prove it."

She'd seen men like him before. Men who didn't take kindly to being called a coward. Who never backed away from a dare. She'd known men like him plenty long enough to know better than to throw down a challenge like that in front of a man like him. Particularly not after he'd been drinking enough to be a little more reckless than usual. No, it probably hadn't been the smartest thing she'd ever done to say that to him. But she'd be damned if she'd take the challenge back.

They stared daggers at each other, electricity crackling and popping between them, building until she thought they were both going to explode. How could one man be so attractive and so damned infuriating at the same time?

Jackson's arms swept around her and he picked her up, carried her over to the bed and dumped her on the mattress. It hadn't finished bouncing before he followed her down, pressing her deep into the soft comforter. How their clothes got off so fast, she wasn't quite sure. But in about ten seconds, she was sprawled out naked beneath him, and his equally naked body pinned hers into immobility.

"Do you just like angry sex?" he growled. His teeth closed on her shoulder and he bit her hard enough to leave marks tomorrow. It felt glorious.

"Not especially," she panted. But it turned out she did like it hot and heavy, apparently. Her leg crept up around his hips, guaranteeing he wouldn't walk away from her this time. She kissed him with abandon, shocked by the wildness he'd unleashed in her.

Her fingernails raked down his back and one of his hands grabbed a fistful of her hair, pulling her head back and exposing her neck to his voracious kisses. Determined to have her due, she turned her head and grabbed his earlobe in her teeth. She bit down hard enough to let him know she wasn't without weapons of her own. Yup, she'd had a secret wild side waiting to come out all along, apparently.

He laughed darkly and rose up over her, kneeling between her widespread thighs. He gripped her knees in his fists, spreading her even more for him, allowing her no escape into modesty. His member was huge and ready, a drop of moisture glistening at its tip. He glared down at her and she glared back up at him.

"Go ahead, Jackson. I dare you."

"You really shouldn't have said that."

Oh, yes. She really should have.

"Protection. Dammit. There are condoms somewhere in my bathroom—"

"I'm on the Pill, and I haven't had sex in forever. I don't have an STD."

"Ditto for me."

He hadn't had sex in forever? That surprised her. "Well, then. We're back to 'I dare you.'" She barely recognized the brazen woman she'd turned into. Had all this lust been bottled up inside her for her entire adult life? Or was it just Jackson who brought it out in her?

He made a sound somewhere between a laugh and a growl. He positioned himself and her internal muscles clenched and released convulsively in anticipation of his invasion. He eased about the first inch into her. Paused. And then plunged all the way to the hilt inside her. Her hips lurched up off the mattress and she cried out at the incredible sensation of being filled to bursting by him.

He started to withdraw and her legs whipped up around his hips to grip him for all he was worth. "Don't you dare walk away from me this time," she ground out.

"I'm not going anywhere," he muttered, driving home again. Powerfully. Completely.

"Again," she panted.

He obliged and she cried out once more. Her hips rocked forward, meeting him thrust for thrust as he set up a deep, driving rhythm that drove her out of her mind. She reached up, grasped his biceps in her fists and hung on for dear life as they flew to the moon and back.

It wasn't pretty or elegant or romantic. It was fast and hard and sweaty. Slapping flesh and pants and grunts. The bed banged into the wall and her head banged into the headboard until Jackson grabbed her hips and yanked her down the mattress.

What it was, was glorious madness. She hadn't the slightest doubt they were going to regret this sooner rather than later, but no way was she pushing him away. Oh, no. She hung on to his big, muscular, sweaty body, surging up against him, crying out, "Yes. Yes. Oh, yes, Jackson!"

It would have made for a horrendously bad porn movie, and she prayed no one else in the house could hear her. But she felt fantastic as he plundered her body, mind and soul. He wasn't afraid to be a man. To treat her like a woman, and to make it clear in no uncertain terms that she was his. She'd had no idea she needed this so badly. She needed to feel small and fragile and utterly possessed, and yet totally safe. And he did all of those things to her.

He grabbed the headboard above her head with one fist as their frantic race slowed. He stared down at her, his eyes blazing with emotions that were too raw to be named, as his body stroked hers more slowly now, more deeply.

Their joining was wet and slippery and hot, and even though her body had relaxed and stretched to accommodate him, he still filled her not quite to the point of discomfort and totally to the point of screaming-holy-cow-right-there-ohmigosh perfection.

Zinging sensations shot around inside her like frantic atoms seeking a way out, gathering and building where their bodies met until she could hardly stand the pressure. "More," she gasped.

Maddeningly, though, he held back. He kept to his steady rhythm, refusing to go harder or deeper or faster no matter how much she begged. The lightning storm climbed her insides until she nearly cried with need.

And then, all of a sudden, without warning, her entire being exploded. An orgasm ripped through her so hard she thought she'd actually disintegrated into billions of individual molecules. She cried and screamed and shouted all at once, and Jackson's mouth was wet and hot on hers, capturing every bit of it greedily for himself.

And still his body moved like a piston inside hers, relentlessly driving her onward. Incredibly, new fireworks started to crackle within her. Sharper this time. Even more electric. Clawing for release, tearing her apart from the inside out.

"I can't hold it back," she gasped.

Jackson grinned darkly. "Don't even try. Give it to me, Ana. Give it all to me."

She arched up into the hard wall of his body, helpless to hold back the explosion that tore through her. Her entire body convulsed around him. He stilled, taking it all in as she came apart around him.

She groaned, "I can't take any more."

"Wanna bet?" he growled. And then he did let go of all that vaunted self-control of his. He pounded into her, and she surged up into him, and they attacked one another like wild animals. Her hair tangled in the perspiration on her face and his lips drew back from his teeth in a grimace of pleasure so intense it looked nearly painful to him. She wrapped her entire body around him, arms, legs, internal muscles, heart and soul, and held on to him like she was never letting go.

He threw his head back, tendons and muscles cording in his neck, and shouted as he surged into her one last time and stayed there, his entire body shuddering violently against hers. She absorbed his orgasm into her own, shuddering along with him and crying out wordlessly.

His elbows landed on the mattress on either side of her head. His chest heaved against hers. She breathed every bit as hard as him as he lifted his upper torso off her to let her gasp for air, too.

Her hands loosened on his biceps and her legs relaxed around his hips, but she didn't let go of him. The expression in his eyes was dazed. He looked nearly as stunned as she felt. What the hell had just happened between them? Something unfettered and fantastic had overtaken both of them. It was…

The only word that came to mind was *magic*. Totally untamed, raw, blazing magic.

"Dammit, Ana. Did I hurt you?"

Her gaze narrowed as she glared up at him. "If you apologize for what we just did, I'm going to have to kill you, Jackson Prescott. Slowly and painfully."

"Okay. No apology. But I need to know. Are you hurt?"

"I will not break at the slightest little bump."

"That was more than a little bump, honey."

"And yet, I'm not broken." Not only was she not broken physically, apparently she was not nearly as emotionally broken as she'd believed. Apparently she was entirely capable of a healthy sexual relationship with a man as long as it was the right man.

"All right, then." The worry darkening his eyes retreated, leaving behind…

She frowned. *Leaving behind nothing.* His expression was closed up tighter than she'd ever seen it. A steady stream of swearing poured out of a heretofore unknown well of despair and frustration in the back of her mind.

What on earth had she been thinking to goad Jackson Prescott into having sex with her? He was so not ready for a relationship with her. Or with any woman, for that matter. She'd played her cards too soon. Pushed him too hard. And on cue, he'd retreated to his mental man cave and completely closed her out. Crap, crap, crap. She knew better than to shove a man into relationship stuff.

This was a disaster.

She had to distract him, and fast. Get him back onto what he considered safe ground. "Any word from Adrian on when production's going to ramp up?"

Jackson blinked. "Yeah. Right away. I'll start handing out fight sequences at the staff meeting tomorrow morning. And you can forget me firing you. I'm keeping you close where I can keep an eye on you. We'll catch the bastard who's targeting you. And when we do…" He trailed off, the tone of his voice gratifyingly threatening. After a short pause, he asked grimly, "You still gonna be okay doing fight sequences with me?"

"Sure. Why wouldn't I be?"

"You know. After this. Just didn't want things to be weird."

"They won't be weird unless you make them weird. I still work with you and for you, and we still have a movie to make."

He cleared his throat. "Right. Glad to hear you're not freaking out on me."

Oh, she was totally freaking out. She just knew not to dump it in his lap unless she wanted him to run screaming for the hills. Men could be such emotional sissies sometimes.

"So we're good?" he asked.

"Yeah. Great." Just flipping great. She could very well have thrown away her one chance for a real relationship with him for one stupid roll in the sack that hadn't even meant anything to him. If only it hadn't meant so blasted much to her. What in the world was she going to do now?

Chapter 9

She woke up early and moved around her room quietly, vividly aware of Jackson sleeping next door. She'd lain awake most of the night in her bed, tossing and turning while her traitorously excellent memory replayed their sexual encounter over and over—and freaking *over*—in her mind. Their epic sex was burned into her soul as permanently as a brand. So was the hurt in her heart when she'd left his bed, and he hadn't said a single thing to get her to stay.

If only he'd shown the slightest hint of emotional response to making love with her. But no. He'd mentally locked down like a terrorist attack was imminent and had gone full defensive.

She crept into her bathroom and examined herself carefully in the mirror. Surely she looked different after last night. Lord knew, she felt totally different. She'd had smoking-hot sex with the legendary Jackson Prescott. And if she didn't miss her guess, not many women could say that. Of course, *no* woman since Vanessa van Bitchy could say that he'd actually fallen for her, either.

If only she knew the first thing about how to attract a man and hold his attention once she had it. She'd spent her entire adult life cultivating the opposite skills. Fading into the background, being invisible, just one of the guys. She was the girl who never wore makeup or dresses or flirted with men. Ever. Heck, she'd even picked up rumors among her fellow students that she batted for the other team and didn't even like men. And she'd done nothing to dispel those rumors.

Truth was, she *didn't* like men, plural. She liked one man. Singular. And she'd even had sex with him. It had rocked her world, but it hadn't even caused a blip on his emotional radar.

She was a complete failure as a woman.

Glumly, she headed downstairs to the kitchen and found Minerva making tea. Ana forced fake cheer into her voice and said, "You're up early."

"I like the stillness of the ocean in the early morning. It's calming. Come outside and have a cup of tea with me, dear. You'll see what I mean."

God knew, she could use a little calm right now. "Your home is lovely, Mrs. Prescott."

"Call me Minerva. Everyone does."

"You've been so kind to let me stay here. Jackson's going to have the studio cut me my first paycheck. Then I can start looking for a place to stay and get out of your hair."

"No rush, dear. Jackson is really enjoying having you here."

Holy crap. If faces could catch on fire, hers just did.

Minerva smiled knowingly. "He says the two of you are going to be working closely together on his movie. Tell me about it."

"We're going to be playing a pair of aliens whose races hate each other's guts. We have to cooperate to defeat a larger enemy. We're slotted to do several hand-to-hand fight scenes. I'll try not to hit him in the nose again."

Minerva chuckled. "Oh, a good wallop is therapeutic for him now and again. Stubborn as a goat, that boy is. Always was."

A goat, huh? In her experience, if a person pushed at a goat, it would push back for no reason other than it was being pushed on. In other words, if she tried to push their relationship to a deeper level, Jackson would likely push back. Reverse psychology then. That had to be her approach. His grandmother was turning out to be a font of information.

Minerva was speaking again. "These fight scenes of yours sound passionate. Will all that passion lead your characters to kill each other or fall in love?"

An apt question. Applicable to more than a movie script. Ana shrugged. "I'm not sure. The shooting script is supposed to be finalized any minute."

"I'll bet it ends up being a love story between your characters. " Minerva clapped her hands together in delight. "Oh, I like it! A cosmic Romeo and Juliet."

"Are you a hopeless romantic, then?" Ana asked the older woman in amusement.

"There's nothing remotely hopeless about my romanticism," Minerva replied tartly.

Ana couldn't help but laugh. "I see where Jackson gets his sense of humor from. He's so much like you."

The older woman reached across the table to give her hand a squeeze. "Why, thank you, darling. That's the nicest thing anyone has said to me in a long time."

"He's really lucky to have you. He dotes on you, you know," Ana responded.

Minerva's eyes twinkled. "I think he dotes on you rather more than his pesky granny these days."

Ana shook her head. "What we have doesn't compare to his relationship with you."

Minerva took a slow sip of her tea and said reflectively, "I'm not so sure about that. I haven't seen him relate to a woman the way he does to you since—"

"Since Vanessa?"

"He told you about her?" Minerva blurted.

"We've talked about her a little. He seemed pretty devastated by her betrayal."

"Destroyed." Minerva took another sip of tea. "And it's not as if most of the women in the film industry do much to inspire confidence in him. No offense, sweetie. It's just that some actresses will do *anything* to advance their careers. Thank God you came along. I didn't think he was ever going to love another woman."

Her and Jackson? Something hungry and wishful fired off deep in her gut. If only. But she knew full well she couldn't force him to love her. It was entirely out of her control. And that was a feeling she didn't like one bit.

Jackson still hadn't taken her over to pick up her car, and Minerva insisted that she take Jackson's bad-weather car to the studio. He drove it when it was raining and he couldn't ride his Harley, apparently. The bad-weather car turned out to be a Viper.

She let the car's power and quickness distract her from the awful feeling in her gut that she'd done a bad thing by daring Jackson to have sex with her. The sports car whipped around a sharp S-curve, hugging the road like it was glued to the asphalt and cornering superbly. Her stunt driving class had made her deeply appreciate cars with this kind of responsiveness.

Sheesh. What kind of man wanted a woman who could analyze the handling characteristics of cars but knew nothing whatsoever about being female, let alone having relationships? She might have successfully goaded Jackson into a one-night stand with her, but she wasn't delusional enough to believe that it meant anything significant.

Hell, the first thing he'd said afterward had nothing to do with being glad he'd discovered her, or that he'd enjoyed himself, or that he liked her in any way. He'd merely checked to make sure she wasn't hurt. Sex with her hadn't been any more significant than just another day at the office for him.

Jackson woke up slowly. Something was different this morning, but it took him a second to regain enough consciousness for it to register.

Ana. Last night. Sex. Correction: great sex. He inhaled the faint vanilla scent of her on his pillow and a smile broke across his face. That would henceforth and forever be the scent of epic sex to him.

Still. Ana? What the hell had he been doing sleeping with her? He knew better. He had no business jeopardizing everything with her by introducing sex into the equation. Hollywood and his mother had taught him that one long ago. What an *idiot* he was. He liked her, dammit!

And now, everything would be ruined. She would start acting all weird and possessive, and he would feel suffocated, and she'd get needy, and he'd resent her clinging, and they'd start to fight, and before long she would quit her job, storm out of his life and leave him high and dry, wreck the movie, take down the studio and…

…dammit, and him back to being his lonely, isolated self.

Oh, sure, he had friends. But no women. After all, how many women looked past the glam exterior to see the real man beneath?

He'd gotten swept up in the moment and had made a colossal mistake last night. He *knew* better than to have sex with Ana and all her emotional baggage. She was already shaky enough about doing the movie. The last thing he needed to do was chase her away. She had no idea how talented she really was nor how much the camera loved her.

Although last night she bloody well hadn't been shaky. She'd been sexy and curvy and passionate, and she'd drawn him into her body and soul with an abandon that left him breathless. She'd been strong and wild and generous—no doubt about it; that was the best sex he'd ever had. By a mile.

It had been surprising that she'd responded so casually afterward. Was she actually okay with using sex for business purposes? He'd been vastly relieved, though, when she didn't demand instant declarations of true love.

But this morning, it wasn't sitting quite so well in his gut. Somewhere deep down, he'd been pretty sure she'd had a major crush on him. But now, he wasn't so sure. It was disconcerting not knowing where he stood with her.

They would go back to the studio that morning to work out a fight scene and run lines like nothing had happened between them. She would joke around with him, and things would settle back to normal. If she wanted to chalk up their roll in the sack as a one-time anomaly, he could live with that. He really didn't want to lose her from the film. In fact, he kind of liked the idea of being friends with her. She struck him as the kind of person who would make a good one. She would be loyal and funny and supportive. Yeah, that was it. He would become friends with her.

Except when he went downstairs, she'd already left the house. And his Viper was gone. Rosie didn't know where Minerva was, either. Unaccountably grouchy, he chowed down a bagel and tossed back a cup of coffee before heading out on his Harley.

He stomped into the movie studio, irritated that Ana hadn't waited to have breakfast with him or to ride in to work with him. He'd been looking forward to having her plastered to his back on a 1500-cc vibrator.

"Jackson! I'm glad you're here! You must have read my mind," Adrian Turnow exclaimed when he walked onto the soundstage.

"Why's that?"

"I've just finished building a tentative shooting schedule. I'm starting filming with you and Ana in two weeks, if you think she can be ready by then. We'll start with the green-screen work. The CGI guys are going to need all the time they can get to work on the alien scenes— starring you two—so we're shooting those first. I'll do the stuff with live actors later, while your scenes are in production on the computer-generated imagery."

"Uh, great. Ana and I will start running lines and rehearsing right away then."

The director nodded. "The green-screen set is yours as long as you need it."

"Hey, Adrian. Last night Ana offered to leave the crew for everyone's safety. It's possible someone's out to harm her, and she's worried that someone else will get hurt. She thought you and I might want her off set until her stalker issue is resolved."

"Are you okay having her around?" Adrian asked soberly.

"Yes. Even if she's being targeted, I'd rather have her here where we can look after her."

Adrian nodded in agreement. "I'll hire some extra security and we'll press on. We need her on this movie."

Great guy, Adrian. Loyal. Decent. And sane. Jackson added, "I'd actually like to set up a trap to catch her stalker and stop the shenanigans around the set."

"Is she okay with that?" Adrian asked, frowning.

"I'm not going to use her as bait or anything like that. But I want to catch this guy, not just scare him off."

"Okay," Adrian said a little doubtfully. "I'll leave it up to you and the security team. Let me know if you need anything from me."

"Thank you."

Adrian waved away the thanks with an impatient hand. "Sheila, have we sent the revised scripts over to Jackson's house yet?"

"Not yet," the director's beautiful brunette assistant said from behind him. "I was just about to call the courier service."

"Since he's here, why don't you just give them their scripts now, so he and Miss Izzolo can get to work."

"Ana's here?" Jackson asked, surprised.

Sheila answered, "She got here nearly an hour ago. I think she's working out on the main stage where we moved the green set to."

As the assistant turned away, Jackson called after her, "If you'll get me two copies of the script, I'll take Ana's to her."

Adrian said, "As soon as you two are ready to shoot a scene, let me know. If you want to take test shots or rehearse scenes with me, give me a couple hours' notice so I can pull in a shooting crew."

Jackson nodded, startled. He wasn't used to having an entire movie crew at his beck and call. Usually, he was one of the ones becked and called. "We'll get right on it. Would you rather have us rehearse one scene at a time, shoot it and move on? Or would you rather have us prepare the whole thing and come in to shoot it all at once?"

"Whatever's more comfortable for you two."

He had no flipping idea which way would be more comfortable for Ana. "You won't let her come off looking like a rank amateur, will you? Or me, for that matter," he added with a grin.

The director smiled broadly. "I will not. I promise."

"Thanks. I'll talk to Ana and let you know how she wants to do this."

Sheila brought him the scripts and he headed over to the main soundstage where the temporary greenscreen mat was set up. After yesterday's lighting accident, Adrian was having all the riggings checked before he let anyone back out on that stage.

Ana was out in the middle of a padded spring floor running through a complicated martial arts sequence, kicking and spinning and air-punching an invisible foe. Her movements were graceful, fluid and powerful. Like she'd been last night, wrapped round him in the throes of sex.

She caught sight of him, broke off her practice and

walked over to him, panting. She was wearing one of those camisole things again. It clung to all her curves and had skinny little straps that left her shoulders bare. Perspiration glistened on her skin, and an urge to lay her down and lick it off her washed over him. *Get a grip, man. Last night was a one-night deal.* A colossal, unforgettable, one-night deal.

"Hey, Jackson."

Dammit. She sounded as detached and professional as the day they'd met. Like last night had never happened. Just like he had hoped she would sound. Why, then, did it piss him off so much? Was his ego so overinflated that he'd expected her to swoon at the sight of him this morning? *Jeez, Prescott. Catch a reality check.*

"What's up?" she asked.

"Here's the shooting script. Adrian wants to film our green-screen scenes first, like in two weeks. Do you want to rehearse them and shoot them as each scene is ready, or wait and shoot all the scenes at once?"

She shot him a blank look. "No idea."

He suggested, "Why don't we have a look at the script and see if anything suggests itself to us? Once we start shooting, the expenses will mount fast, and we'll need to stick closely to the final schedule Adrian builds for us."

She nodded and plopped down on the floor to read her copy of the script. He did the same beside her. Or at least he tried to. She was doing that pretzel thing again, moving from one stretch to another as she read. Each contortion was more distracting than the last, and he couldn't help thinking of creative ways to incorporate the poses into hot, sweaty sex. Jeez! He was a mess!

In spite of her maddening flexibility, he finally finished the script and turned back to the beginning to go through it again, this time to make some preliminary notes on the changes.

Adrian would go over the script in detail with the cast and crew in the next few days, entering into endless coordination meetings to go over any additional ideas they came up with to enhance his vision of the film. After he and his crew had settled on the movie's settings, costumes, makeup, stunts, lighting, staging and a thousand other details, then production would kick up into high gear.

He'd heard Adrian comment before that directors didn't film movies these days as much as they managed movies up onto the silver screen. The guy was not wrong.

Ana looked up from her script, apparently finished reading it, as well. "There's a lot of fighting. And kissing."

"It *is* a space Western." He was eager to get started choreographing their fights. Or maybe he was just antsy to get his hands on her again. *Perv.* This was a damned job. No sexual overtones authorized. Hell, no sexual undertones were authorized, either.

"I need to talk to you after work today," she announced without warning.

Quick alarm jumped in his gut. Here came the psycho-girl reaction to their sex last night. He asked cautiously, "About what?"

"Your grandmother."

Minerva? Ana had managed to surprise him. She'd knocked him completely off balance more times in the past few days than he could recall any woman ever doing. Except maybe his mother. "What about my grandmother?"

"It can wait."

In other words, Ana didn't want to talk about it here. He frowned, but nodded. "Later, then."

"Shall we get to work on the first fight?" she asked briskly.

He studied her closely. Her expression wasn't giving a thing away. Leave it to him to sleep with the only woman in Hollywood who didn't wear her thoughts and emotions on her sleeve. No, wait. That was good, right? Why was he bugged that he couldn't read her, then?

"You have stunt hand-to-hand combat training, right?" he asked her.

"Yup. I've even caught a couple of jobs as a fight extra," she answered. "Do you need to stretch out and warm up before we get to work?"

Work. Got it. She didn't want to talk about anything personal. Probably a good call on set. These places had flipping ears. The speed with which gossip flew on movie sets still shocked him, even after his many years in the business.

"Okay," he said, matching her briskness. "We've got the dialogue that becomes an argument. We can learn that later. When it blows up, you'll need to step forward and threaten me."

Ana stepped right up to him, chest to...well, stomach. He was a lot taller than her. She reached up and poked him truculently in the chest. Grinning, he commented, "You're so cute down there. Adrian's gonna love that."

He shoved her shoulder in response to the poke. But the second his palm made contact with her, the silken slide of her skin beneath his hand slammed into his consciousness. Her bones were delicate. More than he'd ever registered before. Her entire frame was petite, in fact.

"You need to knock me off balance, Jackson. Shove me harder."

He pushed a little harder on her shoulder.

"C'mon, you can do better than that. Really give me a good shove."

He frowned. He didn't want to break her, for crying out loud. "Why can't you fake the loss of balance and just step back?"

"Because it's not that big a deal to do it for real, and then it'll look more authentic on camera. Stunts 101, Jackson. If you can do it for real and not die, do it for real."

He scowled, ticked off at her for being right, and more ticked off at himself for being so damned messed up in the head this morning. "Fine."

He gave her a hard shove that made her stagger back a couple of steps. And immediately, he felt remorse and concern. "You okay?" he asked quickly.

"What the hell is wrong with you? A few days ago you swung a baseball bat at me with all your strength and didn't think twice about it."

He glared down at her. "You know exactly what changed between us."

Shock flashed in her eyes. And something else that disappeared as quickly as it appeared. But for a second there, he thought that might have been hurt in her stare. She ground out low, "We're at *work*. Focus, for crying out loud."

That was usually *his* line to his female costars. Particularly once he'd bedded them. Jaw clenched, he nodded tersely. Using every ounce of self-discipline he possessed, he forced his mind back to the fight at hand. "Okay. You've staggered back. You'd lower your head and charge, don't you think? Plant your head in my stomach."

She gritted her teeth and did as he ordered. He grabbed for her arm and missed, ending up with a handful of her left breast. She gasped. He yanked his hand back as if she'd burned him, and they both suddenly found distant objects incredibly fascinating.

Finally, he mumbled, "How about we just walk the fight through and don't actually go hand-to-hand today?"

"'Kay," she mumbled back.

Crapcrapcrap. They couldn't even work companionably anymore. He'd ruined everything by jumping at her dare to have sex with her. He'd had no idea how much pent-up lust for her he'd been holding in check. It just couldn't wait to burst forth. The second she'd thrown down that sassy dare, he'd leaped all over it like a starving man on steak. God, he was an idiot. There was obviously a lot more going on in his subconscious regarding her than he'd ever let himself acknowledge.

No more dares for him.

Ana toweled dry in Jackson's private office bathroom. The day had been a never-ending nightmare. Jackson hadn't been any more focused than she had, and they'd both been massively awkward and uncomfortable with each other. Office romances sucked even worse than she'd been led to believe.

Of course, a one-night stand with her boss didn't rise to the level of an actual romance. The knowledge was bitter in her mouth.

She dressed, discouraged, and trudged out to the parking lot to head for her motel and Officer Westmore of the Serendipity P.D., who was going to meet her there and take her statement about the vandalism of her room. Not that she had a whole lot to say. She'd come home and her room was trashed, nothing apparently taken. End of statement.

Still, it ended up taking over an hour while he took a million photographs, lifted fingerprints off the door-knob and photographed the dried remains of the boot print on the front door. Westmore had a partner with him tonight. Big husky guy named Callum something. The guy seemed skeptical when she claimed to have no ex-boyfriends. He actually had the gall to ask her if she had a pimp or drug dealer. Jerk.

He did phone the North Carolina authorities and verify that Chandler LaGrange, the kid who'd tried to strangle her, was still institutionalized. Although she was on the list of people to be notified if he was ever released, it was still a relief when the California cop confirmed that Chandler was still locked up.

She dragged herself down the stairwell and out to the parking lot, a fistful of papers in hand that she would need for her insurance claim. Lord, she was exhausted. It was late and getting dark, and she was dog-tired after air-fighting all day. It was almost more tiring than actual fighting because each movement had to be both thrown and stopped before contact was made with the oppo-nent. Not that she hadn't been mighty tempted to haul off and slug Jackson for real after the way he was tiptoeing around her like she would break at the slightest bump.

Something moved ahead of her and she looked up… *Drat.* Jackson was waiting beside the Viper on his Harley.

"You heading home now?" he asked evenly enough.

"I thought I might try to find a shop to do some main-tenance on my car while I have access to alternate transportation," she lied. Now, why had that come out of her mouth? Was she that desperate not to look desperate?

A shadow passed through his eyes right before his emotional shutters slammed down. "You've had a long day. Tomorrow's soon enough to get your car fixed. I'll introduce you to the best mechanic in town. And besides. We need to talk."

No kidding. She sighed. "Here?"

He looked around the parking lot. "I want a shower and some hot food in me before we do it."

Lord, it sounded like talking to her was worse than a prison sentence. "I'll head back to your grandmother's place then."

Without another word, he cranked up his motorcycle and rode it out of the parking lot. It felt like a chunk of her heart ripped out of her chest and dragged along on the asphalt behind him. Like toilet paper stuck to the bottom of his shoe. Yup, that was her.

Last night had been a dreadful mistake. They couldn't even talk to each other today, let alone work together or be friends.

When she pulled into Minerva's garage, she was surprised to see that the Harley wasn't there. Where had Jackson gone off to? He'd been the one who'd wanted her to come straight back here so they could talk. Frowning, she stepped into the kitchen.

"There you are, dear," Minerva practically sang. "I have a surprise for you and Jackson tonight."

Alarm slammed into her. "I'm not sure this is a good night for surprises. Jackson had a rough day."

"Did you slug him again?"

"No!" Although the thought had crossed her mind.

Minerva waved a breezy hand. "No need to worry about Jackson."

"I happen to hate surprises, too, Minerva," she said warningly.

"Perfect!"

Huh?

"All will become clear shortly. Dinner will be ready in a half hour, and my special guest will arrive shortly thereafter."

A guest. Okay, she could deal with that. She just didn't need Minerva interfering in the crazy mess that was currently her nonrelationship with Jackson. She went upstairs to change clothes and put on some makeup before supper.

Whoa. Since when did she wear makeup on a daily basis? Since she'd had sex with Jackson and really, really liked feeling like a woman, apparently. She shook her head at herself and called herself all kinds of names for doing it, but she still changed into a casual dress and started putting on makeup.

The more she thought about facing him again, the more nervous she got. And the more nervous she got, the more makeup she gooped on her face. Eye shadow. Liquid liner. Mascara. Blush. Lip liner. Gloss. Desperate, she rooted around in the makeup case that had appeared in her bathroom, compliments of Minerva. Was there anything else in here she could put on?

Eventually, it dawned on her what she was doing and she threw down the eyebrow brush in disgust. Clown face and all, she marched downstairs to face the music.

"You look spectacular, Ana," Minerva declared.

"I look like a freak," she snapped.

"Let's see what Jackson thinks and then decide," Minerva said smoothly, amusement humming in her voice.

She could see how the woman's meddling got on Jackson's nerves sometimes.

Jackson's Harley rumbled into the garage just as Rosie was serving up dinner on the veranda. He strode out into the fiery glow of the sunset and Ana's breath caught at the sight of him, his broad shoulders filling out his black leather jacket, his powerful legs braced apart and his hair lifting in the breeze coming up off the ocean. How was it possible for one man to be that hot?

He caught sight of her, and she could swear his eyes actually had little flames shooting from them there for a second. "I rest my case," Minerva murmured in triumph.

Meddler. But something feminine and wild responded with excitement deep in her gut to that momentary look of lust in his eyes.

"There you are, dear. Just in time for supper." Minerva waved him to his seat.

"I thought you wanted a shower," Ana murmured.

"The studio called. Had to swing by to review the new security setup. Then part of the crew invited me out for a beer. I couldn't say no to them."

But he could bloody well put her on the back burner, apparently. If there'd been any doubt in her mind what his opinion was of her, he'd just laid it to rest once and for all. A beer with the guys was a lot more important than a serious talk with her.

Jackson slipped into his chair and Minerva took over the conversation, bubbling with excitement and chattering on about nothing at all. Which was just as well. Ana didn't know what the hell to say to Jackson anymore. He'd been completely weird all day at work—stiff, stilted and flamingly uncomfortable with her. And now this slap in the face.

Jackson seemed content to let Minerva dominate the talk with her meaningless patter. Ana surreptitiously watched him eat. He was unnaturally quiet tonight. Great. He was still weirded out. He appeared to be studiously avoiding making eye contact with her. When they reached simultaneously for a bowl of green beans and their fingers bumped, he jerked his hand away and actually muttered an apology.

She was tempted to kick him under the table.

Minerva rushed Rosie through serving dessert and even insisted on helping the woman carry in the dishes after the meal was over. Vividly aware of the French doors to the kitchen standing wide open, Ana refrained from demanding to know what the hell was wrong with him. Barely.

The doorbell echoed through the bowels of the house and Jackson looked up in surprise.

She commented, "You missed Minerva's pre-dinner announcement that she's expecting a special guest this evening. Your grandmother's tremendously excited to have you and me meet whoever it is."

"Oh, Lord. Not another one of her fortune-tellers," he groaned.

Minerva was into mediums? Okay, that explained a little more about where Jackson's mother had gotten her wild, creative streak.

He rolled his eyes and rose to his feet. Apparently, he didn't inherit the wild part of it from his own mother. Jackson held her chair for her as she also rose, but she expected it had more to do with ingrained good manners than actually wanting to show genuine courtesy to her. God, she was getting cynical in her old age. She followed him toward the sound of voices, and it took them to the library in the front of the house.

"There you two are. Come in. Come in," Minerva directed eagerly. "This is Yogi Surhan. He's a tremendously talented seer. Foretells the future. I was just telling him about you lovebirds."

Lovebirds? And a seer? Color her confused. Ana threw a questioning look at Jackson, and he shrugged back.

"Yogi Surhan, this is my grandson Jackson and his girlfriend, Ana."

The turbaned man, who looked about a hundred years old, and shockingly like a raisin, stepped forward. He was even shorter than Ana, which was saying something. The man held his hand out to her as if to shake hands, and Ana grasped it politely. He didn't let go, though. In fact, he took a step closer and laid his free hand on her stomach without warning.

"Hey!" She tried to jump back, but for a tiny raisin of a man, Yogi Surhan was shockingly strong. Heat from his hand permeated her dress and sank into her belly.

"What the hell? Take your hands off her, buddy. You're making her uncomfortable," Jackson declared. When the yogi ignored him, he demanded of his grandmother, "Who is this guy?"

The yogi not only ignored Jackson's outburst, but he closed his eyes and started humming, a low, nasal sound. For all the world, it looked like the man had fallen into some sort of trance.

Ana batted at the hand on her belly, but the wiry little bastard ignored the slap. She looked up in distress to Jackson for help. But as he took an aggressive step forward, Minerva waylaid him, physically stepping between her grandson and the yogi.

"Yogi Surhan is a world-famous psychic, Jackson," Minerva proclaimed proudly. "He's *never* wrong. Let him concentrate."

The world-famous psychic opened his wizened eyes and looked back and forth between her and Jackson. "I see your baby."

"*Our* baby?" Jackson spluttered, gesturing between himself and Ana.

If Ana weren't so freaked out by this stranger groping her stomach, she might have laughed at the thunderstruck expression on Jackson's face.

Minerva clapped her hands together in delight. "Oh, do tell us. Is it a boy or a girl?"

"Minerva," Ana wailed, "don't encourage this madness!"

Jackson's grandmother waved her to silence. "If you'll just pipe down for a few seconds and let Yogi Surhan focus, he's going to tell us the sex of your baby." She added rapturously, "My first great-grandchild. Oh, I'm so glad I lived to see this day."

Behind Minerva's back, Jackson threw her a bewildered look, and she shrugged in response. He rolled his eyes, and Ana restrained an urge to giggle. She had to give Jackson and his grandmother credit. Their household was never boring.

"Stop laughing and concentrate," the yogi snapped.

"On what?" Ana blurted.

"On revealing the sex of your child to me," he replied indignantly. "Open your womb to me."

Open her *what?* The urge to laugh became almost unbearable.

"You must be calm and focused for me to penetrate the mists of the future and ascertain this child's gender."

This should be interesting. Particularly since she wasn't freaking pregnant.

"Everybody, close your eyes," he ordered imperiously.

Oh, for the love of Mike. Ana closed her eyes reluctantly. Was it legal for her to suffocate Minerva in her sleep with a pillow?

A long silence stretched out as everyone in the room closed their eyes. Eventually, bored, Ana cracked one eyelid open to peek at the yogi. Eyes screwed tightly shut and adding even more wrinkles to his aged face, he looked like he was wishing very hard for something. Or constipated. Her urge to giggle returned. The more she thought about it, the harder it became not to laugh.

She closed that eye and peeked sidelong out of the other eye at Jackson. He was staring up at the ceiling in grand exasperation as if appealing to a higher power for the patience not to kill his grandmother.

"I have it!" the yogi yelled without warning.

Ana jumped about a foot straight up in the air. Jackson gave one last eye roll to the heavens, while Minerva clasped her hands over her heart in anticipation so great she obviously could not contain herself. "Oh, do tell!" she cried.

"The young man and the young lady. They are going to have a boy child."

Maybe in a few *years*. In an alternate universe where Jackson didn't think women were Satan's handmaidens and she wasn't his employee.

"There is no question about it," the yogi announced. She carries a boy." The guy spoke with such authority it was hard not to believe him out of hand.

Jackson gaped at her. She gaped at the yogi. The yogi smiled beatifically at Minerva. Minerva beamed at everyone.

"What the *hell* is going on around here?" Jackson finally demanded.

Ana spoke carefully in a Herculean effort not to dissolve in laughter. Or tears. Did Jackson have to sound so completely appalled at the idea of him and her ending up together? Maybe even having a baby someday? "If Yogi Surhan is to be believed, we're going to have a baby boy."

"What? When?" Jackson looked completely dumbfounded. She had to give him credit for doing a fantastic job of acting genuinely surprised.

"In the future, Jackson. Far, far in the future." Now that she was over the initial shock of the yogi's announcement, Ana was actually starting to be a little amused. Okay, a lot amused. She'd never seen Jackson this flustered.

"A…b-baby?" He was having trouble even saying the word.

"Earth to Jackson. Come in. You need to breathe. You're turning blue, big guy."

Finally, the reality bird pooped on Jackson's head, and he seemed to put together crazy yogi and crazier prediction with the idea of nothing to worry about. A look of the most profound relief swept across his face. God, she would double over with laughter if such a big part of her didn't desperately wish the yogi was right and that she was pregnant with Jackson's son.

He mumbled, "A baby, huh? Um, wow. That's fascinating. I guess congratulations are in order."

He startled her by sweeping her up in his arms and kissing her soundly. And darned if the second his mouth landed on hers she didn't respond like her entire being had just gone up in flames. Passion roared through her, surging forward to consume her, and she threw herself into the kiss without conscious thought. *This was Jackson, and she wanted him worse than life.*

His mouth slanted across hers in response, devouring her like they were never going to be allowed to kiss again. She opened her soul to him, and he filled it, renewing her like floodwaters sinking into parched earth. Her hands plunged into his hair and she tugged his head down closer, stroking his tongue with hers, sucking his tongue into her mouth, hungrily absorbing the taste of him. God, she couldn't get enough of him.

He made a low sound in the back of his throat that she felt more than heard. It rumbled of possession. Of territory claimed. Of lust and passion, gluttony and greed. Her insides melted and her body molded eagerly to his.

Yogi Surhan chortled. "Good thing they've already made the baby, yes? Or we would have to send them upstairs now to do the deed."

The bald comment shocked Ana back into awareness of her surroundings. The library. Minerva. Raisin Man. And Jackson. Oh, Lord. She was crawling all over him like stripes on a tiger. Guiltily, she unwrapped herself from him as he straightened. The poor guy looked nearly as flabbergasted as she felt.

What the heck had *that* just been? They'd barely spoken to each other all day and all hell had broken loose between them the second they'd touched each other.

"My work here is done," the yogi announced. "I wish you all felicitations from my heart. This baby, he will be healthy, strong and wise."

This *hypothetical* baby. She only hoped Minerva hadn't paid this charlatan seer a whole lot for that bogus act.

Minerva showed the little man to the front door, gushing over him every step of the way. Jackson, who had never actually let go of Ana's hand after that incendiary kiss, dragged her into the foyer after his grandmother.

The front door closed and Jackson announced firmly, "Ana and I are going to go upstairs now and have a conversation."

"I'll turn the television up loud, dear," Minerva said blithely.

Ana's jaw dropped and her face flamed with hot shame. Jackson's grandmother thought they were going to have sex? Loud, raucous sex? Ohmigod, she would never be able to look the woman in the eye again.

"C'mon, Ana," Jackson ground out, bodily dragging her up the right staircase. "We need to have that talk you mentioned earlier. Now."

Chapter 10

Jackson turned to face Ana. She looked like a guilty child standing in the middle of his bedroom staring down at her toes. He wanted to make love to her so badly he could hardly stand upright. That kiss in the library had been out of this world. If he so much as touched her, he would lose whatever modicum of control he had and fall on her like a beast.

Being careful to stay well out of arm's reach of her, he took tight hold of his surging lust and asked low and grim, "What the hell was that circus downstairs all about?"

Ana exhaled hard. "You tell me. I had no idea your grandmother was into fortune-tellers and soothsayers."

"Exactly what triggered all of that?"

"I have no idea. This morning, she did bring up the subject of wanting a great-grandchild. I didn't say anything to lead her on, though. It's not like I told her I'm pregnant or anything."

Holy Mother of God. Just hearing those words out of Ana's mouth did crazy things to his gut. The idea of a baby—their baby—was shocking, and strangely... exciting.

Not good exciting, he told himself hastily. Scary exciting. Yeah, that was it. That knot twisting in his gut was an instinctive threat reaction. That was all. It wasn't possible that Ana was pregnant. Well, technically, he supposed it was—

Alarm slammed into him. "Last night. *Christ.* You *are* using birth control, aren't you?"

"Yes, of course," she answered quickly, matching his alarm. "I'm on the Pill. It helps keep my...my cycle... regular."

His gut twisted at how appalled she sounded at the idea of actually having his kid. He wasn't that bad a guy, was he? He wouldn't be the worst choice on the planet to be a father. Not that he blamed her for not wanting to be saddled with a baby. She was single and just starting a demanding career. A baby would be a huge inconvenience for her.

Thank goodness she wasn't one of those women who would use a pregnancy to trap a star into coughing up millions in child support...or worse, demanding a wedding ring. No child deserved to be used that way.

God knew, he'd been an inconvenient child, himself. No way would he do that to any kid of his. After his father died, his mother had drifted without an anchor. He and his siblings had bounced from crash pad to crash pad with Linda while she got stoned and tried to sleep her way into acting jobs, when she was cleaned up enough to know what day it was. Had Minerva not finally stepped in and taken them away from her, had his grandmother not given them stability and fierce love, who the hell knew how things would have turned out for any of them. If he had a kid, by God, he would be there to raise it.

The idea of watching his own son or daughter—son if he was to believe Yogi What's-his-face—grow up was seductively appealing. Good thing there was still plenty of time for him to settle down. To have kids later.

Ana was talking again. "I'm sorry I didn't warn you about Minerva having arranged a surprise before she ambushed you."

"This isn't the first time she's pulled a stunt like this. Don't beat yourself up over it." He paced the length of the room, unaccountably restless.

"Are you okay?" she asked in a small voice. "Do you need me to leave and go stay in a hotel until I can find a place of my own?"

"I'm fine. And no, I need you to stay."

"I've never seen your grandmother happier than when that nutball told her I was going to have your son. She *really* wants a great-grandchild. I think she's genuinely worried you won't ever get around to having a family on your own. And now that I've seen how focused you are on your career, I have to say I agree with her."

Great. Just what he needed: *two* women meddling in his personal life. As if one wasn't enough, now Minerva had help.

He opened his mouth to tell Ana to butt out, but something inside him prevented the words from coming out. After all, he'd been the one to insist that she come here to stay.

She was speaking again. "It's going to kill Minerva to

find out I'm not your girlfriend, let alone pregnant with your baby. I think we should nip this in the bud and dash her hopes now, before she gets too much more invested in the whole us-dating thing."

They *weren't* dating? They were sleeping together but not dating? He opened his mouth to protest before he thought better of it. This was every bachelor's perfect situation, right? Hot girl is happy to jump in the sack with you but wants no emotional commitment whatsoever?

"My impulsive grandmother? That ship has sailed. She's convinced you and I are headed for happily ever after."

"I'm sorry," she said in a small voice.

"Nothing to apologize for, Ana. Everything's great." Except he didn't feel great as she turned silently and returned to her own room without a backward glance for him.

Ana dragged herself out of bed reluctantly. Every day for the past week, she and Jackson had been rehearsing, running lines and practicing fight scenes with each other and with the stuntmen in the movie. Each day had been worse than the last. Jackson seemed to have relegated her to finished business in his mind and was treating her like one of the guys. Distant. Professional. Impersonal. He still had trouble hitting her properly, though.

At least something had come out of their onetime romantic interlude. He'd figured out that she was a girl. And now he was totally hinky about punching her. But apparently, she wasn't woman enough for him to be interested in having an actual relationship with.

She'd been hunting for a place of her own each day after work, but the price of housing in this exclusive beach community took her breath away. And it was just possible that she didn't really want to move out of Jackson's house and sever the last tentative emotional tie she had to him.

As for who had mugged her and trashed her motel room, no obvious suspects were forthcoming. The local police seemed to think it had been some sort of domestic dispute, and that she was refusing to hand over the name of whoever'd done it. As if she would ever protect some man who would act like that. Hah!

She kept getting the feeling that she was being watched, but she kept her suspicions to herself. The sensation of being followed was bad enough to make her sleep terribly and feel cranky when she was awake. For the first few days, she whipped around to look behind her when the sensation overcame her. But eventually, she started to feel crazy and forced herself not to react anymore to the feeling of a malevolent glare boring into her shoulder blades.

She knew that it was perfectly normal to experience heightened sensitivity and anxiety after a traumatic experience. The shrinks taught her that after Chandler had nearly killed her. But just because her head understood it, that didn't mean her gut was listening to reason. At all.

It wasn't listening to her regarding her hunky costar, either. She had to find a way to survive the agony of living in close proximity to Jackson at his grandmother's house and yet being so very distant from him. The worst of it was that he didn't seem to think anything was wrong.

He chatted pleasantly with her at breakfast, worked with her and the other members of his crew during the day, and wished her sweet dreams every night when she went up to bed, inevitably well before him. She'd known he would have to work hard both producing and acting in this movie, but she'd had no idea how hard movie-making was.

Despite how late he came home most nights, she was still awake when she heard him come into his room. She tossed and turned, tangling herself in the hot sheets most nights, too, her lust ragingly unsatisfied. If only she could creep next door in the middle of the night and make love with him one more time. Although, she suspected one more time wouldn't be nearly enough for her. She would never get enough of him. The man was an addiction she wasn't likely to kick anytime soon.

The good news was that Jackson didn't seem to be sleeping any better than she was. She heard his mattress creak and groan for hours sometimes as he tossed and turned. What kept him awake in the wee hours? She would give anything for it to be fantasies of her. Of course, it was more likely issues at work weighing on his mind. She was neither naive nor stupid, and she knew Jackson was done with her.

After one of those nights where neither she nor Jackson had gotten any rest at all, Ana stumbled downstairs in the morning to the sound of rain pounding at the big picture windows ocean-side. The gray, gloomy weather fit her mood perfectly.

Minerva announced cheerfully over breakfast in the not-sunny sunroom, "I have a surprise for the two of you. It was just delivered."

Ana looked up at Jackson in quick alarm. He looked as unpleasantly surprised as her as he ground out, "Please tell me that yoga guy isn't back."

"He's a yogi, dear. And no. He's not back. We already know the sex of your baby. Come with me."

Perplexed, Ana rose from her seat and followed Jackson and Minerva into the kitchen. The older woman opened the garage door with a flourish, announcing, "A gift. For the two of you."

Jackson was first to step into the garage. His voice floated back to her in outrage. "What the *hell?*"

Ana stepped outside and spied a chunky maroon minivan beside the Viper. The new vehicle looked like a beached whale parked next to a barracuda.

"Look," Minerva said excitedly. "It's already got a baby seat preinstalled and everything. And the rear row of seats folds down automatically. The man at the dealership said you can fit all kinds of baby gear in the back. Playpen. Stroller. Even a high chair. It's perfect for when the baby gets here. You can't exactly put an infant on a Harley, and the Viper has only two seats and no storage room at all. It was totally impractical for a young family."

Shocked to her core, Ana turned to stare at Jackson, who was noticeably pale. The man looked like he'd just been run over by a freight train.

"Since it's raining today, you two can drive it to work and see how you like it." Minerva held out the key fob and Jackson took it, staring numbly at the little black device in his hand like he'd never seen an electronic car key before.

"You need me to drive, big guy?" Ana asked, amused. "There's no shame in not knowing how to drive a mommy-mobile."

"I can drive the damned car," he snapped. Color was returning to his face. A lot of it. Fast.

"We should name it, don't you think?" Ana said cheerfully. "Any ideas, Minerva?"

"Oooh. Something cuddly. The Hugster."

"There will be *no* Hugster in this house. Is that clear?" Jackson declared forcefully.

Ana slapped a hand over her mouth to stifle her laughter. He was too pissed off to see the humor in the moment just yet. If she wasn't mistaken, Minerva's eyes were glinting with something evilly akin to humor as the woman sailed into the kitchen with a wave of a hand. "You two enjoy the ride. Let me know how it goes."

The kitchen door closed behind her, and the garage fell silent.

Ana tiptoed around to the passenger side of the luxuriously appointed minivan and slid into the heated glove-leather seat. It actually was a pretty snazzy vehicle with all the latest bells and whistles.

Jaw set, and steam all but shooting out his ears, Jackson adjusted the driver's seat back to accommodate his height and strapped himself in. He backed out of the garage and into the rain, his movements precise. Tense. She had to give him credit for being a great grandson. He was going to drive the minivan once for Minerva.

He pulled out of the driveway onto the main road and the car behind them honked as it ran up on their slowly accelerating tailgate. Ana had to choke back a giggle yet again.

"I'll kill her," Jackson growled.

That was it. Ana dissolved into gales of laughter as he grasped the big steering wheel in angry fists, his foot jammed to the floor on the accelerator.

"Aw, c'mon," she chortled. "You wear the Hugster well. It looks great on you."

"Shut up, Izzolo. This is not funny."

"Yes. Yes, it is. Just think. You can fit six…" she turned around to count seats "…no, five—because of the baby seat—drunks in here when you go out partying. You'll be the most popular guy on set. Designated driver forever. On guys' nights out, you can call it the Shaggin' Wagon."

"That'll be enough out of you."

"Minerva's just twisting your arm a little. That's why you're so mad. She one-upped you. I have to give her props for this one. I didn't see it coming."

Jackson fumed in silence most of the way across town to the studio. As they turned onto the long drive that led back to the big soundstage, he surprised her by commenting, "I've been staying late at the studio for the past week in hopes that your stalker would show up there again and try to sabotage something else."

She blinked over at him, startled. *That* was why he'd been coming home so late every night? He wasn't trying to avoid her?

"You're positive the guy who tried to kill you is still locked up?" Jackson asked.

"Yes. Positive. Brody and Callum verified it last week. Besides, I'm on the list of people to be notified if he's ever released."

"Have there been any rumblings about him getting out?"

She shrugged. Privacy laws being what they were, she wasn't granted much access to Chandler's medical records. She shared what she did know, though. "The way I hear it, he had a complete schizophrenic break and has never shown any signs of rejoining reality."

"Okay, so we rule out LaGrange as a suspect," Jackson commented.

"Have you learned anything more about the studio accident?"

"No amateur would know how to set the specialized charges that brought down the light track. I've been going through the roster of all the employees to see who might have past training in handling explosives. Of the guys who know how to make cutting charges, none of them have any connection to you. I gotta say, I'm stumped as to who's coming after you."

"And you're sure it's not just a random thing? That I wasn't in the wrong place at the wrong time and the victim of a random crime?"

"Not three times in a row. I don't believe in that kind of chance."

Neither did she.

Silence filled the Hugster until they pulled into Jackson's spot in the studio parking lot. A couple of crew members were lounging out front on a covered porch, smoking. They guffawed at Jackson's new wheels and razzed him about his sexy ride.

During the morning, she might have accidentally let slip something about the factory-installed baby seat in Jackson's new minivan. Before long, the entire crew was giving him holy hell about his hot ride. As pranks went, Ana had to give Minerva credit for sheer, evil genius.

Today, she and Jackson were supposed to rehearse their first scene with Adrian. She was already nervous, and now Jackson was in a royally foul mood to boot.

She changed into a lime-green bodysuit with white dots strategically placed all over it. Apparently, the dots were used by CGI artists to tie their computer graphics to film of her body movements. Although today was only a screen test of their fight choreography, Adrian made a policy of staging every screen test just like a real film shot. That way, if today's take was better than anything he got later, he'd still have usable film.

She spied the tall, lime silhouette of Jackson heading across the green carpet. Yup. He was still pissed. She knew that set of his shoulders and the way his jaw was rippling with clenched muscle. Not that he was the type to randomly spew his temper at the people around him. He was too good a boss for that.

"All right, guys," Adrian said cheerfully from the edge of the mat. "Let's see what you've got."

She and Jackson duly went through the argument lines leading up to the fight sequence. They actually grappled today, and she knew immediately that it wasn't working. Jackson was holding back and refusing to really engage in the fight with her.

They tried a couple of takes, and finally, as lunchtime came and Adrian dismissed the cameramen to go grab a bite to eat, the director came over to the two of them privately. He asked quietly, "Is there something going on between the two of you that I should know about?"

Ana looked up at Jackson, blatantly punting the question to him. He said, "What do you mean, Adrian?"

"You're off your game. It's like the two of you are afraid to hit each other. Did one of you get walloped again during rehearsals or something?"

"Nope. Nothing like that," Jackson answered evasively.

"You need to get over whatever's making you guys so cautious. Go have sex or something. Get your hands on each other and get comfortable with each other like you were a few weeks ago. I'll meet you back here in an hour."

Ana's jaw dropped as the director turned and strolled away from them. *Go have sex?*

"My office. Now," Jackson muttered.

She followed him to his office, which was small, neat and functional. Not all the lavish Hollywood star's digs she'd expected. She closed the door and turned to face him expectantly. She might be the amateur actor, but even she knew he was the problem.

His mobile features conveyed deep chagrin. "Look, Ana. It was a mistake for us to sleep together. We have to find a way to get past it and get back to the initial working relationship we had."

He might as well have stuck a dagger in her heart and twisted it. Her impulse was to crumple up in a little ball until she found the strength to slink away and never come back. But then anger poured through her. She was nobody's victim, and she didn't slink away from anything or anyone.

She stood up straighter and glared up at him. "I happen to disagree. I do not think it was a mistake. I don't regret it for one second. The sex rocked and I'd love to do more of that with you."

Shock—and heat—began to fill his gaze.

She continued more forcefully, "However, you obviously are emotionally stunted and trapped in your hurt feelings from years ago. You aren't mature enough to handle a real relationship with any woman, and you certainly don't deserve me. I'm not about to stick around waiting for you to get your head out of your ass and realize how awesome I am and how much I care for you. I've signed a contract to do this movie, and I'm going to do my level best on it. But after that, I'm out of here, Jackson."

"But—"

"But nothing. You're an idiot."

She turned and marched out of his office without a backward glance. *God, that felt good.* She'd needed to say that to him for a while. He *was* an idiot for not seeing how much she loved him and what a great girlfriend she would be—

Oh. My. God. She'd just admitted to him that she had serious feelings for him.

And as if that weren't horrendous enough, she'd also just told him to go to hell. What in the world had gotten into her? She didn't do emotional outbursts. Ever. It hadn't been her style even before Chandler tried to kill her, and it still wasn't her style. She was calm about her interactions with other people. Thoughtful. She analyzed and examined things from every angle before she decided how she felt about them. She didn't just blurt out that she cared for a man in one breath and inform him in the next breath that she hated his guts!

She held it together until she hit the ladies' locker room. And then she fell apart. Totally. Tears and all. It was official. She'd lost her mind. And apparently, she'd lost Jackson, too.

Chapter 11

Jackson stared at his office door as it shut behind Ana. What in the hell had just happened? He'd brought her in here to apologize to her for holding back this morning, and she'd gone completely postal on him! He'd apologized for having sex with her because it was what he thought she wanted to hear from him! Hell, he thought the sex between them had been epic, too.

He shoved a distracted hand through his hair and fell into his desk chair. She *cared* for him? Equal parts terror and exultation roared through him. Did he care back? Cripes, he was too shell-shocked right now to have the slightest idea how he felt about her.

Where had calm, steady, dependable Ana gone to? Since when was she emotional and volatile? Genuine worry for her filled him. But if he wasn't mistaken, he'd just been told in no uncertain terms to butt out of her life. He frowned. If she were any other woman, he might put it down to some sort of massive hormone surge and ignore the order to buzz off. But he had *no* idea how to proceed with Ana.

Shocked at himself for doing it, he pulled out his cell phone and dialed Minerva.

"Hello, dear. Is everything all right?"

He leaned back in his chair and closed his eyes. "I don't know. I need some advice."

"About what?"

"Women."

"Ahh. You and Ana have a fight?"

"I guess so. Not exactly. She had a fight with me."

"Big emotional blowup where she vented stuff she's been hanging on to for a while?" Minerva asked perceptively.

"Yes, actually. That's pretty damned accurate. Do you know what's up with her?"

Has grandmother laughed gently. "Yes, honey. It's called pregnancy hormones. Hers are raging out of control right now. It'll get worse before it gets better. Your job is to be patient and understanding and not take any of it personally."

He mumbled something incoherent and got off the phone fast.

Huh. If Ana were actually pregnant, he'd be all over doing what Minerva had suggested. But she wasn't pregnant, and he had no earthly idea what had caused her to flip out. He'd been doing everything in his power to get things back to the way they'd been before they'd had sex because that seemed to be what she wanted, but nothing had worked.

Hell, he probably should have dragged her to bed the

first time things got weird between them and kept having sex with her until they were totally at ease with each other. Even Adrian had suggested they just have sex and get it over with.

Did the director see the attraction between them, then? Did everybody else see it? Was *he* the only one who'd been blind to it all this time?

He wasn't particularly prone to long bouts of introspection and self-examination, but he did close his eyes and cast his mind back over the past months of working with Ana. Had the signals been there the whole time?

It wasn't that he didn't find her attractive. He actually did. Who wouldn't? He hadn't been lying the other night when he'd said he *had* noticed she was a girl. She was pretty, funny, smart, easy to be around. And she looked great in a tight T-shirt. But he'd been so busy trying to be a good boss that he'd strangled any reaction he might have had to her as a woman. In his own defense, he'd been working eighteen- and twenty-hour days trying to get the movie rolling and catch whoever had sabotaged his set. It wasn't like he'd had time to do anything about his attraction to her.

Speaking of which, he had a bunch of set stills to approve. The photos were taken of newly constructed sets to check how they would look on camera. He stuck the pictures under his desk lamp to study it more closely. Son of a bitch. These had been taken during yesterday's rehearsal, and he and Ana were in a bunch of the shots. He was looking off into the distance, but she was looking up at him. Staring up at him adoringly, to be more precise.

He pulled out another picture of them together. And another.

In every one of them, her attention riveted on him.

Jesus. Had she been doing that all along? How had he missed it?

Talk about feeling like an idiot. He deserved the moniker from her. What about him? How *did* he feel about her? It wasn't like he'd ever really stopped to think about it. Visions of her wearing dresses and makeup, sitting across the veranda table from him looking so tasty he could eat her alive, flashed through his mind.

And the night they'd made love…sure, she'd provoked him. Hell, she'd dared him outright to have sex with her. But he hadn't been in any big hurry not to take her up on it. He wasn't some raw kid to allow himself to be manipulated like that. If he were to be brutally honest with himself, he'd been all over jumping in the sack with her.

It had freaked him out a lot worse than he'd expected, though. The emotional connection between them had been too intense for him.

Be honest, dude.

Okay, fine. Their emotional connection had scared the hell out of him. He never opened up to other people that way, male or female. But she'd blown right past his defenses and looked deep into his naked soul.

And I pushed her away.

When he'd wanted to tell her how amazing she was and how great she'd made him feel, he'd asked her instead if she was hurt and promptly started to talk about work. He'd fled for safe ground because he was a damned coward.

He swore under his breath. Which left them…where? She apparently hated his guts now, and planned to go as far away from him as she could as fast as she could. The thought caused panic to rip through his gut.

Two weeks. That was about how long the remaining filming of their scenes together would take. All the time he had left to break through whatever barriers she'd thrown up regarding him. A couple months from now, Adrian might need to do some retakes, but knowing the accomplished director, he would get all the takes he needed the first time around.

Two weeks wasn't long to fix things between him and Ana. Particularly since he didn't have the foggiest idea how to make things better. The first order of business was to find her. Talk to her. Salvage this afternoon's shoot, somehow.

He left his office and looked all over the set for her but couldn't find her anywhere. Eventually one of the female prop girls said something about seeing her in the ladies' locker room. Hiding perchance? Since when did Ana hide from anybody? Frowning, he made his way to the locker-room door.

He cracked it open enough to call through it, "Ana? Are you in there?"

"Go away."

So not happening. He pushed open the door and strode into the forbidden land of estrogen. It looked about like the men's locker room, but it smelled better and the discarded towels were mostly in the laundry bin by the showers.

"Jackson! Get out!"

"Is anyone else in here?" he asked tersely.

"No. But—"

"Great." He turned around and locked the hallway door. "We need to talk."

"I've said all I need to say."

"Yeah, well, I haven't."

Ana glared at him through watery eyes.

"You're right. I'm an idiot. I should have noticed a long time ago how you felt about me. But I didn't see it, and I can't change that. For better or worse, you've taken me by surprise. I need a little time to process it all and figure out how I feel. And in the meantime, you and I have a movie to shoot. We've got to set aside our personal feelings and get the job done."

She shrugged. "What do you think I've been doing for the past couple of weeks? You're the problem in that department, not me."

It stung to hear her point it out. "Fair enough. I'll do my best. I just need a little reciprocity from you. Can I count on that?"

"Sure. You can always count on me. Good ol' reliable Ana. That's me."

"Look. I know you're mad. You probably have a right to be. But can we at least try to keep this civil?" he asked.

"Actually, no. I don't think so."

He stared, stunned. What the hell had gotten into her? She *never* acted like this!

"It's time for us to head back out to the mat, Jackson. I need to stretch before we fight again. My back's been a little tight the past few days."

She sailed out of the dressing room while he stared, dumbfounded, at the door as it swung shut behind her. *She'd lost her mind. Totally lost it.*

Ana did, indeed, need to stretch her back. It had been aching right between her shoulder blades. Those damned push-up bras she'd bought back when she thought she had a chance with Jackson had made not only her back hurt but also made her breasts ache. Her poor girls weren't used to being smushed and pushed quite so aggressively. It didn't help that she'd been sleeping like hell, either.

Screw him. Even when Jackson was trying to make nice and calm her down, he said not a word about returning any of her feelings. What. A. Jerk.

The tiny voice in the back of her head rather hesitantly brought up the possibility that she might be overreacting a teensy weensy bit, but she mentally snapped at the voice to sit down and shut up. Thankfully, it did.

"Okay, kids," Adrian announced jovially. "Let's fight."

Actually, that sounded like a great idea. Eyes narrowed, she stepped forward to face Jackson. If he refused to fight with her, that didn't mean she couldn't vent her frustrations on him. In fact, a good hard fight might be just what the doctor ordered.

Adrian called for the cameras to roll and she closed in on Jackson, spitting and snarling like the feline-based alien she was portraying. Her glare was entirely real as she leaped at him.

Jackson fended off her first attack, and a look of genuine surprise crossed his face. They hadn't choreographed that leap.

She pounced again. This time, though, he was ready for her. She bounced off his hard forearm thrust and crouched low, circling him angrily, looking for an opening to attack again.

Jackson ground out from behind unmoving lips, "What the hell are you doing?"

"Acting."

The guy's physical defenses were impenetrable. Time to improvise, especially since they were totally off the choreography already. She eyed the ledge behind him and maneuvered him toward it with a series of feints and retreats. When he was in the right position, she took a running start and ran up the inclined ramp beside the structure, onto the ledge itself and took a flying leap at Jackson, pouncing on his back.

"Jesus, Ana," he grunted. "You're way off script."

"Screw you and your damned scripts," she growled back in his ear.

He whirled fast, almost dislodging her. She reached across his chest and raked her hands across his upper torso. Letting go of all her rage, she bent her head and grabbed his earlobe between her teeth and bit down. Hard.

"Ow!"

He bent over hard from the waist, slingshotting her over his shoulder to slam to the mat. He jumped after her, but she scrambled aside just in time to avoid being flattened. He did snag her around the waist with his outstretched arm, though, and dragged her up against him, squirming and swearing.

She pummeled him with her fists until he captured those with his free hand. He pulled her wrists high over her head and backed her into the closet-size structure she'd jumped off in the first place. Using his body, he pinned her against the wall, effectively immobilizing her.

Then, in an impressive display of strength, he lifted her by her wrists until her feet literally dangled off the floor and she was face-to-face with him.

"*What* is your problem?" he ground out.

"You are," she growled back. "You're a big, clueless jerk who can't see what's right in front of your eyes."

"Maybe you should give me a little time to take a damned look at it first."

"You're out of time, buddy."

They traded glares that could not have been any more fiery if actual flames had shot from their eyeballs.

"Dammit," Jackson bit out just before his mouth closed on hers and all hell broke loose.

What was it about kissing him that made her completely lose her mind? Before she knew it, her arms and legs were wrapped around him while his powerful arms crushed her against him. They didn't kiss so much as they attacked each other, biting and sucking and smashing lips and clacking teeth. It was wild. Unbridled. Angry. And so passionate she was pretty sure her hair caught on fire.

"And...cut."

Cut—huh? Startled by the male voice nearby, Ana pulled back sharply from Jackson. He looked similarly disoriented.

"I'm so sorry," she breathed. "I lost control—"

"Oh, my God, I love it!" Adrian exclaimed from close enough to make her jump.

Jackson let her body slide slowly to the floor and she stumbled back from him guiltily. Unable to bear looking at the molten lust in Jackson's stare, she turned to face the director. "I'm so sorry, Adrian. That was totally uncalled for. I went completely off script. It's my fault—"

The director cut her off with a sharp wave of his hand. Jackson started to say something and was cut off the same way by Adrian. She waited apprehensively beside Jackson while the director stared off into space, his formidable mind clearly in overdrive.

"Yes. Let's do it," he declared without warning.

"Do what?" Jackson asked cautiously.

"Let's go with that."

"Um, with what?" she asked, cautious in turn.

"Fight morphing into steamy embrace. This film is

gonna be a blockbuster if you can generate heat like that in every scene. We'll need to tweak the script to account for the fights turned love scenes… Sheila! Get me the script doctor on the phone!"

The director turned away and left Jackson and Ana staring at one another in shock.

"What just happened?" she asked in a small voice.

"No idea. But he's the boss when it comes to creative decisions. Whatever he wants, he gets."

Adrian called over his shoulder. "Sex. I want more sex from you two."

Flabbergasted, she looked up at Jackson. He looked positively stunned.

"I've got to go," he said suddenly.

And just like that, he strode off the set.

She was left alone to endure the ribbing of the crew. Which sucked, by the way. No matter how many times she told them it was just acting and they should all grow up, it didn't seem to have the slightest effect on anyone. The entire crew was hooting with glee over the two of them all but having carnal knowledge of each other on film.

And no matter what Jackson said, it *was* her fault. She was the one who'd picked a real fight, and she was the one who'd provoked Jackson until he finally responded in kind. One thing she knew about him: he hated being humiliated. He was never going to forgive her for this. Could she possibly screw up things between them any more?

The ride home in the Hugster was quiet. Really quiet. As in totally silent. Another thing she knew for sure: she had to get out of the house and away from him, fast. Even if she had to eat and sleep in her car until she found an affordable place.

Maybe it was her tension with Jackson, or maybe it was just her stress making her paranoia worse than usual, but she got the feeling someone was watching her while they were sitting at Serendipity's only stoplight. She twisted around in the passenger seat to peer out the back window of the minivan, but it was impossible to differentiate one car from another in the line of vehicles behind them.

"What's up?" Jackson asked alertly as she turned back around to face front.

She shrugged, reluctant to admit her silly fears to him.

"Why were you looking back there?" he asked. "And why are you still staring at the rearview mirror like it's going to attack you any second?"

"Sometimes I get the feeling I'm being watched. It's no big deal. It's just heightened nerves after the stuff that happened to me all at once."

Jackson went all macho and protective on her, exactly like she'd feared he would. "When do you get the feeling? Have you ever seen anyone tailing you? What times of day do you get the feeling? Does it happen in the same places?" he demanded.

"It's nothing. There's never anyone there, and it's just a little post trauma anxiety. Stand down, Mr. Commando. It's okay."

"In my experience, intuitions should be listened to—"

"Not in this case," she interrupted. "I'm telling you. You're overreacting."

He scowled at her and muttered, "Maybe you're underreacting." But thankfully, he dropped the subject.

Lord, that man could be overpowering when he chose

to be. And it was as sexy as hell. She had to get out of here if she was ever going to break free of his spell on her.

As soon as she got back to her room at the seaside mansion, she started packing her meager possessions. She probably ought to leave behind all the beautiful clothes Minerva had purchased for her, but she didn't want to offend Jackson's grandmother, who'd been genuinely kind to her, and who'd gotten a big kick out of Ana wearing the elegant, feminine clothing.

"How are you doing, dear?" Minerva asked in concern the second Ana showed her face in the kitchen.

"I'm fine," she answered as politely as she could. It wasn't his grandmother's fault Jackson was an ass.

"Are you sure? Jackson was pretty worried when he called me today."

That stopped her in her tracks. "He called you?"

Minerva laughed "Can you believe it? He asked me for advice on how to deal with a woman. I never thought I'd live to see the day."

"Advice? What kind of advice?"

Minerva loaded up a plate with turkey breast, mashed potatoes, gravy, a big pile of steamed vegetables and cranberry relish, which was giving off a heavenly orange aroma. "Here, Ana. You're not eating enough."

Her appetite *had* been off the past few days. Although she couldn't tell it from her waistline. Rosie was an amazing cook who was going to wreck Ana's figure if she stayed here too much longer.

"Do you want to talk about what an ass he's being?" Minerva asked sympathetically.

"No. That's okay. I pretty much expressed my opinion to him earlier."

"Just remember, dear. Hate is not the opposite of love. Apathy is. As long as you have passionate feelings of any kind for each other, your love is alive."

Hah. The two of them must feel enormous love for one another if the passion between them was the measuring stick. Except Jackson had never once even hinted that he knew what love was, let alone that he felt it toward her.

Ana carried her plate upstairs to her room and picked at it unenthusiastically. Minerva was right about one thing: she was not over Jackson. She doubted she would achieve apathy where he was concerned for a very long time. If ever.

She drew designs in her mashed potatoes idly with her fork. Was she ruined for anyone else? Like Jackson? After Vanessa van Buren, he was apparently done with love, forever. Would that be her fate, too?

She'd thought it was a wee bit self-indulgent of him to swear off love for as long as he had. She might even venture to say he was being overly dramatic. But here she was, guilty of acting the exact same way. Of course, in her case, she'd had hang-ups about guys before Chandler ever came along—

Huh. Was it the same for Jackson? Had his mother's emotional abandonment and early death given him issues about women before Vanessa had come along to mess with him? It wasn't like she was going to ask him about it outright, of course.

Okay, fine. So she needed to start dating again, and Jackson had shown her that she could handle it with the right guy. Too bad she wasn't the right girl for him. Why did it have to be so darned complicated? Why couldn't he just return her feelings and be done with it?

Appetite wrecked, she pushed the plate away from

her and crawled into bed. It was barely 8:00 p.m., but she was exhausted by the day's roller-coaster emotions.

Jackson knocked quietly on Ana's door. They really needed to talk about what had happened between them on the set. Not that he relished the idea of dragging out their emotions and putting them under a microscope, but it wasn't as if he had any choice in the matter. Over dinner—which Ana was notably absent from—Minerva had told him in no uncertain terms that if it came to a breakup, she was keeping Ana and the baby and ditching him.

Dammit.

He knocked again. Still no answer. Alarmed, he tried the knob and it turned under his hand. He slipped inside the darkened room quickly. She wasn't so distraught she would do something drastic, was she?

He looked around frantically until he spotted the long lump of her in bed. Wow. She was already asleep? He moved over to the bedside to stare down at her. In the scant light seeping in around the curtains, she looked like a fallen angel. Her hair formed a halo around her face on her pillow, and he studied her bone structure for a long time. She was a genuinely beautiful woman.

Quietly, he picked up her plate of cold food and headed downstairs with it.

"How's she doing?" Minerva asked him.

Buttinsky. "Asleep."

His grandmother nodded sagely. "Most women are usually tired in the first trimester." She glanced down at the largely untouched plate of food. "And they're picky eaters, too."

He was half tempted to dump the plate of food over

Minerva's head. Of course, he was also tempted to blurt out that Ana was not freaking pregnant. But there was no need to lash out at Minerva just because he was ticked off at himself.

Bored, restless and feeling caged, he ended up going to bed early. His only other option was to get stinking drunk, and he had a production meeting with Adrian first thing in the morning. He couldn't afford to show up hungover.

But sleeping was a joke. He tossed and turned all night while visions of Ana danced in his head. Working with her. Laughing with her. Making love with her. Even fighting with her.

She was so different from cool, contained and, ultimately, calculating Vanessa. Ana was plainspoken. Down-to-earth. Real. Totally unlike the string of ambitious actresses he'd serial-dated since Vanessa.

Was Ana right? Was he stuck in the past? Hell, he doubted Vanessa even remembered his name. Knowing her, she was on her second or third husband by now. Ana emphatically wasn't that kind of girl. She'd said it herself: once her feelings were given, they stayed given.

It wasn't that he didn't think Ana was great. She was. It was just that he was scared stiff of committing to a forever relationship. There hadn't been too many forevers in his life. Except for Minerva, of course. But was his grandmother enough to compensate for his missing father, a mother who abandoned him and a cheating, lying ex-fiancée?

Was there something wrong with *him* that made people not stick around for him? Or was he the ass who didn't stick around long enough for anyone else to get a chance to love him?

He made the mistake of letting his mind drift to his and Ana's on-screen tussle earlier in the day. What on earth had been wrong with him? The second he got his hands on her, all hell had broken loose inside him. All he could think about was getting more, and yet more, of the taste and feel of her. He probably ought to just drag her off to bed and not let her out of it until she got over whatever was ticking her off so bad.

Yup, that pretty much did him in for sleeping the rest of the night. His raging hard-on wasn't abating anytime soon. And, short of storming Ana's room and begging her for some release, nothing was going to help him.

Sure, he could go take a shower and ease his misery. But there was something fitting about him being in pain, his body rock hard and throbbing insistently. Ana would say he deserved it. And she would not be wrong.

When dawn began to creep in his window, he was relieved to get out of bed and head out of the house. He severely needed a long ride on his Harley to clear his head before he went in to work.

Ana lay in bed and listened to Jackson's motorcycle roar out of the driveway at the crack of dawn. Her dreams had been troubled and mostly involved her and Jackson crawling all over each other having gnarly sex, their naked bodies colored bottle-green.

How had things gotten so messed up between them so fast? If only he was a complete jerk. And if only she didn't dissolve into a blob of fiery lust every time he laid a finger on her. Maybe she ought to tie him down and have her way with him until he gave up resisting the chemistry between them. *If only.*

She made her glum way downstairs for breakfast and

was surprised to see Minerva up at the crack of dawn. "What's got you up so early?"

"Big plans today, dear. Are you off to work early?"

"Yes. But I heard Jackson leave already. Mind if I take the Hugster? I'm hoping to do some apartment shopping on my lunch break today."

"Not at all, dear. I got the minivan for you and the baby."

Ana couldn't help wincing. Somebody had to convince Minerva that the yogi was a fake and that she was not pregnant, but she wasn't about to do it. The woman was Jackson's grandmother. He should be the one to tell her the truth.

The production meeting between Adrian and Jackson finished about when Ana got done with her usual morning stretching and conditioning workout. The senior members of the crew emerged from Adrian's office talking shop. In a blatant effort to avoid seeing Jackson, she darted into the women's locker room to change clothes. She shrugged into her Lycra bodysuit and headed out to the green mat. Jackson was already there, looking thunderous.

"Meeting go bad?" she asked low.

"Nah. I just slept lousy."

A half dozen stuntmen strolled out to the floor just then and commenced harassing Jackson. Mercilessly. Apparently, in this morning's meeting, Adrian had screened yesterday's footage of her and Jackson fighting. He'd said it exactly captured the mood and tone he was looking for in the movie.

Great. So everyone in the crew who hadn't caught their performance live yesterday was aware of it now, anyway. How special. Knowing the crew, they would never give it a rest. Even if Jackson's patience was clearly wearing paper-thin.

She caught a few jabs, herself, but Jackson was quick to intervene and redirect the banter at himself. She was grateful but also perplexed by the gesture. He was possibly less amused by the ribbing than she was.

Thankfully, Adrian showed up before long and saved them both from any more teasing. The director asked briskly, "All right. Cameras, are we ready to go?"

"Yes, sir," the director of photography replied.

"Jackson? Ana?"

"We're good," Jackson answered grimly.

"All right. Places. Quiet on set. Test shot one of fight sequence two. Roll cameras if you please, gentlemen."

Ana gritted her teeth. She really didn't need an audience of her peers for this. But it wasn't like she had any choice in the matter. She focused on Jackson's big body moving toward her, stalking, circling.

He jumped and she dodged, chanting the step sequence in her head. They stayed on script for a little bit, but every time she slipped through Jackson's grasp—which was choreographed to happen several times—the frown on his face got more thunderous.

Finally, his pent-up emotions seemed to get the best of him, and it was his turn to go off script. Whether his feeling got the best of him, or he was just tired and forgot the routine, or he did it intentionally, she couldn't tell. But all of a sudden, she was trapped in his arms, wrapped in a grip that crushed the air out of her.

She dropped to her knees, slipping the grip, and it was *on*. Like yesterday, the fight turned real, and they demolished the breakaway tables and chairs that had been set up to simulate the bar the scene would take place in.

They stalked each other, leaping and swinging at one another like savage animals.

She spied the opening she'd been looking for. She feinted left, he dived right, and she jumped onto his back like she had yesterday. Except this time she anticipated his attempt to flip her over his shoulder and wrapped her legs around his waist before he could throw her off. She didn't anticipate his flexibility, though, or the way he was able to reach around behind his back and peel her off of him by main force, dragging her around to his front.

He smashed his mouth down on hers and everything else disappeared. The catcalls and whistles of the crew, the cameras, the set, everything. It was just him. His mouth. His hands. His glorious body.

All of a sudden, she was crawling over him like she wanted to get inside his green suit. She kissed him with abandon, and he threw himself at her just as freely. Their kiss turned into wrestling, their wrestling into dry humping, their dry humping into an all-out fight. They flowed from sex moves to fight moves and back again seamlessly.

It was as if the two of them took their work and their relationship and mixed both in a smoking-hot mash-up they totally lost themselves in. In reality, it was more a case of neither of them being able to control their reactions to one another. At all.

It took a while, but eventually, through superior strength and size, Jackson subdued her. She thudded to her back on the floor with him straddling her hips suggestively. His eyes blazed with passion, and her belly burned just as hotly for him.

And then he wrapped his hands around her throat. It made sense in the fight scene, but all of a sudden, real panic ripped through her. She tensed and froze. And abruptly Jackson realized what he'd done.

"Oh, God, Ana. I'm so sorr—"

"Cut!"

Humiliated at panicking like that, Ana looked away from Jackson's stricken stare.

"That was spectacular," Adrian declared, grinning from ear to ear.

Jackson threw his leg off her hips and stood up. He offered her a hand, which she ignored, and climbed to her feet by herself. She was so embarrassed at losing it like that she could hardly see straight.

Not to mention that blatant display of lust. At least their show seemed to have temporarily silenced the gaping crew. Of course, she'd just sexually assaulted Jackson in front of them all. On film. In revealing bodysuits that left *nothing* to the imagination.

Speaking of which, Jackson was gritting his teeth and seemed in an inordinate hurry to sit down in one of the tall canvas chairs offstage. *Oh.* A raging hard-on in a stretchy bodysuit must suck.

"Playback?" Jackson gritted out.

One of the computer guys obliged, setting up a laptop on a tall table in front of Jackson. The technician pulled up the digital recordings of the scene and commenced replaying all four shots in split screens on the monitor.

Ana leaned on one arm of Jackson's chair to watch while Adrian leaned on the other. It looked like a can of lurid green paint had fallen over the set of a porn movie as the two of them went at it like animals on-screen.

"God almighty, that's hot," Jackson muttered under his breath.

She nodded, too embarrassed to speak.

Jackson added, "If anyone asks, Adrian, we were just acting."

He might as well have stabbed her in the belly with a machete. "Right. Acting," she managed to mumble in agreement.

Adrian was, in a word, delirious about their performance. He went on and on about how fantastic the scene was, even better than yesterday's, and something inside her cracked. She couldn't do it. She couldn't stand here and listen to Adrian rave about their chemistry and how the lust and desperation between them leaped off the screen.

She whirled and left the set, mumbling something inane about having to go to the restroom. Her stomach heaved and she had to break into a run to make it to the toilet before she barfed her entire breakfast into the commode. It had just been Jackson. Yes, he had put his hands on her neck, but he would never, ever harm her. It was okay. She was okay.

Dammit. She was supposed to be past all this reaction-to-her-attack stuff. It had been years, for crying out loud. The shrinks had said she might have flashbacks for the rest of her life, but it had been a long time since she'd had one.

She flushed the toilet and stared down at the swirling water, frowning. Was it just being in a relationship of sorts—as broken as it might be—with a guy that was triggering this? Was she really that freaked out over Jackson grabbing her neck for a few seconds?

An ominous foreboding took root within her and grew with every second she stood there staring down into the damned toilet. She was in trouble. Big, big trouble.

Chapter 12

When Ana got back to the mansion, she headed straight upstairs to take a shower. She stepped into her bedroom—

What on earth?

Was she in the wrong room? The furniture was all gone, the carpet torn up and a pair of men hard at work building some wooden platform thing on the far side of the room. She backed out into the hallway to check her location. No, this was her room. Or at least it had been when she'd left the house this morning.

Was Jackson kicking her out of the house? Stunned, she headed for the stairs and met Minerva coming up them.

"Oh, there you are, dear! I'm so excited about the new project. I'm going to need a lot of help from you with it, of course. Are you surprised?"

That was a word for it. She managed to mumble, "Where's my stuff?"

Minerva waved a hand "Oh, that—" She broke off when Jackson's voice greeting Rosie in the kitchen drifted up to them. "Perfect. I can show both of you at the same time."

"Jackson!" Ana shouted. "I think you'd better come up here."

He came on the run, bounding up the stairs three at a time. "What's wrong?" he demanded sharply as he joined her and Minerva at the top of the stairs.

"Your grandmother has another surprise for us."

On cue, Minerva turned and headed down the hall toward the back of the house. "Come with me, kids, and let me show you. You're going to love it."

"Christ. Now what?" Jackson grumbled under his breath.

Ana rolled her eyes at him. "That would be exactly the appropriate tone of voice to take, based on what I've already seen."

Minerva threw open Ana's former bedroom door with a flourish. "Voilà! The new nursery for your son!"

Jackson screeched to a stop in the doorway. "What the hell have you done, Gran?"

"I've decided to convert this room to a nursery for my great-grandson. Your bedroom is plenty big enough for the two of you, and it has the best view in the house. I know you love that room, Jackson. So I figure you two can use it as your bedroom and then this adjoining room will make for a perfect nursery."

Jackson's mouth opened. Closed.

Yup, Ana knew the feeling. She was pretty damned speechless herself. Minerva dismissed the workers for the day, and Ana watched in dismayed silence as the carpenters packed up their stuff and left the room.

As soon as they were gone, Minerva blithely ignored her and Jackson's shock and launched into an enthusiastic guided tour of what some interior designer, whose name Ana didn't catch, had come up with for the room. Vaguely, Ana registered where the crib would go, how the antique rocking chair Minerva was having restored would sit by the window, and something about a daybed. Ana went into mental overload and tuned out entirely when a changing table entered the woman's narrative.

Finally, Minerva drew breath long enough for Ana to get a word in edgewise. "Minerva, this is…spectacular. You really, *really* shouldn't have. But in the meantime, may I please know where my clothes are?"

The older woman laughed gaily. "They're all moved into your room with Jackson, of course. Rosie and I took care of getting you settled with him today. It really has been sweet of the two of you to use separate bedrooms while you've been here, but this is the twenty-first century. I'm totally fine with the two of you sleeping together. You're in love and expecting a baby together, for goodness' sake."

Ana's gaze snapped to Jackson, and his snapped to her, as well. Her body went first cold, then hot, as she stared up at him. What was that expression lurking in his stare behind the shock? Dismay? Betrayal? Sheer horror? Whatever it was, it rendered his beautiful eyes a turbulent, muddy color. *In love. Expecting a baby.* She didn't know whether to wish it true or guffaw with laughter. Or maybe cry.

Jackson spun away from her abruptly. He demanded incredulously, "You moved her into my room?"

Minerva strolled past him, pausing long enough to pat his cheek fondly. "You're welcome, dear. There's no reason for you not to sleep with your girlfriend. This is your home, too, after all, and the two of you are consenting adults. And speaking of which, how about I give the two of you a little time alone together to take in the new nursery and talk over the design? If you want to make any changes to the layout, now's the time before we get too far along with the renovation."

And with that salvo, she left the nursery, closing the door behind her.

Ana stared at Jackson, so bombarded with emotions she didn't know which one to react to first. Finally, she said in a small voice, "Wow."

Jackson replied drily, "Welcome to Hurricane Minerva."

"She definitely is a force of nature."

Jackson just shook his head.

"You've got to talk her down off this delusion of hers before it goes too much further."

He frowned, matching her expression of concern. "I've never seen her like this. She seems genuinely convinced of this whole baby thing. You haven't said anything to her to lead her on…"

"Of course not!" Ana exclaimed. "Speaking of which, where am I going to sleep tonight?"

He exhaled hard. "You might as well bunk in with me. Knowing my grandmother, she's had Rosie strip the sheets and blankets off of every other bed in the house. Hell, I wouldn't put it past her to do a bed check and chase you into my room if you attempt to crash anywhere else. She's determined to throw the two of us together."

Ana was pensive through supper. How in the hell was she supposed to spend the night in the same room with Jackson and not end up having sex with him again? As frustrated as she was with his inability to get in touch with his feelings, there was no denying the chemistry between them. It was freaking incendiary.

Jackson seemed to be laboring under the same question. As the sun dropped low in the west, he asked her abruptly, "Wanna go for a ride, Ana?"

She retorted wryly, "Gonna take the Hugster out for a spin?"

He scowled. "No. The Harley. Thought I'd head up the coast. You interested?"

Was that sexual innuendo intentional? His eyes gave away nothing as her gaze collided with his. "Sounds fantastic," she murmured.

She suspected he had an ulterior motive. Like getting out of the house and out of earshot with Minerva to have a serious talk about how they were going to deal with his grandmother.

Jackson jumped up from the table, antsy to get out of the house, whose walls were closing in on him mercilessly. He grabbed Ana's hand and dragged her through the mansion almost at a jog.

When they reached the garage, he passed her a helmet and started the Harley. As it rumbled to life, she threw her leg across the seat behind him and snuggled up against him. His usual Harley hard-on was noticeably harder than usual as he headed north on the Pacific Coast Highway.

It was a cool evening and the sky was darkening rapidly to midnight-blue. Venus was a bright and steady light overhead, and the ocean was restless and black on the rocks below. But nothing could distract him from the way Ana's chest rubbed against his back, or the way her hands twined low around his waist. He fantasized about her hands dipping lower to caress the bulge in his jeans, and his hard-on grew even more uncomfortable.

They passed through a few enclaves of stupidly rich celebrities and moguls, continuing north until the houses fell away and it was just the two of them, the bike, the first stars of the night and the ocean. He opened up the throttle and let the bike fly. Ana's thighs tucked up underneath his and her arms wrapped even more tightly around his middle. They moved in perfect unison, synced to the bike's swaying turns and straightaway accelerations. All of it turned him on until he could barely sit upright.

Ana leaned forward and shouted in his ear, "Look!" She pointed off to their left, and he followed the direction of her outstretched finger. In the new moonlight, a school of porpoises raced along the coast, flying through the water nearly as fast as the Harley was skimming along the highway.

She laughed in exhilaration as he adjusted his speed to pace the porpoises' joyous leaping and rushing through the surf. The bike hit a bump, and her lips accidentally touched the back of his neck. At least he assumed it was accidental. Either way, he about jumped out of his skin. Worse, her hands had been dislodged from his waist and landed on the upper reaches of his jeans' zipper.

Fantasies floated through his head of her hands sliding lower, slowly undoing the zipper tooth by tooth... working their way inside his fly...grabbing his...

He broke off for fear of crashing and killing them both in his raging lust. His fists tightened on the handlebars, and the bike roared forward as his right hand twisted the throttle convulsively.

Her fist would slide up and down his shaft, and his hips would surge forward into her hands. Her fingers would trace the length of him and then... Oh, yes...creep lower...

The bike swerved a little and her fingers retreated to his waist. He swore to himself and steadied the bike.

He wanted to be inside her so bad he could hardly see straight. His fantasy was going to get them both splatted all over the highway if he wasn't careful. He spied a scenic overlook sign and nearly cried in relief. He slowed the bike and turned off the highway. He parked the bike at the highest spot in the lot, overlooking a mighty cliff with huge waves crashing up against it. Salt spray peppered his face. The velvet blanket of night to settle gently around them.

He reached behind his back with one arm and snagged Ana's waist the same way he had earlier in their fight scene. He pulled her around in front of him, straddling the metal gas tank between his thighs. Her legs draped over his, and the position was overtly sexual. Her breathing hitched and accelerated as she took off her helmet.

The bike idled, rumbling beneath them as he pulled her hips closer. She shocked him by rocking her pelvis forward, bringing her own jeans into contact with the bulge barely containing his raging flesh.

"I don't know what it is about you," she murmured. "The second you put your hands on me, crazy things start happening inside me."

"Where inside you?"

"Down low. Deep in my belly. And, um, lower."

"What things happen? Tell me."

Her gaze slid down and fixed on a point somewhere

on his chest. "Things start throbbing," she whispered. "And getting hot. And wet. And, um, swollen."

"Mmm. I know the feeling well."

A convertible honked several times and a bunch of kids shouted their approval as the vehicle sped past. Ana jolted, and he merely grinned at her and kept her seated firmly on his lap.

"What do you want, Ana? Right now. In this moment."

"I want…I want to pull down your zipper and take off my pants and feel you inside me. Filling me. And… and making love with me."

Without comment, he grabbed her left leg and swung it across the bike in front of him. "Take off your jeans, baby."

"Really?" she squeaked.

He lifted an eyebrow. "You're not chicken, are you?"

"Oh, you did not just dare me," she declared, laughing.

"Did so. I double dare you."

Her gorgeous eyes glinting with humor, she shimmied out of her jeans and panties and threw her leg back across the bike while he unzipped his jeans. His male flesh leaped free eagerly.

"Ooh! That's cold!" she squealed as her rear end came into contact with his bike.

"Get off the metal gas tank, Einstein, and try riding something a little hotter."

She swatted him on the upper arm as he lifted her hips in his big hands. Slowly, slowly, he lowered her onto him. After the cool twilight air, her body was scalding hot. He groaned aloud at how good she felt, gloved tightly around him.

She rocked her hips experimentally. He groaned, and she sighed blissfully. She did it again. In a few seconds, she had set up a lazy rhythm of rock, retreat and impale that was going to drive him stark raving mad in about thirty seconds. His entire body tightened sharply in need and he sucked in a hard breath.

He pulled her down onto him and held her still while he fought to regain his composure. It felt so damned good to be buried in all her wet, hot, tight heat, he could sit here all night like this. He rocked his hips forward and down, and used his hands to spread her cheeks as he planted her pert little behind on the gas tank. The *vibrating* gas tank.

She lurched hard into him. "Ohmigosh, Jackson." She cried out as her first Harley orgasm slammed into her harder than the waves crashing into the rocks below.

"Ride it, baby," he groaned. "Ride me."

Her whole body shook around him as another orgasm slammed into her almost immediately after the first one. She rocked on the bike and on him, completely lost in the engine's rumble, the pounding surf below and him surging into her.

He grinned and revved the engine. Her hips undulated faster and harder as a one-hundred-fifty-horsepower chrome-and-steel vibrator worked its magic on her body. She cried out again, her internal muscles clutching at him as if she was never going to let him go.

She groaned, her face buried against his neck. "Ohman, ohman, ohman, ohman," she moaned in a desperate, endless prayer to the Harley gods. It was the most beautiful thing he'd ever heard. Hell, her coming apart all over him was just about the most beautiful thing he'd ever felt.

He revved the throttle hard, and the massive engine beneath them roared like a lion. Ana threw herself onto his erection like a warrior impaling herself on a sword, and he surged up into her with a mighty roar of his own. His orgasm exploded out of him like a rocket and he shouted his pleasure, the sound torn away by the wind and surf and flung to the dark heavens.

Ana collapsed in his arms, sucking wind like she'd just sprinted a mile, her head lying on his shoulder limply. He held her boneless body close. Good grief, he knew the feeling. He felt like a wrung-out washcloth. She'd pulled every drop he had to give from his soul.

Slowly, slowly, she rejoined the living. Her lips moved softly against his neck. Her hands crept around his waist. Her chest lifted and fell in a contented sigh.

"Shall we continue?" he murmured.

"You're ready to do that again?" she blurted in disbelief.

He laughed. "I was referring to our bike ride, but if you give me a few minutes, I can be up for round two."

"I'm not sure I'd survive another round of that," she murmured. She sounded like a cat who'd just finished lapping up a bowl of cream. Sated. Supremely contented. Just the way he liked his woman.

Whoa. Since when did he have a "his woman"? And since when was she his? They were faking all of this. But what they'd just done on his bike sure as hell hadn't been fake. She'd just screwed his lights out on the side of the Pacific Coast Highway for God's sake.

He thought he'd heard a couple cars honk their horns in approval as they drove past. But at the end there, he wouldn't have heard someone standing three feet away shouting at him through a bullhorn.

Ana slid off the bike—her legs wobbly, he noted with satisfaction—and pulled on her panties and jeans. She slipped onto the seat behind him and he gave the throttle a quick twist. Her hips rocked forward involuntarily, and he grinned over his shoulder. "Like that?"

"If you don't get moving right now, I'm going to climb on you again for that round two you offered me."

"Stay where you are right now," he instructed her, "and turn on your helmet mike. I want to hear every orgasm you have between now and the house."

Her thighs tightened against his, squeezing the seat a little more tightly. Then they relaxed and opened, letting her weight settle more deeply onto the vibrating seat. Her breath caught and then she exhaled on a shuddering groan. Grinning, he released the brakes and the bike leaped forward beneath him. He guided it back toward the mansion, taking the road and the woman at a leisurely pace.

Ana could hardly stand by the time they got back to the house. Her expression was dazed and her body limp from excessive pleasure. He poured her into his bed and, well satisfied with the evening's work, strolled into the kitchen for a midnight snack. He'd worked up an appetite blowing Ana's mind with pleasure. Yup. A tough job, but somebody had to do it.

Minerva was making herself a cup of tea at the kitchen counter.

"Rosie gone for the night?" he asked her.

"She left hours ago. Can I make you a cup of tea?"

"Sure. Lemme just whip up a sandwich for myself." He made himself a quick snack from the platter of deli meats and cheeses in the refrigerator.

"Ana's a lovely girl," she commented. "I approve of her."

He grinned broadly. "Me, too."

"She makes you happy, doesn't she?"

The question stopped him cold. Ana *did* make him happy. Hell, giddy. Giddier than he'd been since he fell hook, line and sinker for Vanessa, come to think of it.

"Are you two thinking about marriage?" Minerva asked.

The old panic gripped him. Images of his bride, the woman he'd loved, walking down the aisle with another man. Beaming at another bastard. Hell, sleeping with the guy while she was still engaged to him—

He broke off the bitter thoughts abruptly and glanced up at his grandmother, frowning. "We haven't talked about it," he answered shortly.

"Well, you should. Not only is there the baby to think of, but you're not getting any younger. She's perfect for you, and she's obviously crazy about you. She'd make you very happy."

"Oh, so now you're a relationship expert?" he retorted sharply.

"I know you, Jackson. She's the one."

He grabbed his plate and stood up, agitated. "Keep your nose out of it. This is my life. I'll do what I see fit with Ana. I need you to back off of all this baby stuff and of throwing the two of us together. Let me do this my way."

"Don't let her slip away while you're dithering, Jackson Prescott. Lots of men would give their eyeteeth to have her. They won't wait around for you to figure out what you want, and neither will she." And with that parting salvo, she sailed out of the kitchen and upstairs.

Dammit. Minerva had put her finger directly on what was worrying him. How his grandmother managed to find his raw nerves and stomp on them so effectively was a complete mystery to him. A hum of unease remained in his gut even after he stormed out of the house and plunked down on the veranda with a bottle of whiskey and his sandwich. Tea be damned—he needed a real drink.

A mental image of Ana and some other guy on a Harley blurred. Became Vanessa and her sleazy doctor boyfriend screwing their brains out behind his back. In both pictures, he was the one standing on the outside, alone, looking in. And that was what scared the hell out of him.

Would Ana really bail on him if he didn't make a move soon to lock down an official relationship with her? She'd said she was going to leave as soon as the movie was done filming. Would she really do it? Somehow, she didn't strike him as the kind of woman to drop empty threats. He had two weeks to give her so many orgasms she couldn't even think about walking out on him.

It was a lame plan, but it was better than no plan at all. And God knew the fringe benefits were phenomenal.

Hell, he didn't even know if she was interested in a relationship with him anymore. For all he knew, she saw this whole thing as an extended friends-with-benefits deal.

He poured himself a shot of whiskey but set the glass back down on the table without tossing it back. Funny, but he didn't feel like drowning himself in booze tonight. The lure of the woman sleeping upstairs in his bed was too much to resist.

He slipped into his bedroom and undressed in the dark. It seemed a little redundant to wear clothes to bed after the bike ride earlier, so he slipped under the covers naked. It was a risk, but that two-week window was going to slam shut in the blink of an eye. He had no time at all. He had to take risks if he wanted her for himself.

And the more he thought about it, the more he was coming to that exact conclusion. He did want her.

Ana stirred, rolling over and taking most of the blankets with her. The air conditioner was running full blast tonight, and in a few moments, the chill in his room became uncomfortable. Gently, he reached for the blankets and tugged them back in his direction.

Not only did the covers come back his way, but Ana's sleek body abruptly draped itself across his. He lay beneath her, stiff as a board from head to foot, for several minutes. He had a long-standing policy of never sleeping with the women he had sex with for this exact reason. It was too damned intimate.

Ana settled more comfortably on his chest, and it became clear she wasn't going anywhere soon. Inch by inch he forced his body to relax, lecturing himself all the while. This was Ana. She was his friend. His colleague. His equal. A woman he was seriously considering pursuing a real relationship with.

Considering, his ass. The decision was made. She'd just screwed his lights out on a Harley, and pretty much made every fantasy he'd ever had on that bike come true. She was funny and kind and smart to boot. How could he say no to a woman like that?

On top of that, she got him. She understood the demands of his work, and where he was calm, she was impulsive. Where he was careful, she was bold. She drew him out of his shell, and he slowed her down just enough to be safe. They were a good match for each other.

His arm came up around her, and she snuggled a little closer on his chest. He had to admit this cuddling thing wasn't half-bad. He felt cared for. Coveted. The human contact was…nice.

He closed his own eyes and drifted off to sleep with a bizarre and unfamiliar sense of contentment welling up inside him. Just maybe this whole relationship thing would turn out better than he'd expected, after all.

Chapter 13

Ana straightened in the green bodysuit, panting. Jackson wore an identical bodysuit, his face painted the same bright soda-bottle-green hers was painted. The ubiquitous white dots covered their faces and bodies like chicken pox.

"That was awesome, guys!" Adrian called from off set. The director strolled forward onto the mat. "I think we've got what we need for this scene. You two have fantastic chemistry. I'll look forward to seeing what you come up with for the next scene."

She grabbed the towel someone handed her and followed Jackson off the floor.

"So, guys," Crash Mashburn murmured to them as they headed for the locker rooms, "I hear you had a nice ride up the coast last night."

Jackson whipped around shockingly fast to stare over

Ana's shoulder at the head stuntman and professional driver. "Come again?" he rumbled low and warningly.

"Apparently, someone's been posting pictures of you two on the internet. Mostly on set. A few at your grandmother's house. This morning, pics went up of the two of you at a rest stop on the Pacific Coast Highway."

Horror washed over Ana. She felt hot and faint and sick all at once.

For his part, Jackson went still. Something far too cold and dangerous to be mere anger abruptly emanated from his big body. "Show me," he bit out. "My office."

She took a step as if to follow him, but he snapped over his shoulder at her, "Not you. Go take a shower. I'll take care of this."

When she emerged from the locker room a half hour later, Jackson, Crash and Adrian were standing in a cluster just outside Adrian's office conversing too low for her to hear. They broke off talking as she approached them.

"Hey, guys. Everything okay?"

"Just fine," Jackson replied promptly. "The pictures are down, and our security company is tracing the ISP address and identity of whoever posted them."

Adrian piped up, "In the meantime, I'm hiring more security for the set. Whether someone's out to harass you, Ana, or just has a thing against the movies in general, is anyone's guess. But I'm done having my crew's privacy, and possibly safety, compromised in this studio."

"Thanks, guys," she mumbled. God. Talk about guilt. How much money was she costing them, and how much danger was she putting the entire crew in? She hated this. She hated bringing a taint to the people around her. She had no business being in a relationship with anybody for this exact reason.

The next few days settled into a pattern. Jackson was underfoot pretty much 24/7. On set, if Jackson wasn't around, Crash always seemed to be in the vicinity. Pairs of wandering security guards were always lurking around the studio now, and the crew had to check in with a guard at the front door, as well. But at least no more pictures of her and Jackson in compromising positions showed up on the internet.

As for their work, she and Jackson blocked out scenes one by one, rehearsed each to their mutual satisfaction, got dressed up in green from head to toe, and filmed until Adrian was satisfied with every angle and every nuance of the action.

Between Adrian and Jackson giving her a crash course in acting, she didn't feel like a complete klutz. They put her entirely at ease and then made suggestions that were so clear and logical that it was a snap to do as they instructed. No question about it, acting was a whole lot harder than it looked. But under their tutelage, she was gradually getting the hang of digging into her character and bringing the alien warrior babe to life.

She fell into Jackson's bed exhausted each night, but as soon as his hands found her in the dark, magic happened. She couldn't get enough of him. He was an amazing lover—strong and gentle, aggressive and playful, a little crazy and a lot imaginative. She walked around in a continual haze of arousal and sexual delirium that she sincerely hoped never cleared. It was hard to imagine that she'd threatened only a few days ago to leave him and their steamy hot nights together for good.

The good news was they'd been channeling all that simmering sexual energy into their scenes with Adrian, who'd actually been forced to close the set because the crew had given the two of them so much grief over their sizzling chemistry.

It didn't actually bug her one way or the other. No matter how embarrassing the catcalls got, the second Jackson touched her, the wild magic exploded and nothing else mattered. Heck, nothing else even registered.

She knew she was an idiot for allowing herself to get sucked into the fantasy of being Jackson's serious girlfriend. Minerva had thrown them at each other, and they were scratching a mutual itch. Lust, although fantastic, was a far cry from love. And with regards to Jackson Prescott, she'd do well not to confuse the two. But still, the fantasy of him having real and deep feelings for her was lovely.

At least until the movie shoot ended and he got on with his regularly scheduled life. And left her choking in his dust.

Minerva, thankfully, had backed off of their cases. The woman was completely absorbed in supervising the renovation of Ana's old bedroom into a nursery. For a boy, of course. A combination biker-sailor theme dominated, and Ana had to admit it was adorable.

About a week after that unforgettable Harley ride culminating in her moving into Jackson's bed, they came home from work and he helped her off the Harley in the garage with a slow, lingering kiss. He surprised her by murmuring, "Are you busy Saturday night?"

"No. Why?"

"I'd like to take you out on a real date."

Date? Him and her? As in going out in public? She opened her mouth and only garbled mumbling noises emerged.

He must have interpreted the sounds as acceptance of

his offer because he kissed her again, turned and strode into the house to take a quick shower before dinner. He'd spent the afternoon outside shooting a scene that she was not in, and it had been a cool hundred degrees in the shade.

She'd been fortunate to be inside the air-conditioned studio all afternoon, training with a bunch of female extras as Crash Mashburn taught them the rudiments of bar fighting.

She'd finally gotten a call from the manager of the only semiaffordable apartment complex in town, and a tenant had moved out without notice. As soon as the apartment was cleaned, she could have it.

The guy didn't ask her if she was still interested in the place, and she avoided the question, as well. Things were going great with Jackson this week, but would the same be true next week? Next month? Was he really capable of committing to a relationship or was what they had now just spillover from their movie roles?

They had only two major scenes left to film together— one was the big love scene where their aliens finally got together, and then some kind of wrap-up scene where they got their happily ever after near the end of the film. If only it was that simple. Fall into bed with the hot guy, have great sex, and he adores you for the rest of your life.

She ought to be over the moon. She'd landed a dream movie role that had the possibility of launching a full-blown movie career for her. And even if Jackson's attentions were fleeting, she'd at least earned his temporary affection. It was better than nothing, right?

Adrian's voice cut across the near sex Jackson was having with Ana like an unwelcome blast of cold air. For this scene, his alien had taken her alien out on a romantic date to an isolated location—Adrian told them to picture a high cliff with a panoramic view and a starry sky with multiple moons. They were supposed to finish the meal and then make dessert of each other.

He and Ana had spent the morning eating food the special effects department had gone to town on. Much of it had been marshmallows sculpted and air brushed to look like alien foodstuffs, and he was pretty much done with sugar for some time to come. During a break in filming, Ana had looked nearly as green as her bodysuit. He'd thought for a minute there that she was going to have to excuse herself to go throw up. But she'd pulled it together and they'd launched into the end of the scene. Which was to say the on-screen sex.

He'd griped before in interviews about how totally unromantic filming a love scene actually was. But he had to say, doing one with Ana was hot as hell. Her flimsy bodysuit did little to disguise her body, and her alternately soft and athletic curves were delicious beneath his hands. He never got tired of caressing her. What his hands couldn't feel, his imagination and recent experience in bed with her filled in.

He couldn't seem to touch her without the two of them going up in flames, and today had been no different. They'd been panting with real desire as they crawled all over one another, mimicking the act they'd been doing every night for the past week or more. On camera, they fell into the rhythm of their lovemaking without thought and their bodies writhed in perfect simpatico as they rolled across the remains of the alien picnic. Their limbs tangled together, their panted breaths mingled and they locked stares with one another as a sexual firestorm built between them.

Adrian called a cut, and Jackson abruptly pushed up and away from Ana. He sat upright beside her while she continued to sprawl beside him, catching her breath. He had a raging hard-on. He grabbed a towel from someone, ostensibly to mop the sweat off his face, but mostly he covered his crotch with it as he stood and moved over to a high canvas seat by the playback monitors.

Ana stumbled to the chair beside his, looking as dazed as she usually did when they came up for air after one of these passionate scenes. He was probably an ass for taking satisfaction in that look in her eyes, like she didn't quite know where she was. But so be it. He enjoyed kissing her into oblivion.

The playback looked nearly as hot as it had felt, and Adrian grinned broadly. "I ought to work with first-time actors more often. Ana, love, you take direction like nobody's business. And Jackson, I have to say this is the best work you've ever done. The heat the camera pulls out of the two of you—crazy fantastic."

Jackson didn't want to burst the guy's bubble. Fine director though he surely was, Adrian's instructions to pretend to be in lust with each other had nothing to do with the real and towering sexual tension between him and Ana.

The playback ended, and everyone watching was momentarily silent, which Jackson took as a supreme compliment from the crew. But then, the teasing and comments started to fly. They were worse than usual today. Not only had that scene been the closest to on-set sex of any of his and Ana's scenes to date, but most of the film's cast and crew happened to be in the studio today.

He had no choice but to take it in good humor, but he did console himself with the fact that he was the guy who got to take Ana home that night and sleep with her for real. The rest of them could only go home and jerk off alone while fantasizing about her.

Crash muttered from beside him, "Can you stand up yet, buddy?"

Jackson scowled at the stunt coordinator, but the guy smiled and shrugged. "I wouldn't be able to get through a scene like that without getting pretty turned on. Ana's one hell of a firecracker." He added thoughtfully, "Never thought you'd be the one to light her off, though."

"Can it. She's just doing her job."

"Just a job. Right." Mashburn grinned. "Of course, if I were you, I'd stake my claim on her pretty damned fast. After today's scene, every guy on the crew's gonna be gunning for a piece of that action from her."

Jackson barely refrained from grabbing the guy by the shirtfront and telling him to back the hell off.

Rather than make a complete fool of himself, he and the wadded towel in his lap stomped off to his office to take a shower. A cold one.

The worst of his frustration abated, he dried off and dressed thoughtfully. Crash did have a point. The other guys were going to come after Ana hard now. And there was no way he would allow it. He didn't even want to think about the feeding frenzy in Hollywood once the film premiered.

Shy of putting a stamp across Ana's forehead that said in big red letters Taken, he doubted that anything would likely back other men off. They all knew he was a confirmed bachelor. They would assume she'd be a free agent any second if she wasn't already. He couldn't afford to lose any of his other actors or primary crew members going into the bulk of production on this movie, and Adrian didn't need strife in his crew over a woman, either.

The alternative wasn't much better, though. If he made it clear he was dating Ana, how would the cast and crew react? But if he pretended not to be dating Ana, then open season would be declared on her, and he was back to the beginning of his argument. He swore luridly at the entire situation.

The ride home cleared his mind. As he slowed to turn into his driveway, a shocking thought occurred to him. What would be so bad about telling Ana how he felt about her? That he wanted to change their arrangement. To upgrade their on-screen relationship to a real, off-screen one. That the two of them needed to formalize their relationship to avoid the appearance of favoritism with the cast and crew.

What the hell "formalizing" entailed, he had no idea, and he frankly shied away from wanting to define it. Images of a white dress and church pews flashed through his head, and he banished them hard.

Ana would go along with the plan, right? She'd had a crush on him since they'd met. And either she was the greatest faker in history, or she was as addicted to what they had going on between the sheets as he was.

The more he thought about it, the more he liked the idea of making the two of them official. They had a ton in common. He genuinely enjoyed being with her—in and out of bed. Minerva would shut up and quit pestering the two of them. Even better, Ana was gradually driving the demons out of his head. Maybe someday she would actually succeed at driving them out of his heart, too. And the sex…well, the sex was epic.

Yup, he had a plan. Now to implement it. When he

got home, he heard the shower running in his and Ana's room. Perfect. He headed downstairs to recruit Rosie and Minerva to help him finalize his plan for a perfect, romantic date. Tomorrow night. Him and Ana.

Chapter 14

Ana started getting ready for her date with Jackson hours before it was time to go. But she was so nervous she couldn't sit still. He'd been kicked out of their room for the day and had retreated to some other guest room to do whatever guys did before they went out on a date. He wouldn't tell her anything except to dress up.

Three new and gorgeous cocktail gowns had appeared as if by magic in the closet last night. Make that Minerva magic. The woman really was a loving and generous soul, even if she was a meddler.

Ana heard Jackson's motorcycle roar out of the garage right about when she was despairing of ever getting her toenail polish right. As if on cue, a knock on the door turned out to be Minerva offering to help her get ready. Thank God. She was losing her mind in here alone.

"Okay, I need a spy report," Ana declared. "What does Jackson have planned for tonight?"

"I'll never tell," Minerva replied playfully.

"Huh. Some help you are."

"Here. Give me that nail polish. You're going to look like chiggers attacked you if you get much more of that red polish on your ankles."

Ana gratefully relinquished the little bottle into more capable hands. "Can't you at least give me a hint?"

"Nope. My lips are sealed." But Minerva's eyes twinkled merrily. She was pleased with whatever Jackson had cooked up for tonight, obviously.

Drat. "Can you at least tell me which dress you think I should wear?"

In short order, she had to try on all three dresses and model them for Minerva.

Eventually, the older woman declared, "The white one. No question about it."

"You don't think it's too...well, bridal? God knows, Jackson is jumpy as all get-out about anything that remotely reminds him of Vanessa."

"It's high time he got over that. It happened years ago, for goodness' sake. At some point, a person's got to pick themselves up and move on. I never liked that girl much, anyway."

"Really? She sounded just about perfect from what I read. At least up to the part where she cheated on Jackson and didn't bother to break up with him before she married that doctor."

"She was cold. Controlling. That girl had Jackson dancing on a chain like a trained dog most of the time. It wasn't good for him."

"How so?"

"I'm sure Jackson's talked to you about his childhood." Ana nodded and Minerva continued. "That kind of start in life doesn't build a lot of confidence in a child. I don't think he ever felt good enough for Vanessa. He thought he was the one reaching above himself in the relationship, but in truth, she didn't come close to deserving him."

"Jackson's always struck me as self-confident and at ease in his skin."

"Acting has been good to him. Not only has he had a lot of success, but he's grown up. Discovered something he's really good at."

She could think of more than a few things he was good at. A flash of Jackson blowing her mind in bed momentarily distracted Ana.

"Can I help with your makeup, dear? In my day, most actresses had to do their own stage makeup. I've got a fair hand with it."

Ana laughed. "Be my guest. Anything you can do will be better than what I can."

At six o'clock, Jackson got back from the Chesshire Hotel, where he'd checked to make sure the finishing touches on the evening were in place. He'd rented one of the venerable resort's private villas for the night. Long a destination of Hollywood stars seeking utter seclusion for their most private rendezvous, the villas were opulent and aching romance.

He went upstairs to shave and put on the tuxedo his grandmother occasionally drafted him into wearing when he took her to various charity functions. For once, he was glad he owned the damned penguin suit.

He combed his mostly dry hair into place, gave his bow tie one last tug to straighten it, and headed downstairs to the veranda. He checked his watch. Almost seven-thirty. He poured two glasses of the expensive Mosel white wine Minerva had insisted on donating to tonight's undertaking from her private stock of collector wines.

There. Everything was perfect. He looked up as the French doors opened. Forget what he'd just thought. Now *that* was perfection.

Ana stepped outside into the gathering sunset and paused to take in the view…and him. A slow, hesitant smile unfolded on her face as she sought his gaze. She walked across the stone terrace toward him, and they never broke eye contact. He drank in the sight of her with a combination of awe and delight.

He wondered if Minerva had given her a heads-up about what he'd done to the villa, because her vintage dress was white. Thin spaghetti straps held up the unadorned bodice. It cinched in tightly to her waist, and the skirt flared in layered petals of chiffon that skimmed her tanned legs like dozens of butterfly kisses. Her blond hair framed her face in a golden nimbus that made her eyes look huge and dark and mysterious in the wash of crimson sunset.

She glanced up at him sidelong as he handed her a glass of wine. "Would you like a glass of wine before we go?"

"We're not staying here?" she asked in surprise.

"Of course not. We eat here every night. It's a beautiful spot, but I promised you something special."

"You did? I thought you just promised me a date."

He grinned as he led her through the mansion to the tall front doors. He opened them with a flourish. "In my world, a date means something special."

Ana gasped in delight at the white limousine waiting

in front of the mansion. He smiled indulgently, enjoying her pleasure. Wait till she got a load of the rest of the evening's surprises. This date of theirs was going to be so romantic, and he was going to sweep her off her feet so thoroughly that she couldn't possibly say no to being his for real.

He guided her into the spacious limo and topped off his glass with the wine, which he'd brought along. Somehow, Minerva had discovered that Ana didn't care for champagne, hence the white wine. Although Ana's glass looked like she'd barely touched it.

"Don't like the wine?" he asked. It was good, though even he had to admit it didn't taste much like wine. He started to reach for the limo's built-in bar.

"The wine's fine," she said quickly. "I'm just a little nervous. Butterflies in my stomach aren't liking alcohol right now."

Fair enough. Nerves and butterflies boded well for his plan. "A toast," he murmured. "To us and to many, many more nights just like this one."

"To us," she murmured. She touched the glass to her lips while he took a sip of the German wine. It was crisp and fresh and as elegant as the woman seated across from him.

He kept the conversation light during the ride to the hotel. Ana gasped in delight as the limousine turned into the lush drive of Serendipity's iconic seaside hotel. He commented, "It's the movie-star treatment for you tonight."

"Ooh, this is going to be fun."

She had *no* idea.

They strolled through the tropical garden that provided privacy for the row of villas, and she gasped again as he turned down the private walk to one of them. He pulled out the key and opened the door for her. It had taken a refrigerated truck to get all the roses here earlier this afternoon.

He'd chosen Caroline de Monaco roses—white, tipped in pale pink—for her. They were pure with just a hint of naughty, like Ana herself. And they were everywhere. Dozens upon dozens of them, tucked in corners, displayed on mantles, resting on tables, floating in crystal bowls. And where there weren't roses, there were candles. Thousands of them. The hotel had devoted a half dozen staff members to arranging the flowers and lighting the candles for him this afternoon.

Even he was blown away by the effect. It was like an enchanted fairy bower. As he'd requested, a table for two was laid with white linens, fine crystal and sterling silver. A single perfect Caroline de Monaco rose lay across Ana's plate.

Jackson seated Ana at the table with a smile and a light kiss on her cheek.

"My goodness, Jackson. When you said a real date, I didn't think you meant all of this!"

He shrugged. "Never let it be said that I do anything halfway."

She laughed lightly as she spread her napkin. "Duly noted, sir."

A waiter in a tuxedo and white gloves served them each course. They lingered over the magnificent food and chatted about nothing and everything. Watching her eat a piece of double chocolate devil's food cake was a sexual experience in and of itself. Who knew that solid, sensible Ana was such a sucker for chocolate?

It dawned on him eventually that this was the first

time he'd seen Ana eat well in a while. She'd even been picking at Rosie's delicious cooking for the past week or two. Poor girl was under a lot of stress. But all things considered, she was holding up remarkably well.

He had to hand it to his grandmother. He might not have ever found Ana if it weren't for Minerva's pressuring and interference. Being with Ana had definitely been good for him. He only hoped he'd been good for her, too. And not just in the "I gave her a big break" way.

"What's on your mind, Jackson? You went quiet all of a sudden."

He smiled across the intimate table. "I was thinking about us."

Unaccountably, her expression abruptly went serious on him. Tight. Tense. Fearful, even. She'd barely touched her wine, and he suddenly wished he'd been able to get quite a bit more of the liquid relaxation down her.

"Are you sorry you took this role?" he asked.

Her brow twitched into a momentary frown. "The movie role? Of course I'm not sorry. It's the chance of a lifetime. Heck, I hit the career lottery. I'm thrilled beyond belief."

That wasn't the role he'd been thinking about. He'd had in mind the role of real girlfriend to him.

He opened his mouth to explain, but she interrupted him, blurting all in a rush, "There's something I have to tell you. I'm too nervous to listen to anything you have to say until I tell you what I have to."

He smiled indulgently. "Of course. What's on your mind that's making you so nervous?"

"You."

His smile widened. "There's nothing to be nervous about with me. We're colleagues, friends and lovers.

Pretty much what you see is what you get with me. And we've gotten to know each other extremely well. You can tell me anything."

"God, I hope so." She took a deep breath that threatened to spill her swelling cleavage out of the top of her dress in the most distracting and sexy way. "Here goes."

What on earth had her wrapped so tightly?

She exhaled hard. "Jackson, I'm pregnant. For real."

Chapter 15

Ana winced as Jackson looked like his brain had just exploded inside his skull. His face turned dark red. Heck, even his ears turned red. "You're *what?*" he demanded with terrible intensity.

Ana flinched, even though he hadn't raised his voice, not one decibel. "You heard me. I'm pregnant."

"How in the *hell* did that happen?"

"Um, the same way it usually does. You had a health class in high school, right? Insert Widget A in Slot B and all?"

He shoved back from the table violently and surged to his feet. Emotions blasted across his face like artillery bursts. Shock. Dismay. Fury. Chagrin. *Betrayal.*

Her insides felt as if he'd reached down her throat and torn her heart out. This was supposed to be a happy moment. One shared by a loving couple excited to have created a new life between them. *The beginning of a forever family...*

"How could you?" he threw at her.

...or not.

"Excuse me," she retorted frostily, "but you were there, too. And a willing participant in the act, I might add."

"You said you were taking birth control pills."

"And I was."

"Then how?"

"I'm just as stunned as you are, Jackson. Statistically, the Pill is ninety-eight percent effective or something like that. Apparently, we're part of the two percent."

"Lucky us."

He might as well have stabbed a knife in her heart. She *wanted* this baby. His baby. *Their* baby. But he was acting like she'd just declared a death sentence on him.

"God. The press is going to have a field day with this. I've spent *years* trying to avoid exactly this sort of scandal. Not to be a tabloid joke, like my mother!"

He paced the living room in agitation, kicking aside rose petals angrily as he went. She watched warily. Too many emotions and thoughts were flying across his face for her to decipher them all. But the bottom line was that he was furious. And he blamed her.

She was willing to tolerate a little bit of that, initially. This news had hit him out of the blue, after all. But at the end of the day it had taken two of them to freaking tango. He could step up and take responsibility for his part in making this child.

The longer he paced, muttering to himself, the less patience she had with his reaction. Sure it was a shock. It had been a hell of a shock to have her suspicions confirmed, too. But she'd moved on to the practical considerations a hell of a lot faster than he was doing now.

"I suppose you expect me to marry you," he flung at her. "That you've won the lottery and forced my hand."

That did it. She planted her palms on the linen-covered tabletop and surged to her own feet. "I don't expect a damned thing of you, Jackson Prescott. And for the record, you're behaving like a complete ass."

She was *not* going to cry in front of him. She raced outside and ran down the sidewalk until the main hotel came into view. Heading for the lobby, she asked for a cab, and in under a minute was riding down the lush drive. *And he didn't try to stop her.*

She did cry then. So hard she couldn't see, let alone think. No way was she going back to the mansion. She had no family to turn to. What friends she had were back in Los Angeles. She had nowhere to live. Most of what she owned had been trashed in the motel. Hell, her whole life was trashed.

Was she crazy to consider going through with having this baby? Should she think about terminating the pregnancy and saving her and Jackson a whole bunch of life-changing adjustments? Despair at the notion of giving up on Jackson's child—and on Jackson himself— washed over her.

She directed the cab to the movie studio. It was as close to an actual home as she had right now. Adrian Turnow's car was in its reserved spot out front, and she punched in the security code to unlock the stage door. The security guard at the front desk nodded a hello to her and waved her into the studio.

For his part, Adrian looked up in surprise from the bank of computer monitors as she stepped out of the shadows and onto the deserted soundstage. "Nice dress. What brings you here at this late hour?" he asked her in surprise.

"I, uh, was thinking about a fight sequence and I needed a bungee harness to try out a new move."

He nodded rather distractedly and went back to work.

She probably did need the workout. It had always been her best form of stress relief. She changed out of the lovely dress that was as close to a wedding dress as she was ever going to come, and changed into leggings and a sloppy T-shirt in the trunk of her stuff that she kept in Jackson's office.

She'd been jumping around like a kangaroo for a while in a bungee harness and actually had worked out a very cool combat sequence when Adrian called from by the exit, "Check out with the guard when you leave, okay?"

"You've got it," she huffed back.

When she'd finally exhausted herself enough to sleep, she took a shower, changed into a clean set of sweatpants and a T-shirt from the stash of clothing she kept in her locker, and made her way to Jackson's office.

She crashed on his couch. The way she figured it, he owed her a night in his office after being such a self-centered jerk earlier. She'd had such high hopes for him. He'd seemed to be coming along so nicely at committing to a relationship. And then tonight's freak-out.

That was how it always was with him. He would let her draw close to him but not so close that he actually had to give up any part of himself to her. As soon as that threatened, he ran screaming in the other direction.

Not that she could blame him entirely for flipping out. If only he'd gotten his head out of his ass long enough to think about her for even a second. But he was too broken, too scarred, to see beyond his own fear of abandonment, his own terror of commitment, apparently.

She couldn't stop the tears when they came again, this time more quietly. A pregnant woman was allowed to cry whenever she felt like it, right? She grieved for herself and for the hurt little boy inside Jackson. And she vowed silently that she would never, ever let her son feel so unloved or insecure, no matter how big a jackass his father might be.

The clean masculine scent of said jackass rising from the blanket she huddled beneath nearly did her in, though, before she finally managed to cry herself to sleep.

Something moving in the hallway outside his door made Ana jerk awake sometime later. Probably just the security guard. Except the guy was moving awfully quietly. She'd heard the roving guards' boots slapping along earlier, and that wasn't what she heard now. Maybe there'd been a shift change while she was asleep. She opened the door to let the new guy know she was here.

But when she threw Jackson's door open, the hallway was pitch-black. That was weird. A few lights were always left on at the end of each hallway and on the sets. There were too many wires and too much equipment lying around at any given time that people could get hurt on, so the place was always partially lighted.

Her impulse was to call out to the guard, to let him know she was there, but some instinct warned her to be silent. She crept out into the hallway cautiously. It had sounded like the guard was headed for the main sound-stage. She followed the quiet shuffling sounds ahead of her, speeding her steps to catch up with him as the weight of the darkness pressed in on her.

She caught sight of a shadow slipping behind one of

the big trolley cameras across the set. She opened her mouth to call out to the guy, but then she heard another sound. A faint groan.

What the—

And then another sound reached her. A sound she knew all too well from her martial arts classes. The sound of knuckles slamming into flesh.

Holy crap. The shadow had just slugged something—someone—lying on the ground over there.

She ducked down fast behind a table full of computer monitors, her adrenaline screaming at her to run for her life. She eased around the edge of the table to peer toward the sounds. A door opened quietly and then clicked closed. Had the attacker left the set? Or was that a ploy to make her think he'd left? But a ploy would mean he knew she was here. Stay or go?

Panicked, indecision paralyzed her until it dawned on her that someone was down and possibly hurt behind that camera. Worry for whoever it was galvanized her into motion and she crept around the edges of the set, sticking to the shadows and hiding behind big equipment as she cautiously made her way toward where she'd heard the groan and the punch.

She reached the camera trolley and crouched down beside a big cloth curtain designed to absorb echoes. Was that a man lying on the ground in a heap over there? She crept forward, heart in her throat. Surely, if the guard had knocked out a bad guy, he'd have handcuffed the intruder, turned on all the lights and called the police.

Which meant the downed man had to be the security guard, and the bad guy was still roaming around the set. Was it her mugger, returned to set up another "accident"?

She forced her feet into motion and eased forward,

hugging the curtain and the deep shadows shrouding it. The unconscious person came into sight. Oh, God. It was a guard. She recognized the uniform. And as she drew closer, she recognized the face of the guy who'd checked her into the studio earlier.

With a last furtive glance around, to be sure they were alone, she moved to the guy's side and felt for a pulse in his throat. He was alive. And that was when she saw the ugly gash over his right ear and the black puddle of blood under his head.

She felt in his hair for the wound. It didn't feel like it was bleeding anymore, but she had to get help right away! She fumbled at her jeans pockets. Crap. Her cell phone was back in Jackson's office. She fumbled at the downed guard's pants pockets and was relieved to feel the hard rectangle of a cell phone in one of them. She pulled it out and dialed 9-1-1.

She whispered when the dispatcher answered, "I need police and an ambulance at Starstruck Studios, Stage 4. There's an intruder in the building and I'm with an unconscious and injured security guard at the back of the main stage."

The dispatcher efficiently told her to find a bathroom to lock herself in and that emergency services had been summoned and would be there in under ten minutes.

Ten endless minutes to crouch beside this poor guy, her hand pressed over his wound to stop the seeping blood, and pray that the intruder didn't swing back this way to check that the guard was still unconscious.

Unable to take the suspense, she dialed Jackson's phone number.

"Hey, Bart," he answered. "What's up?"

"It's me," she whispered. "I'm at the studio and someone knocked Bart out. There's an intruder."

"Take cover, Ana," Jackson ordered tersely. "Don't make any more noise by talking but stay on the line. Find a spot to hide and don't come out until I tell you it's okay. I'm on my way. I'll be there as soon as I can."

He sounded calm, but she sensed terrible urgency in his voice.

And then she heard a movement behind her. The door the intruder had disappeared through was opening again. She dived for the acoustic curtain and rolled underneath it. She plastered herself against the concrete wall behind it and prayed she wasn't making a bump that the intruder would spot. Her heartbeats sounded like booming bass drums in her ears. Surely the intruder could hear them.

She realized she was panting in terror and held her breath sharply.

In terror, she watched a pair of black work boots walk over to the guard's body and stop. *Oh, God.* The guy wasn't more than six feet away from her. One boot drew back and kicked the unconscious guard viciously in the mouth, and she had to bite her lips to hold back a gasp of horror.

In the distance, she heard a siren and it rapidly grew louder. The boots half turned and then took off running across the soundstage.

She lifted the edge of the curtain to see if she could get a look at the intruder, but it was too dark. All she saw was a large shape fleeing out one of the side exits.

"He ran, Jackson," she breathed into the phone. "And I hear the police."

"Stay where you are, baby. Don't move. Don't make a sound. The bastard may not be alone."

Crud. She hadn't thought about there being more than one intruder. She settled back behind the curtain. Her hands instinctively cradled her belly, protecting the tiny spark of life there. No way could she get rid of this baby. She already loved it and was fiercely protective of it.

The studio was as silent as a tomb around her. Only the screams of approaching sirens disturbed the thick blanket of night. She'd never felt so helpless as she crouched there, watching blood drip from the poor guard's mouth.

She started when Jackson's voice sounded in her ear. "I'm outside the studio with about six cop cars. We're going to come in now. Where are you, Ana?"

"Back side of the main stage behind the acoustic curtain. About six feet from Bart. He needs an ambulance."

"Got it. Don't move. We'll be there in a sec."

The studio's lights went on all at once and noise erupted everywhere as police barged into the building from every direction, clearing the huge studio loudly. And then, without warning, the curtain lifted away from her. Her hands whipped up defensively as a big, dark shadow reached for her. *Jackson.* She flew into his arms and all but knocked him over in her relief.

"I've got you, Ana. You're safe," he muttered into her hair. He wrapped her in a hug so tight she could barely breathe. But then she returned the favor and practically strangled him himself. He eased her backward, drawing the acoustic curtain around both of them until they were blanketed in darkness once more.

He placed his mouth on her ear and breathed, "We're going to stay here until the police declare the building safe."

She nodded against his chest, registering vaguely that he'd turned her until she was pressed against the wall and his body created a living shield between her and the rest of the movie set. She was nestled in his arms, safe once more. She always felt safe with him.

In a few minutes, the police shouting back and forth declared the building clear, and paramedics rushed over to take care of the unconscious security guard.

Jackson kept her plastered against his side as they watched the EMTs pack the guard's mouth with gauze, collect the three teeth that had fallen out of the guy's mouth and put them in a jar, and transfer the now moaning guard onto a stretcher.

And then the police descended upon her. She wished she could tell them more, but she'd been more concerned with staying alive than with spotting the intruder.

Adrian showed up on the set, his clothes akimbo. "What the hell's going on?" he demanded of Jackson. "The police called and said there was an intruder."

"Ana's stalker came back. The police and our security guys are going over the set with a fine-tooth comb to make sure the bastard didn't successfully sabotage anything before Ana scared him off."

"I didn't scare him off. The police sirens did that."

"You called 9-1-1," Jackson declared.

"Thanks, Ana," Adrian chimed in.

She just shook her head. She was no hero. But she was getting sick and tired of being scared stiff. "We need to catch this guy and stop him," she declared. "If not for me, then for everyone else in the crew."

"I'm working on it," Jackson replied, his voice grim. "Adrian, a few of the stunt guys are ex-Special Forces types. I'd like them to rig a few trip wires and booby traps around the studio with your permission."

"Done," Adrian declared.

Jackson growled, "Next time this bastard tries anything around here, he's gonna get the surprise of his life."

Jackson drove her home to the mansion and deposited her in bed without much conversation. He seemed distracted. Probably was busy planning how to trap the intruder at the studio. Too bad his protectiveness didn't change anything from earlier. He still wasn't prepared to have an actual relationship with her. And he damned well wasn't ready to be a parent. And on that unpleasant note of harsh reality, she went to sleep, alone in his big bed.

In the morning, Ana woke sore and stiff from last night's excitement. She rolled over, rubbing her stomach in disbelief. It was hard to believe a new life was under way inside her, and that she and Jackson had created it.

No matter how gigantic an idiot he'd been about it when she'd told him, she was secretly over the moon about this baby. She had no idea why she felt that way, but there it was. Apparently, she had some heretofore untapped female instinct for baby adoration. Who knew?

If Jackson had come to bed at all last night, there was no evidence of it. He was already out of the house when she strolled downstairs to nibble on dry toast and sip a little weak tea. They seemed to be the only things her stomach would tolerate in the morning anymore.

When the hour advanced enough for businesses to open, she called her insurance company to get an update. It turned out they were prepared to write her a check for the full amount of her renter's insurance, which would cover the security deposit on an apartment with enough left over to buy a few pieces of furniture. The timing of the news could not have been better. She arranged to have the money wired to her checking account and headed out to rent herself an apartment.

She waited until she knew Jackson was in a meeting to call his cell phone. Relieved when it kicked over to voice mail, she left him a brief message to let him know she had moved out of the mansion. She disconnected the call and officially declared herself a big ole chicken.

She didn't need a confrontation with him just now. Not when she was this fragile emotionally. She would deal with him later, when she had her feet under her. The two of them weren't scheduled to shoot again for a couple of days. Plenty of time to fortify herself to face him. They had just one more scene to shoot together. She could get through one lousy scene, right?

By the end of the day, she'd settled into her tiny studio. No matter that it would fit inside the bathroom in Jackson's suite. It was hers. She needed to impose some order on her life, and continuing to live with Jackson and his grandmother was not going to help her do that.

She cooked her first meal in her own place and settled down to nest a little. Except the apartment didn't feel safe. After last night's scare, her paranoia was working overtime. A call to a locksmith had a man at her place installing a pair of hefty dead bolts on the front door and security bars in all the windows that made her feel marginally better.

She would have to figure out how to get her personal stuff from the mansion later, but she couldn't face Jackson or Minerva just yet. It was too painful to see what could have been every time she was around them. If only Jackson had been able to overcome his demons regarding women and trust.

Not that she had any right to cast stones in that department. She'd spent plenty of time not trusting men, either. But now, with a baby on the way, she didn't have years to wait around for him to figure things out. She had her own life to live and another one to look out for, and it was high time she got on with both.

She had just finished hanging curtains in the living room when a knock sounded on her front door. Cautiously, she peered out the peephole and saw a distorted image of Jackson standing there, looking thunderous. She cracked open the door a tiny bit without taking off the security chain. "What do you want?"

"I was worried about you when you didn't come back to the house for supper," he ground out.

She opened the door but didn't invite him in. "I left you a message that I moved out."

"Yes, but you didn't leave me an explanation why."

"I don't owe you any explanations. You made it perfectly clear you don't want a relationship with me. It's high time I get on with my own life."

His jaw muscles rippled in irritation but he said evenly enough, "One of the guys drove over here with me so I could drop off the Hugster for you. I thought you might need a car to get to and from work."

She might have grudgingly thanked him, testing the waters to see if it was a peace offering or not, but the hurt over his rejection was still too fresh. "Thanks, but I don't need it. Crash is giving me a ride over to the garage to pick up my Bug when he gets off set this evening."

The simmering irritation in his gaze erupted into full-blown anger. She really, really didn't want to talk to him while he was in this frame of mind. She'd gotten her fill of that at the Chesshire Hotel.

In her experience, people were most honest when they were caught off guard like he had been that night. No matter what he said now, she'd gotten a glimpse of his real feelings about her. He didn't trust her and thought she was capable of trapping him in a relationship with her.

"Avoiding me?" he bit out sarcastically.

"Hell to the yes," she snapped back. "I've got nothing to say to you, and I damned well don't want to hear what you have to say while you're in this snit."

"This is not a snit—" He broke off as Crash came bounding up the outdoor stairs, jangling his keys noisily.

"Hey, Jackson. C'mon, Ana. We gotta roll. Garage will close soon."

"You got it, Crash." She stepped into the breezeway, locking the door behind her. "Go home and have a beer, Jackson. You look like you could use one. I'll see you on set Friday."

She blew past him quickly, making sure to stay to the far right of the steps and not give him any opportunity to grab her and subject her to a grand chewing-out. She truly didn't want a confrontation with him. If nothing else, he was her boss, and she needed to be able to get work after this film wrapped more than ever now that she was going to have to support a child.

Jackson was so tense he all but vibrated as she hurried past him, but thankfully he didn't make a scene. He was still standing on the steps staring grimly in her direction as Crash's car pulled out of the parking lot.

"Good news, Izzolo," Crash announced. "I see your wreck out back. It must be finished."

She climbed out of the car and looked where Crash pointed. Sure enough, there was the Bug Bomb. And she looked better than she usually did. The mechanic must have washed and waxed the old gal.

"That car would be worth a little bit if you restored her

properly," he commented. "Vintage Bugs have come back in style." Given that he was the resident car expert on the stunt crew, she was inclined to believe he was right.

"I just need the transportation, and she was cheap when I bought her."

He shrugged. "I've got a little garage and a lift at my place. I'd be happy to work on her some more, if you like. You pay for parts and I'll throw in the labor."

Ana stared at him, shocked by the generosity of the offer. "You don't have to do that, Crash."

"I know I don't have to. But tweaking cars relaxes me, and I'm not working on one right now. It would give me a project to play with."

"Thanks for the offer."

"I've got a buddy who tows classic cars. Just let me know when you can spare your baby for a few days."

She jolted at the reference to babies and looked over at him sharply. He was staring at the Volkswagen, thankfully.

The six-hundred-pound gorilla lurking in the corner of her brain stirred. *What the hell was she going to do about raising this baby?* If Jackson wanted to be part of his child's life, she couldn't very well keep him out of it. God knew he had a whole lot more money than she did if it came to a custody fight with lawyers involved. Panic at the idea of him taking her baby away made her a little light-headed.

Where on earth did a shared child leave the two of them?

Chapter 16

Jackson tossed and turned sleeplessly as the moon rose outside his window and eventually set again. *What the hell am I going to do about a baby?* And about its mother, for that matter.

He was a little shocked to discover that he wasn't all that upset about the existence of a baby. But, Lord, getting pregnant was just the sort of thing his mother would have done. Except she'd have used a baby to trap a big movie star purely for the publicity, or even just to advance her career. He'd sworn long ago to cast off the taint of his famously wild, drug-addicted mother in Hollywood. But apparently, blood won out in the end.

Ana was being completely irrational and wouldn't even speak to him, for God's sake. It was not in his nature to avoid problems, but clearly he was going to have to give her a few days to cool down before he tried to talk with her again.

He punched his pillow and the faint scent of her vanilla perfume rose to meet his nose. His body stirred instantly. Dammit. Even the smell of her turned him on. Truth be told, everything about her turned him on. Even the fiery glint of anger in her eyes today had been sexy as hell.

Everything had been going so right for them. How could it all have gone so damned wrong so damned fast?

Before dawn, he gave up on pretending to sleep and went downstairs. He made his way out to the veranda as sunrise started to make the sky pink behind him. A tall mug of coffee did nothing to lighten his mood, nor did it offer up any answers to him about women and their incomprehensible ways.

He turned sharply at the sound of crunching in the driveway. He knew that particular tenor of thrown gravel. That was the Hugster. *Ana's home. Thank God.*

He raced through the kitchen and punched the garage door opener on the wall impatiently. The big panel slid up achingly slowly as he waited to see her face again. To take her in his arms. To tell her how much he'd missed her and that he wanted to take care of her and the baby and wouldn't abandon them.

The minivan pulled into the garage, and the door opened…

…and Crash Mashburn got out.

Damn, damn, damn. "What are you doing here?" Jackson demanded.

"Ana asked me to return the van to you. She's got her Bug back, and it's running." He added ominously, "For now, at least. Thing's a piece of crap. Needs a major engine overhaul…"

He tuned out while Crash listed the things that needed

fixing on her car. Cold-sweat terror erupted in his gut. *It was already starting.* He and Ana had one fight, and the circling sharks moved in. Crash was a decent enough guy, but Ana was carrying *his* baby, God damn it. *Doesn't that somehow make her mine?* He barely caught the keys Mashburn casually tossed him. *Apparently not.*

"Sweet ride for a minivan," Crash announced drily. "Needs a suspension adjustment, though, if you're planning to corner it hard. Rear axle's running a little loose."

Jackson scowled, and the stuntman said more seriously, "I assume you won't mind giving me a ride in to work this morning since we both have the meeting with Adrian at nine?"

Work. Meeting. Adrian. He swore under his breath. "You had breakfast?" he asked reluctantly.

"Nope."

"Come on in," he said in resignation. "I'll fry us some eggs."

He managed to restrain himself until after he'd plunked down a plate of eggs, bacon and toast in front of Crash. Then he blurted, "How's Ana doing?"

Crash answered around a mouthful of eggs and toast, "Settling into her place. Seems a little outta sorts, but the kid's under a lot of pressure what with this being her first big acting role and all. And those attacks were rough. She's tough, though. She'll bounce back."

Jackson made a noncommittal sound of agreement. He probably couldn't get away with questioning Crash any more on the subject of Ana without rousing the guy's suspicions. Mashburn was sharp as a tack and didn't miss much that went on around him.

They'd arrived at the studio in the cursed minivan and were walking in from the parking lot when a call came in to Crash's cell that turned out to be related to Mashburn having Ana's car delivered to his place so he could work on it for her. Jackson couldn't keep his mouth shut any longer. He put a restraining hand on Mashburn's arm and the guy turned questioningly to him.

"Ana's been through hell, Crash. Back off and give her some breathing space. She's not ready for a major relationship right now."

Mashburn snorted. "That's hilarious coming from you. Maybe you should take your own advice, there, Jackson."

"I'm serious, man."

Crash took a step closer and stared him hard in the eye. "So am I. Ana's a great girl. Boss or not, I'm tellin' you. Don't screw with her head." And on that note, he whirled and strode ahead of Jackson into the studio.

What the hell had she told Crash about the two of them? Had she rebounded into the former race-car driver's bed already? His blood boiled at the idea of her sleeping with Crash—hell, with any other man. His teeth were still grinding together when he sat down with Adrian.

He struggled through the whole damned meeting to keep his mind on the topics at hand. Mostly, he failed. The saving grace was that Sheila, Adrian's blessedly efficient assistant, had printed up copies of the shooting and production schedule that most of the meeting was devoted to going over. He would look at it later when he wasn't dying to bury his fist in the face of the guy across the table.

Was Crash right? Had he taken advantage of her emotional fragility after a big scare and the huge shock of diving into moviemaking headfirst? Was *he* the villain in this scenario?

* * *

It felt strange being on her own again. Ana found herself watching her rearview mirror carefully and looking over her shoulder often, just like she used to. Weird how safe she'd felt after Jackson had come into her life.

Had she seen that tan sedan earlier in the day? The car looked familiar. She ran a red light trying to ditch it and earned a chorus of honking horns before she declared herself crazy and shook off the silly paranoia. Chandler LaGrange was locked up in a mental institution and couldn't come after her. And even if he did get out, she lived on the other side of the country now.

Still, she couldn't forget the firecracker sounds before that lighting rig had nearly crushed her. The police never had figured out who'd broken into her motel room. The intruder had probably worn gloves because he left no fingerprints behind that the police could discern. And, given the number of people who stayed in short-term motel rooms like that, there was no way to sift through the other forensic evidence to figure out who the last person in the room had been. Brody Westmore had been helpful but explained there was nothing more the police could do.

She saw the tan sedan coming with just enough time to brace herself against the steering wheel, but that was all. The speeding car smashed into her door with enough force to spin the little Bug all the way around.

Her body slammed violently against the seat belt and shoulder harness. The car was far too old for air bags. *Oh, God, please let that not have hurt the baby.* She undid her seat belt and pushed at the door, but it was a mangled mess bowing in toward her. She crawled over the center console to the opposite door and pushed it open. The frame of the car was bent and she had to give it a good heave with her shoulder, and she half fell out of the Bug as the latch gave way.

Righting herself, she climbed out of her car to check the other driver. Other drivers had stopped and were running her way.

"You okay, lady?" one of them asked.

"Yes, I'm fine. Check the other driver."

She followed the Good Samaritan around the front of her vehicle to the tan sedan and stopped in her tracks. *There was no driver.* The driver's side door was wide open, and *no one* was in the car. The engine was still running, but the car was empty. Who would slam their car into someone else and then just take off? An illegal alien? A criminal? *Her stalker?*

She felt her jeans pocket, and her cell phone was still in it. She pulled it out and dialed before she could stop to question her choice of phone numbers.

"Ana. What's up?" Jackson sounded surprised. Pleased, maybe.

"I was just in a car accident, and the other driver fled. I thought you might want to call your security guys and have them respond."

"Where are you now?" he responded tersely, in full crisis mode. "Do you need an ambulance? Have the police been called?"

"I definitely don't need an ambulance. I'm fine."

"Sit down and don't stand up again until I get there," he ordered.

She actually did as he'd said to when she started to feel a little dizzy and faint. *Please God, let nothing be wrong with the baby.* She'd die if she lost this miracle now.

The police arrived on the scene before Jackson—

Brody and a guy she'd never met on the Serendipity police force—and questioned her in detail about the other car and driver. She wasn't much help, though. She'd barely seen the car before it hit her, let alone the driver's face. A man. Wearing sunglasses and a baseball cap. Not much help to the police.

All any of the witnesses could tell the police was that it had been a man. The descriptions declared him medium in every way. Medium height. Medium build. Medium brown hair, average features. Which was to say, no one had seen a thing.

Jackson was more decisive with the police when he got there. He was not amused when the police failed to find any fingerprints on the steering wheel after a dusting for them that he insisted on.

After the complete lack of prints, Brody's partner came back to press her harder for any ideas she had regarding who might be out to harm her. She reiterated that she had no enemies, no ex-boyfriends and no idea whatsoever who could be targeting her like this, but this officer was even more skeptical than the last ones had been.

She was near tears in her frustration when Jackson finally stepped in to end the interrogation. "I'm taking her to the hospital now. You can call her tomorrow if you have any more questions."

"I don't need to go to the hospital, Jackson," she protested.

"You're pregnant. Indulge me," he retorted in a voice that brooked no disagreement. When she tried to protest, he merely said, "Don't make me invoke the insurance clause in your contract. I can legally force you to go."

It took them a couple of hours of sitting around to get an ultrasound and get it read, but a doctor finally declared both her and baby hale and healthy. She didn't know who was more relieved—her or Jackson.

"I'm taking you back to my place," he declared.

"You most certainly are not!" she retorted sharply. "I'm going home. To *my* home."

"Ana—"

"Don't argue with me," she warned him. "I'm in no mood for a fight tonight."

Surprisingly, he took a deep breath and exhaled it slowly. Much more calmly than she expected, he said, "Fair enough. But here's the thing. You're carrying my child, and someone just tried to kill you. No way, no how, am I leaving you alone tonight. I'll sleep on your couch or outside, leaning against your front door. But, honey, I'm not going away, and I'm not going to fight with you about it."

She subsided and let him drive her back to her place… and honestly, it was nice to have a big strong man look out for her a little. The accident and disappearance of the driver had rattled her worse than she wanted to let on.

He ended up bunking down on her couch, and surprised her by not asking to join her in her bed. Which was just as well. She didn't want to have to deal with him—or more accurately, her feelings for him—tonight. If only he wasn't so damned dependable and decent in a crisis. He made it hard to hate him.

She took a long soak in a warm tub to ease the aches and pains she was going to feel tomorrow after the accident, put on her fuzziest pajamas, called it an early night and went to bed.

The nightmare shouldn't have surprised her, she supposed. But it was worse than usual. The hands around her neck were tighter and more real than they'd been in a long time. She woke with a jolt, sitting bolt upright in the dark, shaking from head to foot in terror. Maybe she should think about calling her psychiatrist back home in the morning. This was getting out of hand.

What was happening to her? Who was doing this to her?

Jackson would come in here in a heartbeat and hold her the rest of the night. All she had to do was call his name. But dammit, she was going to have to learn to live on her own sooner or later—likely sooner given the state of affairs between them now.

She lay back down and pulled the covers all the way up over her head. That lasted until she decided she'd rather see her attacker coming and have a chance to defend herself. It was one of the hardest things she'd ever done not to ask Jackson to come sleep with her. She missed him all the way down to her bones. Every cell in her body ached to be with him. But they could never be a couple. Not in the way she wanted—committed, loving and real. Her eyes burned with tears that refused to come.

She pulled the covers back down under her chin and stared gritty-eyed into the corners of her bedroom for the rest of the night.

Chapter 17

Ana sat on a wooden bench in the women's locker room at the studio. Rats. She was going to puke again. And this time it wasn't the combination of dry Cheerios and morning sickness making her stomach heave. It was knowing that, in a few minutes, she was going to have to go out and fake a love scene with Jackson.

Today was their last scene together. After filming wrapped this afternoon, they would be done with each other in every way. No more ties would be left to bind them together...except a child he didn't want. An urge to cry like a baby washed over her, tightening her throat and making her eyes swim in unshed tears. *Get a grip!* Like it or not, she had a job to do.

How in the hell was she supposed to film a steamy love scene with him when they weren't even speaking to each other? He'd waited until she was up and around this morning and had slipped out of her apartment without a single word to her. A security guard from the studio had been waiting outside her front door when she opened it and had given her a ride to the studio in what rode like an armored SUV.

How did actors and actresses have on-set romances and get through the end of films after their temporary romances blew up and they'd gone their separate ways?

She jumped as a loud mob of young women burst into the locker room, making more noise than a flock of chickens. She'd forgotten that today was an open casting call for bit-part actors. Which meant there'd be a huge audience to witness her humiliation with Jackson. Great. She zipped the green bodysuit up to her neck but left the hood down. Might as well get all smeared in green facial makeup and get her facial dots glued on before she put on the hot, uncomfortable hood. Glumly, she headed for makeup.

Tyrone Cozier, one of the top makeup artists in the biz, waved her into his chair this morning.

"Hey, Tyrone, how do I rate the star treatment from a fancy makeup artist like you?"

He laughed and commenced turning all her exposed skin green. "I'm not too proud to do grunt work, girl-friend." He worked in silence for a minute and then murmured, "So why are you already green before I've started putting makeup on you, hon?"

She sighed. He had a reputation for being freakishly observant. It probably came from studying human faces in minute detail all day long. "I'm not feeling great this morning."

"You don't look hungover. Eyes aren't bloodshot

enough. Did you catch the stomach flu that's going around?"

"Yeah. That must be it. Or maybe I ate something weird last night. I did have seafood." It was a lie, but no way was she admitting to him that she was pregnant with Jackson's baby.

Tyrone nodded, but doubt lingered in the guy's dark eyes. Entirely too observant, he was.

"Okay, sweetie. You're all done. Take care, and I'm here if you want to talk."

Ana smiled her thanks weakly. She dared not dwell on the makeup artist's kindness, or she'd cry for sure. She made her way over to the green stage. Jackson was already there, looking better than any man had a right to, wearing a full-body leotard that was entirely too informative about his physique. The guy didn't carry one spare pound anywhere on his muscular, fit frame, and it showed in the suit.

A bevy of girl extra wannabes giggled off to one side and seemed to be enjoying the sight of Jackson far too much for Ana's peace of mind. But, hey, it wasn't like she had any say in who ogled him. He was just the boss…

…and the father of your freaking baby.

She was really getting tired of that little voice in the back of her head editorializing about everything having to do with him.

Jackson turned around as she stepped out onto the mat. He looked grim as hell beneath his covering of green makeup and white polka dots. "How are you feeling today?" he asked quietly.

"I've been better," she answered honestly.

"Is anything wrong with…you know?" he asked with concern.

"Nothing that a bunch of saltine crackers can't cure," she muttered back.

Comprehension lit his eyes. "Ah. Sorry. Wish I could be there to hold your hair out of the toilet."

The sentiment startled her. He *wanted* to experience the joys of morning sickness? She had no time to examine her reaction to his statement, though, because Adrian stepped out onto the floor just then.

"Jackson, Ana, if you don't mind, I've asked the young ladies who've gotten callbacks for the movie to observe your green-screen work today to get an idea of what will be expected of them if they get a role in the film."

Like she was going to say no to the director. Personally, she wasn't the least bit thrilled to have an audience. Getting through this scene was going to be hard enough already. How in the hell was she supposed to fake having happily-ever-after sex with Jackson in front of a bunch of giggling strangers?

Jackson didn't look any more thrilled than her.

It dawned on her, though, that Adrian couldn't possibly have missed the tension between her and Jackson. She would bet he'd arranged for an audience to keep the two of them behaving professionally and keep their minds off their personal problems.

Adrian walked over to the close-in camera, took a quick peek through the viewfinder and gave the lighting guys a thumbs-up. "Whenever you're ready to go you two, let me know."

Ana took a deep breath. She sat down in the lime-green forest glade setting that had been built for this shot. Jackson sat down beside her and nodded to the director.

Adrian rolled cameras.

She and Jackson went through their lines, which were

blessedly short and easy enough to deliver. And then it was time for the clinch. It was supposed to be passionate. Joyous. But for the life of her, she couldn't summon anything resembling joy. Instead, the hopelessness of it all washed over her. No matter how much she loved Jackson, it would never be enough if he couldn't let himself return her love. They were doomed. This would never work out. The quality of their embrace changed. Took on a sense of desperation. Of lovers about to be wrenched apart by fate, never to see one another again.

To her shock, Jackson met the intensity of her emotion beat for beat of his heart against hers. The tragedy of loss flowed through him and into her so strongly she nearly wept from it midscene. They traded intense, wistful kisses and caresses that communicated a thousand times more loudly than words how keenly each of them felt the loss of what they'd had between them. Did he really feel that way, too, or was he just acting?

How could this be acting? It felt too raw, too painful, to be anything but real. He might be a great actor, but there was a limit to what any actor could do. And truth be told, they'd been getting through this entire series of shoots by wearing their actual hearts on their sleeves.

The script called for a passionate reunion in this scene. Happily ever after. Not this tragic farewell of doomed lovers. And yet, here they were dying in each other's arms.

Jackson went through the motions of making love to her with a gentleness that stole her breath away. She responded from the depths of her soul, begging him with body, mouth, eyes and soul to take everything she was. To remember her and hold a tiny piece of her somewhere in his heart. And he accepted her gift in its entirety, giving her back a piece of his soul in return. It hurt so bad she struggled to draw each breath.

The poignancy of their sweet passion crescendoed and then broke as they collapsed to the mat, breathing hard.

Adrian called a hushed "Cut."

Utter silence fell over the soundstage.

Uh-oh. What had she and Jackson just done? Was it that crushingly bad?

For once, not a single snide joke was fired in their direction from Jackson's guys. Even the teeny-bopper extras were silent and subdued. Crud. When had that giant lump lodged in the back of her throat? Ana risked peeking up at Adrian as he strode over to them, frowning.

"Did we totally screw that up?" Jackson muttered.

"Not at all. It just wasn't what I expected. It's a fascinating take on the scene, though. I wasn't looking for Romeo and Juliet, but I have to say, the star-crossed lovers theme works."

Oh, no. She and Jackson had channeled their real relationship into the scene. Again. Or more to the point, onto film for all the crew—all the world—to see. If there were a real rock nearby for her to crawl under, she'd be there already, hiding in a tight little ball of misery and humiliation this very second.

Adrian nodded slowly. "The hopelessness works. It permeated all your movements and leaped out of the scene. It wouldn't have worked if either of you had committed any less to it. Frankly, I didn't think Ana had the acting experience to pull that off, so I didn't take the story there. But now that you have, I *love* it. *Great* job."

Adrian dropped his next bomb so casually that Ana didn't see it coming until it had already blown up in her face. "I want to run that scene again, but this time let's do it the other way. I want you two fighting to an upbeat, passionate conclusion. Can you make that shift now, or do you need a break to reset mentally?"

Ana squeezed her eyes shut in brief agony. How was she supposed to survive dredging up the full power of the passion she and Jackson had shared…and lost?

Jackson ground out, "Let's just get it over with."

His words only increased her pain. He obviously didn't want to revisit their recent passion, either. At all. She'd known all along that she would lose him eventually, but now that the moment was upon her, it was harder to bear than she'd imagined. The loss cut soul deep.

"Okay," Adrian said briskly. "We'll start with anger and violence and shift over into that fiery passion the two of you are so good at generating." He backed up and moved over to have one last word with his cameramen before they rolled.

Oh, she so had anger wired. She'd been pissed off for days. But as she reached for it now, she couldn't find it in the morass of overwhelming sadness left over from the scene they'd just shot.

"Do you remember the moves we worked out for this sequence in case Adrian wanted to run it as a fight?" Jackson mumbled unwillingly in her general direction.

"More or less." They really should have rehearsed this fight in the past few days, but it went without saying that neither one of them had been keen on the idea of a practice session with everything else that had been going on.

"Places!" Adrian called.

She stepped forward and Jackson did the same. God, he looked hot, even decked out like the Jolly Green Giant.

"You smell as good as I remember," he breathed.

Gratitude flowed through her. The comment made

her think of his bed in the seaside mansion. Their first nights together. It was a generous gesture as an actor to give her a cue to help her find an emotion she was having trouble finding.

Their gazes met as some delay with a camera drew the moment out. Shared misery gradually transformed to wry humor as they stared at one another.

Aw, heck. Desire blazed in his eyes, and an answering eruption of lust flared in her gut. His nostrils flared like he sensed it just as Adrian shouted, "Roll cameras... and, action!"

She leaped in to slap Jackson. Her hand smacked satisfyingly against his cheek, and amusement flared in his eyes. She whirled away, falling into the rhythm of the dance with him as easily as they fell into a rhythm with sex. In. Out. Spin. Get caught. Slip the hold. Dance away. Rinse, lather and repeat.

It dawned on her gradually that Jackson was being particularly careful and considerate of her. He was pulling his punches a little more than usual and grappling with her a little more gently than in the past. It probably wasn't noticeable to anyone else, but she felt his concern and caring every time his hands touched her.

"More intense," Adrian called.

Not. A. Problem. Panting, both physically and mentally, she let go of the tightly leashed frustration she'd been holding at bay the past few days so she could stay good and mad at him. Why wouldn't he admit he loved her, dammit? Righteous fury roared through her, and the next time she leaped in on the attack, she jumped into his arms, wrapping her legs around his waist.

He caught her with easy strength and yanked her face to his. They didn't actually kiss because of the CGI artist's damned dots on their lips, but their breath mingled hotly and their stares locked in a silent sexual battle.

She bit his chin—hard—and he let her fall as she sprang back. But this time, his stalking held a distinctly sexual quality. He was a male on the hunt for his mate. Intent to catch her, subdue her and bend her to his will was written in every aggressive step he took.

About damned time.

She circled him, looking for an opening to swoop in, take what she wanted and dart away from his grasp. An apt analogy for their entire relationship. *Except for the part where you secretly hope he would catch you and make you his forever—*

Shut up, self! God, she hated that little voice sometimes!

The instant's distraction cost her. Jackson pounced and she was a millisecond too slow jumping out of his reach. For a moment, he looked surprised. He wasn't supposed to catch her yet in this sequence. But he went with it and wrapped her up in a tight bear hug from which there was no escaping. She wriggled and fought while he threw his head back and laughed in triumph. He planted a kiss on her that would have melted tempered steel, and a romantic sigh rose from the peanut gallery watching them film.

But then Jackson was *really* kissing her. Dots be damned. And the whole world fell away, leaving them in a lime-green universe containing only the two of them. No sound. No fury. No cameras. Just the two of them and the passion raging between them. *How could either one of them seriously contemplate walking away from this?*

He drew her up against his body until she stood on her tiptoes on top of his feet. His strong arms plastered her against him—not that she needed much encouragement to do some plastering of her own. They could deny it all they wanted, and they could be mad at each other all they wanted, but the basic, core attraction between them was bigger than either one of them. Irresistible.

Through their thin bodysuits, she felt him grow hard and huge, and her own body grew damp and needy in response. Her hips rocked against his, and one of his big hands clenched her rear end, holding her snugly against him. He groaned under his breath. The sound vibrated all the way to her core and lodged there, daring her not to respond to it.

And hoo baby, did she ever respond. The telltale beginnings of an orgasm began to snap and crackle deep within her, and she groaned in the back of her throat. Holding her off the ground, Jackson began a slow twirl with her, turning around and around until she was dizzy and clinging to him like he was the sun and she his own personal moon, orbiting him. Comets and meteors and cosmic explosions of lust exploded off the two of them and poured outward into the universe.

The breath-stealing sensations between her legs grew along with the size of his erection clenched tightly between her thighs. She rocked her hips forward once. Twice. She was going to implode—

"And…cut!"

She jolted as Adrian yelled out from somewhere out of her line of sight. Holy crap. She'd totally forgotten where they were. Movie set. Filming. Audience. Huge erection bulging between her thighs. She looked up at Jackson in distress.

He put her down gently, sliding her down his body and steadying her against him until she was able to turn in his arms and face Adrian. She leaned back against him, affording him a modicum of modesty until he could, uh, calm himself.

"You two are naturals," Adrian crowed. "That was spectacular." He turned to the cluster of crew and extras who uniformly wore slightly awed and totally turned-on expressions. "And that, ladies and gentlemen, is how a green-screen scene is done."

"Sign me up," one of the female extras replied fervently.

Everybody laughed. *Wow. That was a lot of pent-up sexual tension humming among the bystanders.* Ana muttered to Jackson, "If Adrian has a heart, he'll call a lunch break and let the crew hook up with those horny little nymphets for nooners."

She felt Jackson's smile against her ear. "I could go for one of those, myself."

"So I noticed."

Adrian called out, "The caterers have lunch ready. Let's meet back here in an hour."

"My office," Jackson murmured. His voice was nearly as charged as her girl parts. They didn't quite run for his office, but they walked pretty damned fast down the hall, and Jackson never let go of her hand.

He closed and locked his door and turned toward her. Amazing how long it took to pull *on* the annoying tight-fitting bodysuits, yet how incredibly quickly they could be peeled *off* when a girl was properly motivated.

Jackson picked her up and she obligingly wrapped her legs around his waist where they'd left off when Adrian had yelled cut. He murmured, "Now, where were we?"

He surged up into her and she all but sobbed with relief at having his throbbing erection buried deep inside her, touching her womb. She whispered against his neck, "Take me like you mean it, Jackson. I've missed you so much."

He drove upward hard, moving as he went, backing her up against a wall and then ramming into her hard and fast enough to rattle the picture frames beside her head. She groaned her pleasure aloud and grabbed his hair, urging him onward.

Apparently dissatisfied with how deep he was able to reach inside her, he spun and swept an arm across his desk. Notes and schedules went flying in a paper snowstorm around them. He laid her down on the desk and she reached up to grab him, surging up to meet him as he moved over her like a tsunami slamming a coastline. Advance. Retreat. Over and over. Higher and higher he went inside her, and with each thrust her lust built toward something so epic it didn't have a name.

She pushed up on her elbows in a moment of retreat, gained her feet and pushed Jackson backward until he fell onto the couch. She followed him down, impaling herself on him with a massive groan of pleasure as she sought the detonation hovering so close. Her hips were not her own, rocking forward hard against his pelvis over and over, faster and faster. Her entire body clenched around his huge, hot member as she rode it like a bucking bronco.

And then, without warning, the explosion claimed her. Her entire being came apart and little bits of her flew to the ends of the world and back as she screamed against Jackson's neck. The corded tendons and muscles there were rock hard with terrible tension. A quick flex of arms and abs, and she was flat on her back beneath him, still impaled on that hot, throbbing iron.

He growled, "Sing for me, baby. Scream for me.

Admit that you'll never get enough of me and no one else can do this to you like I can."

"Ohmigosh, Jackson—"

"Admit it." His jaw clenched as he pounded her like a piston, stroking her out of her mind as another orgasm ripped free of her body and tore her apart. And another. And another.

"I'm not stopping until you admit it," he bit out.

Yet another orgasm destroyed her from the inside out. She couldn't catch her breath. Her muscles had no strength left. She could only cling to him and let him ravage her to his heart's content…and it turned out to be *her* heart's desire, as well.

Finally, the emotional overload of orgasm after orgasm was so intense, so excessive, that she began to lose the ability to think. To see. She was going to pass out soon. "I admit it," she gasped.

Instead of stopping, his pace increased, the piston becoming a ramrod splintering her defenses and driving home in one last apocalyptic crash of electric, exploding conflagration that incinerated her into a quaking, quivering pile of ash. With a shout of his own against her temple, Jackson convulsed, shuddering and shuddering as a massive orgasm turned his entire being inside out.

His big body collapsed on hers, sweaty and heaving. But even then, he was considerate of her. He propped himself up with his elbows, giving her enough space to breathe. Of course, even if she'd wanted to move, she was too wiped out to lift a finger. She panted herself, at a loss for words.

That had been epic. Freaking epic.

How long they laid there in silence catching their breath, she had no idea. His forehead rested lightly against hers, and the familiar intimacy of it was like a warm blanket, an old friend, wrapping around her.

At long last, he murmured, "Wow. Am I crushing you?"

"Yes, but there's no rush on moving."

Nevertheless, he pressed up and away from her immediately. He moved across his office to the closet and pulled out a pair of jeans. He slipped them on, commando, and they hung low and sexy on his hips as he tossed her one of his T-shirts. She pulled on the oversize thing, which fit her like a baggy dress.

"Ana, we need to talk."

She hmmphed. "Look where that got us the last time we tried that. Maybe we should just stick to epic sex."

"Epic, huh?" a brief smile lit his face. Lord, he was beautiful when he smiled like that. His smile faded. "You and I both know great sex isn't enough to build a lifelong relationship on."

She winced and tried, "But it's not a bad place to start. It's a good indicator of compatibility. And trust. And mutually shared tastes."

His lips curved slightly. "Good point." But then waxed totally serious. "We've got some important decisions to make."

Alarm flared in her gut. "Not really. You make a ton of money on this movie, your studio's funded for the long-term and you move on with your regularly scheduled career as a movie star. I'll have this baby, and he or she and I will get on with our lives."

He glared at her, obviously fighting to control his ire.

She used the pause to dive in with "Look. I realize you had no intention of getting into a serious relationship, and you definitely didn't want a baby out of this. I in no way expect you to become Superdad to a kid you didn't even want. However, I won't, under any circumstances, consider an abortion, so don't even suggest it to me because it'll just make me mad."

"Will you, just once, shut up and let me talk?" he finally got in edgewise.

She reared back, startled.

"I'm not going to hold any grudges about how this baby came to be. It happened, and I should've taken steps to make sure you didn't get pregnant. I take full responsibility for that."

She didn't know whether to scream or cry. He seriously believed she'd gotten pregnant on purpose. That she'd *trapped* him. Or at least tried to. She was so engulfed in rage and grief she nearly missed his next words.

"Marry me, Ana. I want to be there for you and the baby. We can go to Vegas and be married tonight."

Shocked, she retorted, "Why tonight? Are you so desperate to get me respectably wed so when people count on their fingers in a little under nine months they don't throw you funny looks?"

"This isn't about my reputation," he growled. "It's about doing the right thing—"

She threw her hands over her ears, abruptly so furious she could hardly breathe. "To hell with the right thing, Jackson Prescott. You can take your right thing and go straight to hell!"

She stormed out of his office and down the hallway to the crowded ladies' locker room where he would not be able to follow her today. Tears built up violently behind the fragile emotional dam she barely hung on to until she made it to her locker. She drew one wobbly, sobbing breath and—

"Oh, my gosh, ma'am. You were incredible earlier!"

"Where did you get your acting training?"

"Screw that. Do you have that guy's phone number?"

Ana jolted hard. The mob of extra girls. She could not deal with all their perky enthusiasm right now. She yanked on her clothes, scrubbed the worst of the praying-mantis makeup off her face and raced out of the locker room.

She spied Tyrone on her way out and said urgently, "Do me a favor, will you? Tell Adrian I'm sick and have to cancel shooting cleanup shots this afternoon. Tell him I'm really sorry...."

That was it. That was as long as she could hold it together. She whirled as the dam within her broke and tears streamed down her face. She ran for the car and driver the studio had provided for her. Dignity be damned.

Chapter 18

She'd not only turned down his proposal, she'd told him to go to hell. Jackson was stunned. What on earth was wrong with Ana? It was what she'd wanted, right? Why else would she have gone and gotten pregnant if not to wring a marriage proposal out of the confirmed bachelor?

He'd give anything to go home and lose himself in a bottle of bourbon, but he was too damned responsible for that. Instead, he was parked in front of her place in the Hugster, standing watch over her. *Or at least on his child.* Any sane man would give up on the baby's mother after her outburst this afternoon.

Completely flummoxed by Ana's irrational behavior, he let his thoughts stray in a safer direction. He was immensely frustrated by the police's failure to catch whoever was stalking Ana. He got that they had violent crimes aplenty to deal with, but someone was targeting the mother of his child. He was not about to sit back and do *nothing* about that.

He spent much of the long night in the Hugster using the internet to research Ana's past. It took him a while to find the newspaper article detailing her attack—in South Carolina as it turned out. The picture with the article showed Chandler LaGrange in a football uniform, standing with his arm thrown around another football player. The caption said they were cocaptains of the district champion football team. LaGrange was decent enough looking, he supposed, but Jackson recognized the type. The guy's body would run to fat in a few years, and the guy would spend his adult life reliving the glory days of high school while he worked a dead-end job in a dead-end life.

Thank God Ana'd gotten away from the guy, and guys like him. She had so much talent and potential, so much life in her—

Focus, buddy.

He was startled to read, according to a later news article, that LaGrange had been transferred to a mental institution in North Carolina. Apparently, his family had him moved there when Chandler had trouble with the staff of the county mental hospital in his hometown mistreating the lad. Ana must have been well-liked by the locals.

Jackson couldn't condone abuse of a mentally ill teen, even if young Chandler had done his level best to kill Ana while they were in college. He shifted his internet search to North Carolina to learn more about the fate of LaGrange.

There wasn't much. A few release hearings over the years that were declined. Frustrated, Jackson sent an email to the physician of record in LaGrange's case to verify that the guy was still incarcerated and to ask if the doctor thought there might be a connection between the attacks on Ana and the guy's patient.

If not Chandler, then who could it be? One thing Jackson knew: she wasn't leaving his sight again until the bastard was caught, whether she liked it or not. A rental car was delivered to her apartment midmorning the next day, and she used it to drive to a grocery store and back. In the early afternoon, he followed her out to the local shopping mall.

At the mall, he waited for upwards of two hours, parked a dozen spaces away from her car. She must really be going on a shopping spree. Which was a little weird for her. He recalled her commenting before that she hated shopping.

Another hour passed, and he began to get alarmed. Something wasn't right. He dialed her cell phone, but she didn't pick it up. He had to have a chat with her about letting his calls go to voice mail until her stalker was caught. It was going to make her mad, but that was tough. Her safety came first.

He resorted to tracking down a phone number for the mall security office and asking them to check on her. He gave them a detailed physical description and described the clothes she was wearing.

Perhaps fifteen minutes had passed since that call when his phone rang. He snatched it up eagerly. "Ana?"

"No, Mr. Prescott. It's mall security. We've checked all our video feeds and run our guys through the entire mall, and the woman you're describing is not here. We've got footage of her entering the mall a little over three hours ago, but then we lost her."

Jackson's blood ran cold. There was a commotion in the background of the call, and the guard on the phone with him swore. "Can you come inside, sir? There's something we need to show you." The guy then spoke to someone near him. "Yes, you moron. Call the police and report it."

Jackson didn't stick around to hear any more. He sprinted from the parking lot toward the mall.

The security guard showed him footage of Ana walking out of a store and a man approaching her. They spoke briefly, and then the man took her by the arm and led her quickly out an exit on the other side of the mall.

Jackson's heart dropped into his feet. "Can you get a better shot of that man's face?"

"We've got one more shot of them in the parking lot," the head guard replied. "Pull it up," he instructed the technician sitting at the bank of monitors.

"Can you zoom that?" Jackson muttered, staring at the screen.

"Nope. That's all I've got," the tech answered.

There was something familiar about the man's face. For her part, Ana looked deeply alarmed. But she didn't look afraid of the man she was with. Did she know him, maybe?

Brody Westmore arrived at the security office after a few minutes, and Jackson filled the cop in quickly. The mall security cameras had captured a license plate, which Brody relayed to his dispatchers. The police would use their access to traffic cameras in the area to try to spot the vehicle. But it was a long shot. Millions of vehicles transited the Pacific Coast Highway, and Ana's captor had been driving a popular and nondescript model of car.

The cops told Jackson they would keep him updated

and told him to go home and wait for news. *So not happening.*

He headed over to the studio and filled his men in quickly on what had happened. They all offered to help… but they had no place to go, no idea how to help Ana.

Would her stalker try to ransom her back? The police seemed to think it was a simple kidnapping that was financially motivated. They said they would go ahead and notify the FBI, but Jackson felt time slipping away from Ana fast.

Where are you? Why did you go with that guy? What could he possibly have said to you to make you leave with a stranger?

Jackson paced the halls of the studio restlessly. He was missing something. He recognized that guy at the mall. But from where?

Ana glanced over at Adrian's assistant construction supervisor. He was the sort of guy her gaze just slid off of. Bland. Nice-enough looking. But unremarkable. She'd seen Marti Frick around the set a few times before and knew him on sight but had never spoken with him. It was nice of the guy to come get her after Jackson was injured on the set. "And you say Jackson's not too badly hurt?" she asked him.

"Nah, not too badly. He's refusing to go to the hospital for an X-ray of his leg, though. That's why Adrian sent me to find you. He wants you to talk some sense into him."

Ana snorted. "That sounds just like Jackson. Stubborn to a fault, he is."

The car turned the wrong direction to head for the studio and she blurted, "Hey! The studio's that way."

"Road's closed down there. They're patching up damage from last winter's earthquake. We gotta go around."

She subsided for a couple more minutes. But then the guy turned the wrong way again. "Where are you going, Marti? The studio's definitely back the other way."

"Shut up, you bitch."

She looked across the front seat in shock. She lurched when she saw the tiny black bore of a pistol pointed across Marti's body at her. *Oh. My. God.*

"You! You're the stalker! But why? I don't know you from Adam."

"You're so stupid. You never recognized me, and I was right in front of you the whole time."

Her heart rate accelerated to something approaching light speed. She had to keep him talking. Figure out who he was and where he was taking her. She moved her hand an inch closer to her purse and the cell phone inside.

"Should I recognize you?" she asked in as conversational a voice as she could manage. *Gotta keep this guy calm.* The memory of his boot smashing into an unconscious man's mouth with casual cruelty came to her.

His laugh was ugly. Mean. And there was something familiar about it....

"Pete?" she asked in disbelief. "Pete Ricollo?" He'd been the star quarterback of the football team in high school. Chandler LaGrange's best friend, who'd attended college with them. The guy who'd been driving the truck the night that—

"You're the one who's been causing all those accidents, aren't you? And you trashed my motel room. Were you driving the car that hit me, too?" she demanded.

"You never even suspected me, did you?" he ground

out. "No one ever saw good old Pete. The invisible man. That's me."

"You're not invisible. I see you clear as a bell."

"Shut up." As her hand inched a bit closer to her purse, he snarled. "Keep your goddamn hand away from your purse. I'm wise to you. Gonna call that bastard boyfriend of yours, aren't you?"

"He's not my boyfriend," she blurted.

"But he'll still come to the rescue like the goddamn cavalry charging to the goddamn rescue, won't he?"

Jackson undoubtedly would. If he knew she'd been kidnapped and if he knew where this nutcase had taken her. But to Pete, she just shrugged and replied, "I doubt it. We're done as a couple."

"I saw you two dry humping on film yesterday. Didn't look too damned over to me."

"That was just acting," she replied as lightly as she could. "He hates my guts."

"I know the goddamned feeling."

"What have I ever done to you, Pete?"

"I lost my football scholarship because of you. I was gonna get out of that two-bit town. Make it in the big leagues. Get rich in the NFL. And then you had to go and jump out of my goddamn truck and wreck my life."

"How did I wreck your life? I'm the one Chandler tried to kill. No charges were made against you."

"There were questions asked. Rumors. Why didn't I try to stop him? Why didn't I pull the truck over?"

"Why didn't you?"

"You weren't the first girl he shut up, you know."

Shut up, as in killed? Stunned, she asked carefully, "How many other girls were there?"

"Three. You'd have made four. You were the last one. One for the road between friends, you know."

"What happened to the other girls?"

"We shared 'em. Shared everything, me and Chandler. We were even cocaptains of the football team."

Shared the girls how? She asked carefully, "Did Chandler strangle the others ones first, too?"

"Not the first one. Turned out to be a pain in the ass, her hollering and fighting the whole time. We learned with the second one to shut her up first."

"And then what?"

He looked over at her, his lewd stare raking up and down her body. Her skin crawled, the answer obvious before he said the words.

"And then we did whatever we wanted to 'em. Had fun with 'em. Did everything we could think up to 'em."

"After they were dead?"

He shrugged. "The first one was more fun still squirming and screaming, but Chandler liked 'em quiet and cooperative."

"Dead."

"Well, yeah."

"That's sick. Twisted as hell, Pete."

"Shut up. When we get to my place, I'm gonna tape your goddamn mouth shut. And then I'm gonna do all the stuff me and Chandler was plannin' to do to you. You can squirm the way I like, but I'm sick of listening to your yapping."

Jackson, where are you? Why, oh, why, didn't I listen to you and stay with you?

This was all her fault. She and the baby were going to die because she'd been too stubborn to listen to reason. She was never going to see him again. Never going to make mind-blowing love with him. Never share watching their child grow up together. Never have a chance to make things right between them. She'd been an idiot. She should've waited as long as it took for him to be ready to commit to her. But now it was too late.

Oh, God, Jackson. Please forgive me.

Chapter 19

"Mr. Prescott?"

He whirled to face the FBI agent who'd spoken from behind him in the high-tech command center. "Anything?" he demanded.

"We got a hit on her cell phone location. It pinged heading into the mountains. We've got units and local police headed that way, but we'll lose cell phone coverage of the area she's headed into shortly. Do you have any idea why her kidnapper might take her up there?"

"Other than it being isolated and damned near impossible to track people through?" he asked rhetorically.

The FBI agent made a sympathetic sound. "Keep the faith. We'll find her."

Jackson nodded, miserable. Yeah, but would they find her before she and the baby died? Something very bad was happening to Ana. He could feel it in his bones.

Somehow, this *had* to tie in to Chandler LaGrange. His attack on her was the only event in her life of any significance that was in any way tied to violence or wackos. But how were the events of then and now related? He opened his laptop and pulled up the articles about Chandler and the attack again.

And that was when he saw it. The picture of Chandler and his buddy on the football team. Pete Riccolo was the kid's name. The same youth who'd been driving the night Chandler had tried to kill Ana. Who hadn't tried to help her. Who'd kept driving the truck when Chandler attacked her in the back…

"I think I know who her kidnapper is!" he called out.

A bevy of FBI agents went to work as soon as he gave them the guy's name. It didn't take long for the agents to find out Riccolo had changed his name a while back.

As soon as someone at a computer called out the name, Marti Frick, Jackson blurted, "He's a construction supervisor on my movie. He works at my damn studio!"

"We lost her cell phone!" someone called from across the command center.

The agent-in-charge ordered his team to look for any place in the mountains tied to Marti Frick. In seconds, someone called out, "Got it. He's leased a cabin in Big Sur."

"Dispatch a team up there, ASAP. That helicopter still standing by on the roof?"

"Yes, sir."

"You coming with me, Mr. Prescott?"

"Wild horses couldn't stop me."

Ana's panic mounted as the urban sprawl of the coast fell behind Pete's car. This was not good. Not good at all.

She needed to make her escape where there were other people around who could help her.

The highway whizzed by at over seventy miles per hour. Even a stuntman with experience jumping out of fast-moving cars wouldn't attempt it. At this speed the impact with the pavement would kill her for sure.

Terror at the notion of having to jump for her life rolled over her. She might have learned how to jump out of a car, but that didn't mean she'd ever overcome her deep phobia of doing so. Her hand crept to her belly. *Hang in there, Sparky. I'll figure out a way to get us out of this. I promise.*

If only Pete would slow down. But instead, his foot pressed down even harder on the accelerator. It was almost as if he'd heard her thoughts. The miles flew by, and with each one that passed, her hope for a rescue diminished a little more.

Finally, Pete turned off the highway onto a smaller road that quickly turned to dirt. Great. She was going to cut and scrape the bejeebers out of herself when she made the jump. If she could bring herself to do it. If he ever approached something resembling civilization again, and if he ever slowed down below about thirty miles per hour, which would be her safe maximum for taking the leap.

Trees started to dot the arid mountainsides around them. She was so hosed. They would never even find her body out here after this nut was done with her. Poor Jackson. He was going to blame himself. If this didn't put him off of women for good, she would be shocked. And he was such a good man at heart. He'd have made a great father. Such a waste.

The vehicle turned onto a smaller road that wound up a mountainside. And more importantly, the curves forced

Pete to slow down. There wasn't even a hint of other human beings nearby, but she was out of time. Like it or not, she was going to have to jump and take her chances with escaping Pete on foot.

"Almost to the last place we pinged her," the pilot announced. Jackson scanned the road below through binoculars for any sign of a vehicle. He didn't see a car, but he did use a trick he'd learned on a movie shoot and announced, "I've got dust on a side road in our three o'clock position."

The pilot veered right, tracking down the source of the dust trail. They topped a ridge and a valley sprawled before them. And in the distance, a car sped along the road, which tracked along one side of the valley about halfway up. *The right color of car.* Jackson used the zoom feature on his binoculars to take a closer look.

"Tallyho," the pilot called in the traditional phraseology of having acquired his target.

The helicopter raced forward, devouring the gap between aircraft and car in a matter of seconds. The steepness of the mountain was such that the pilot had to run up along the left side of the car.

"That's Riccolo," Jackson announced. "Positive ID."

The FBI field agent moved over practically into Jackson's lap to peer down at the vehicle. "Visual on the victim?"

The helicopter pulled a few feet ahead of the car and Jackson gritted out, "I've got her in sight. In the front passenger seat."

"Let's stop this bastard," the FBI agent ordered the pilot.

The car swerved as the helicopter swooped in low

overhead, but it did not stop. The copter tried again, all but planting a skid in the vehicle's windshield.

"There's a pregnant lady in that car," Jackson ground out. "Be careful, for God's sake."

"We're gonna have to take out the driver," the FBI agent replied. "This guy's not gonna stop." To that end, the agent strapped on a harness and prepared to open the sliding door of the chopper to shoot Riccolo.

"Wait," he bit out sharply. "Ana has stunt training. She can egress that car if we can get it to slow down."

"Any suggestion how we do that, given that putting a skid in the guy's face didn't get him to blink, let alone slow down?" the FBI agent snapped.

"Let me jump on the car."

"Are you kidding me?"

"No. I've got stunt training, too. I do most of my own stunts in movies." He didn't add that he only jumped on cars that stunt drivers were operating and he only jumped out of helicopters flown by stunt pilots.

"That's insane, Prescott."

"Let me try. Worst case, I roll off the car and get a little scraped up, and you can shoot the driver and crash the car then."

The pilot interjected, "Whatever you're going to do, it had better be soon. The end of this valley is coming up fast. Once he climbs into the mountains and trees, we won't get another shot at him."

Jackson stared at the FBI agent, willing him to agree to this plan. If that car crashed, Ana and the baby would be hurt or worse.

"All right. Do it," the FBI man bit out.

Jackson moved into the doorway and stepped out onto the skid. "Lower!" he shouted into his headset. He yelled directions at the pilot to guide the guy into position in front of and above the racing car. Now, if only the driver would keep the speed steady until he jumped.

"On my mark, dip down six feet fast," Jackson called.

"Roger. Standing by," the pilot replied.

"Three. Two. One. Mark!"

Ana watched as the helicopter swerved around overhead and Pete swore up a storm.

"You know this ends badly for you, right?" she asked him. If she could distract him, pull his attention away from the helicopter, maybe he would lose focus and make a mistake. Like slowing down the car. He was tooling along at about forty miles per hour, which was about twenty miles per hour too fast for this rough, slippery gravel road.

"They're going to shoot you if you don't stop," she commented.

"Shut up!"

"Did you know they can land that bird on top of your car? They can force you to stop whether you like it or not."

"I said. Shut. Up."

She grabbed the door handle, ostensibly to steady herself after he swerved again. Dang. The pilot had nearly put a skid through the windshield that time. The problem was, if Pete got too rattled and went off the left side of the road, they would tumble down the mountainside for hundreds and hundreds of feet. She was highly doubtful anyone would survive that kind of crash. Not at this speed.

Shoot. She might have to take her chances and jump even if Pete didn't slow down any more. She tensed, reviewing her training and preparing to force open the door and jump.

The helicopter dipped abruptly and something large and dark flew at them without warning. She screamed as the car lurched and something slammed into the windshield.

A familiar face glared into the car and Pete shouted incoherently. Reflexively, the guy slammed on the brakes. Jackson was thrown off the front of the car, but not before she saw him mouth a single word to her.

Jump.

She didn't stop. Didn't think. She just trusted him and did as he ordered. She threw the door open and jumped. She curled into a ball, hands thrown over her head and neck as she hit the dirt.

The impact was incredible. Her body rolled over and over and over like a rolling stone. And with every roll, some new part of her body slammed into the hard, gravel-studded ground. She rolled so many times she lost track of where up and down were and grew too dizzy to see.

The rolling slowed. The sky righted itself overhead, and the ground was hard and painful beneath her.

Jackson. Ohmigod. He'd been thrown from the car at a much higher speed than she'd come out of it. Was he all right? Had he plunged off the mountain in his heroic bid to buy her an escape?

She pushed to her hands and knees. Her palms burned like fire and it felt like there was no skin left on either knee. She pressed painfully to her feet. In time to see the helicopter ram Pete's car from behind. The car plunged off the road at a high rate of speed. The sound of metal crunching and a cloud of dust rose ahead of her.

She turned to look behind her. Where was Jackson?

She took a stumbling step. Another. Broke into a shambling jog. Coordination returned gradually and she picked up speed, running for all she was worth to where Jackson had been thrown off the hood of the car.

Please be alive. Please be alive. Please be alive…

Chapter 20

Jackson blinked his eyes open and squinted against the glare of the hot sun in his face. Damn, it was bright.

A female voice sobbed from somewhere nearby. Something about thanking God that devolved into a diatribe about stupid heroics that nearly got people killed. But mostly, he registered pain. From head to foot. Not one part of his body didn't hurt right now.

"Ana?" he rasped. "Are you okay?"

"Yes, you big idiot. I'm right here. And I'm fine."

He tried to smile, but the effort was more than he could manage. He sighed and let his eyes drift closed.

Ana sat back on her heels, shielding her face from the flying gravel and dirt as the helicopter set down a dozen yards away from her and Jackson. A man in a dark blue jacket with big white letters announcing him to be FBI ran from the chopper toward her.

"Is he alive?" the agent shouted over the noise of the helicopter.

"Unconscious!" she shouted back.

"You okay?"

"Yes," she yelled.

"Can you help me carry him to the bird?" the agent called.

She nodded and lifted Jackson's limp arm, draping it over her shoulder. The agent grabbed Jackson's other arm, and between them, they horsed him upright. Dragging his dead weight between them, they got him over to the helicopter and dumped him inside as gently as they could.

Jackson moaned, but that was the only indication of life from him.

The ride back to Serendipity went fast—the pilot flew like a bat out of hell—but every minute of it was agony for her. She knew all too well the risks of the kind of fall he'd taken. Broken bones were the least of it. The bigger worries were spinal-cord injury and brain injury. Paralysis. Death.

They landed on the roof of the county hospital, and a trauma team whisked Jackson out of the chopper and onto a gurney with shocking speed. He disappeared into the building as the team sprinted away with him.

That was when she noticed her legs felt kind of weak. And she was feeling a little light-headed.

"Whoa, there," the FBI agent said sharply. He grabbed her around the waist moments before her legs went out from under her. He scooped her up in both arms and carried her toward the same door Jackson had gone through a minute before. Someone came outside with a nice, soft bed, and the agent laid her down on it. Everything faded to bright white light. And then to black.

Ana woke up, disoriented, unsure of what had woken her. There it was again. Something pounding like a hammer on wood. No. Fingers. Drumming impatiently on a hard surface.

She turned her head toward the noise and was shocked to see a hospital room take shape around her as her eyes slowly came into focus. Her eyes closed again.

"Wake up, baby. It's me."

Jackson. With Herculean effort, she did as he ordered and opened her eyes. And there he was, looking more beautiful than he'd ever been on screen, even with scratches and bruises covering one side of his face. She whispered through her incredibly dry throat, "You're real? You're alive?"

"Yup. I've just got a little concussion. Nothing a few aspirin won't fix right up."

Her hand lurched to her belly in sudden alarm. "The baby?"

"Fine. Tough little fella. You executed that jump perfectly. Rolled up in a tight little ball and protected our son from any harm at all."

"It might be a girl," she retorted.

"Yogi Surhan said it's a boy, and he's never wrong."

She rolled her eyes at him, but doing so hurt. "Why am I in here?"

"You fainted. Doctors decided it would be good for you to sleep a little while and they gave you something in that IV to help you rest. You had quite a scare."

"It was Pete Riccolo—" she started.

"Chandler's buddy."

"He said they killed three girls and did…things to them."

Jackson laid a gentle finger over her lips, stopping the flood of horrified words. "He's dead, Ana. He's not ever going to hurt anyone else. You're safe."

Tears came then. Jackson just gathered her in his arms and let her cry all over his shirt. Which was progress for him, she supposed. Usually, he panicked and bolted at the first glimpse of tears. Slowly, she cried out the stress and fear of the kidnapping and her certainty that she and the baby were going to die.

"That jump onto the hood of Pete's car was idiotic," she eventually mumbled.

"It worked, didn't it? Slowed him down enough for you to get out of the car."

"How did you know I would jump?"

"I knew you were brave enough to do it and that you would want to live for me and the baby."

She lifted her head from his chest to glare up at him. "It was a hell of a risk you took."

He stared down at her for a long time before he finally murmured, "You're worth it."

"Are you drunk?" she demanded.

He laughed shortly. "God knows I could use a drink. But no."

"Don't ever do anything that stupid again, Jackson."

"Or else what?"

"Or else I'll have to kick your butt," she retorted.

"You and what army?" he laughed.

"I don't need an army. I'll get Minerva to help me."

"No fair."

"All's fair in love and war," she declared.

The humor drained slowly from their eyes as they stared at one another.

"And which one is this? Love or war?" he asked quietly.

"Which one do you want it to be?" she replied. All of a sudden she felt queasy, and butterflies were sprouting in her stomach.

If only she didn't care how he answered her question. But she did. She always would. Like it or not, this was a man she was always going to love. Her heart would always bleed for him and she just had to get used to it. He pushed away from her and paced the confines of the small hospital room liked a caged animal.

He whirled abruptly and blurted, "I'm glad we're having a baby together, Ana."

She stared at him in shock. She hadn't seen *that* one coming. "Glad?" she breathed. "Why?"

He shoved a hand through his hair. "I think we've established pretty thoroughly that I suck at this relationship stuff. And God knows I'm no artist with words, so I'm probably going to screw up saying this. But hear me out, okay?"

He hesitated, and she took pity, saying gently, "Just spit it out."

"I'm really sorry about how I reacted the night you told me you were having a baby. I had flashbacks to my mother and freaked out. But you're so not my mother, I can hardly describe how different you are from her. I *know* you would never take advantage of me or of an innocent baby.

'I'm sorry I got you into any of this. I should have stayed away from you, but for some reason, I just couldn't. You were irresistible." He sputtered to a stop as he ran out of words.

"Jackson, my life was never going to be the same once we made love, whether I got pregnant or not."

"Why's that?"

It was her turn to struggle for words. "After that first night, I couldn't pretend that I didn't love you at least a little. I've been crazy about you pretty much from the moment we met, but you barely gave me the time of day. I mean, you were nice, but you didn't open up emotionally. I tried to convince myself I didn't care that deeply for you. But after we made love and you knocked my world totally off its axis, I had to admit the truth to myself."

"And now?" he asked soberly. "How do you feel now?"

How in the hell was she supposed to answer that? She would be a complete idiot to lay her guts out first, to declare her love for him without any hint from him about how he felt. The first rule of dealing with alpha males like him was never to give them both the upper hand *and* the lower hand. A girl had to hold out a few cards of her own to play in an emergency.

As if he sensed the reason behind her hesitation, Jackson plunged on. "Here's the thing. I love you, Ana."

"Whaaat?" she squeaked.

"You heard me. I love you. Hook, line and sinker. And it's not about the baby. If you'd lost this baby today, I would grieve with you and then want to try for another one. But I love *you*. Everything about you. Your laugh. Your big heart. How sexy you are. How you try to hide your girliness, even though everyone sees it, anyway. The way you go off script all the damned time."

As declarations of love went, it wasn't half-bad. But

what did it mean? She intently studied Jackson, who'd resumed pacing and turning. Lord, that man was gorgeous. She never tired of looking at him. His power and grace, the self-contained confidence and self-discipline, were addictive.

"Aw, hell, Ana. You would never intentionally get pregnant to trap me. You're too honest to pull a stunt like that. I just said that stuff because I was scared of being like my mother." He paused, then confessed, "I was terrified of how I felt about you."

"And how was that?" she asked cautiously.

"You were right, you know," he declared abruptly.

"About what?"

"About how I was hanging on to Vanessa and my mother and the past as an excuse not to face the future."

Had she said that? She wasn't about to quibble with him about it because she happened to agree with the statement.

"I hid behind the crap they both pulled on me. I used it as a shield to protect myself from getting hurt again. But then you came along."

She frowned. "What? And then I showed you whole new levels of hurt?"

He laughed unwillingly. "No. You showed me that along with the risk of pain comes happiness. That you can't have one without the other, and that neither one will kill me."

"I showed you all of that?" she asked in a small voice.

Another hand shoved through his hair. Poor guy. All this talking about touchy-feely stuff must be really stressful for him.

"Minerva was right. I was never going to get around to coming out of my shell and finding a woman to love or to love me, or having a family for that matter, if she didn't give me a swift kick in the butt."

"God bless Minerva and her meddling," Ana muttered.

Jackson's mouth curved up in a wry smile. "And then you gave me another swift kick in the butt with your news about the baby. I had gotten in the habit of being a self-centered ass, and all of a sudden, life wasn't all about me. I didn't react the way I should have to your announcement."

"Meaning what?"

"Meaning, the second you told me you were pregnant, I should have swept you up in my arms and told you that you'd just made me the happiest and proudest guy in the world. And you did, by the way."

Okay, there went her jaw again. Damned thing wouldn't stay shut tonight.

"Instead of telling you how I really felt, I reacted defensively. I started throwing out accusations because I was too damned scared by those other feelings of happiness and pride…" He exhaled hard. "And love. I love you, Ana. I really do want to marry you."

"Whuh…huh?" *Jaw officially unhinged.*

"Even if you don't want to marry me, I want to spend the rest of my life with you, Ana. I want to have hot sex on my Harley with you and make slow love in bed with you to the sound of the ocean. I want to fall asleep beside you at night and wake up beside you in the morning. I want to argue with you and make up with you. I want to raise this baby with you and make more babies. I want the whole damned shooting match, and I'll do my level best to make you happy for the rest of your life. What do you say?"

He strode up to her and knelt beside the bed, leaving only the top of his head visible. His voice floated up to her. "I didn't get a ring, yet, because I want to pick out one with you. My grandmother has a honking-huge diamond she'll want to give to you, but you'll have to take a look at it and see if you like it or want your own engagement ring. Money's no object. I just want you to love it."

He was babbling. And it was adorable.

"Stand up, you big galoot. I can't see you down there."

He jumped to his feet and looked down at her with such a ridiculously hopeful expression on his face that she had to laugh.

"Will you marry me, Ana? For better and for worse, till death do us part?"

"You'd better not die for a really, really long time, Jackson Prescott. I have a *lot* of ideas I'd like to try with you on your Harley. It's going to take us years to get through all of them."

"Years, huh?"

"I have a good imagination. And I've had the hots for my boss for a while now."

"Good to know. I hear your boss is a bit of an idiot."

"He can be a little slow on the uptake at times," she agreed.

"Then you'll marry me?" he asked carefully.

"*So* slow on the uptake," she laughed. "Of course I'll marry you."

He surged forward, scooping her up against him in the mother of all bear hugs. He lifted her out of the bed and spun her around, then his head dipped to hers.

Their lips met, and like it always did, the wild magic swept over them and wiped everything else away. The hurts of the past. The doubts and insecurities. The misunderstandings. All of it. The only thing left was them.

And a baby. Conceived in love and, apparently, going to be born into love, as well.

"Hey, Jackson," she gasped as they came up for air briefly.

"Hmm?"

"Minerva's never going to let us live it down that her yogi was right."

He half laughed, half groaned against her mouth. "Maybe we'll get lucky and have a girl."

"You don't want a son?"

"I want a whole bunch of kids of whatever gender we get so long as you're their mother."

She smiled and sprinkled kisses all over his face, murmuring, "Minerva can meddle all she wants as long as I have you. Forever."

"Forever," he agreed fervently.

* * * * *